DANIEL'S
FINAL WEEK

DONNA VANLIERE

HARVEST PROPHECY
AN IMPRINT OF HARVEST HOUSE PUBLISHERS

Unless otherwise indicated, all Scripture quotations are taken from The ESV® Bible (The Holy Bible, English Standard Version®), copyright © 2001 by Crossway, a publishing ministry of Good News Publishers. Used by permission. All rights reserved.

Verses marked NIV are taken from the Holy Bible, New International Version®, NIV®. Copyright © 1973, 1978, 1984, 2011 by Biblica, Inc.® Used by permission of Zondervan. All rights reserved worldwide. www.zondervan.com. The "NIV" and "New International Version" are trademarks registered in the United States Patent and Trademark Office by Biblica, Inc.®

Verses marked NKJV are taken from the New King James Version®. Copyright © 1982 by Thomas Nelson, Inc. Used by permission. All rights reserved.

Verses marked KJV are taken from the King James Version of the Bible.

In the novel portion of this book, Zerah, Emma, and Lerenzo read from ESV Bibles, and Elliott reads from an NIV Bible.

Italicized Scripture is author's emphasis.

Cover designer: Faceout Studio, Emily Armstrong

Cover photo © oksart1, Rafael Trafaniuc, Ackab Photography, IgorZh, caesart, Marilyn Volan, Volodymyr Burdiak, Mrs.Moon / Shutterstock

Interior design by KUHN Design Group

For bulk, special sales, or ministry purchases, please call 1-800-547-8979.
Email: Customerservice@hhpbooks.com

is a federally registered trademark of the Hawkins Children's LLC. Harvest House Publishers, Inc., is the exclusive licensee of this trademark.

Daniel's Final Week
Copyright © 2022 by Donna VanLiere
Published by Harvest House Publishers
Eugene, Oregon 97408
www.harvesthousepublishers.com

ISBN 978-0-7369-8049-4 (pbk)
ISBN 978-0-7369-8050-0 (eBook)

Library of Congress Control Number: 2021937792

Printed in the United States of America

23 24 25 26 27 28 29 30 / BP / 10 9 8 7 6 5 4 3 2

For Val Clemente,
who searches the Scriptures
and knows that things are looking up!

OTHER HARVEST HOUSE BOOKS
BY DONNA VANLIERE

The Time of Jacob's Trouble

The Day of Ezekiel's Hope

DANIEL'S
FINAL WEEK

Daniel, I have now come to give you insight and understanding…
After the sixty-two "sevens," the Anointed One will be put to death
and will have nothing. The people of the ruler who will come
will destroy the city and the sanctuary. The end will come like a
flood: War will continue until the end, and desolations have been
decreed. He will confirm a covenant with many for one "seven."
In the middle of the "seven" he will put an end to sacrifice and
offering. And at the temple he will set up an abomination that
causes desolation, until the end that is decreed is poured out on him.

DANIEL 9:22, 26-27 NIV

When they cry to the LORD because of oppressors,
he will send them a savior and defender, and deliver them.
And the LORD will make himself known.

ISAIAH 19:20-21

CHAPTER 1

The heavens shudder and galaxies, long held fast by gravity, retreat as if cowering in fright. Stars shake loose from their orbits and tumble to earth as Satan screeches before heaven's throne. With access permitted by the Most High, the ancient serpent has once again flown through the air relinquished by the first Adam thousands of years earlier and stands before God, condemning those sealed by the Lamb's blood.

"No! No! No!" the great dragon shouts as the heavens tremble, and he grabs his sword as myriad angels sweep over the deceiver of the whole world to fight his demonic legion who, millennia ago, fell from their heavenly place with the father of lies. Beelzebul's wings spread and his face twists in rage as he charges the throne. "I won't let you!"

Michael the archangel tosses the prince of demons aside, and when the lawless one regains his footing, his wings rise high over his head like a black, menacing storm as he flies toward Michael.

"I cast you to the ground forever!"

The Creator's voice thunders throughout the heavens as the god of this age crumples before him, begging for his life. "I am the prince of the air!" Satan pleads. "The earth belongs to me!"

The Righteous One will hear no more. The accuser is barred from heaven forever, and Michael lifts up the murderer and tempter and hurls him to earth as the armies of heaven wage tremendous war against the adversary's vicious legion, throwing them from the heavenlies.

A mighty angel turns to the angelic throng and souls throughout heaven. "Rejoice, O heavens and you who dwell in them!" Together, God's armies watch Lucifer fall as a magnificent star from heaven for good. "But woe to you, O earth and sea, for the devil has come down to you in great wrath, because he knows that his time is short!"

The dragon falls to the bottomless pit, where an infinite number of his demonic horde have been locked away for centuries on end. An angel of God illuminates the penetrating dark, holding a key and looking at the destroyer raging in vengeance. Satan takes the key and unlocks the pit as his hellish army, grateful to their master, shriek on their release, blackening the skies and filling the air with a heinous and incomprehensible evil.

Satan wings his way in fury to Jerusalem, where the wounded or dead are being recovered from the ruins left by the massive earthquake that toppled a tenth of the city, killing 7,000 people. To his horror, the two hated witnesses who were murdered here have risen from the dead and into the skies in front of the watching world. Lucifer knows that if he is to rule the entire planet there has to be one final bloodbath— Israel must be annihilated and the Jews destroyed so his enemy cannot return and reign from there.

The ruler of this world hovers above the city, listening as the swine below cry out in fear and watching as the body of Victor Quade is pulled from the rubble, his head bloody from a monstrous wound. Hearts are broken as news spreads throughout the globe that their hero, the very one who saved them from the devastating plagues and hatred of the two witnesses, appears to be dead. The evil one waits for two days as more cameras and phones are focused on the horror of Victor's wound and seemingly lifeless body before making his move.

Two thousand years ago, he entered Judas and, to his delight, Judas betrayed the devil's great enemy. Satan roared in triumph as his enemy died on a cross outside of Jerusalem, but the enemy rose in devastating victory and today he lives, and his people who reek of Satan's own end live as well. But now, for all eternity, they will die, and he will live forever.

With blackest rage he swoops down through the air and slithers into the body of Victor Quade, who has been laying lifeless for two days. Victor's eyes flash open, his mouth turns up in a smile, and the world gasps.

CHAPTER 2

Jerusalem, Israel

As chaos grips Jerusalem following the earth's shaking, many of the bloodied and wounded stand in awe of what they're witnessing. Victor Quade had been dragged from his hotel ruins two days ago and left lying lifeless atop the rubble. No one could survive such massive injuries; his body had appeared broken and covered with blood. The city had been gripped in fear and turmoil as citizens pulled bodies from the earthquake wreckage, and there had not been a stretcher or gurney available for the remains of Victor Quade, the man who had done more for peace than anyone in history when he confirmed a peace covenant with Israel nearly three-and-a-half years ago, bringing calm to the Middle East like never before. While antisemitism had been escalating throughout the earth, millions of Jews from every nation had immigrated to Israel, where Victor's peace covenant kept them safe. As part of the European 10 (or E10 for short) world governing body, Victor had promised hope, healing, and peace for the entire globe. Without him, what would happen to the planet now?

Following the tremendous assault on the universe, images and videos of volcanoes erupting, meteors falling, and some mountains crumbling and islands moving or vanishing from their spots shared screen time with pictures of this great man's mangled and bloody body. Victor Quade's gaping wounds had been shown on every screen throughout the universe as his corpse lay next to thousands more atop the city's ruins for the world to see and mourn. The globe had been covered in dark shadows as it grieved, and every eye had looked on in despair at his seemingly deceased form.

But from the shadows of death, a flash of his eyes and the twitch of a finger sets the Internet and news outlets ablaze. When Israeli prime minister Ari hears the crowd scream, he stops the interview he is giving with several international news correspondents and pushes his way through the wall of people, his heart pounding at the sight. Victor Quade, the man responsible for peace in the Middle East and for the rebuilding of the Jewish temple, is alive!

"Our Messiah," a woman next to Ari whispers through tears.

Several in the crowd hear her and begin shouting and crying. "Our Messiah lives!" "Our Messiah has come!"

Prime Minister Ari stumbles over the rubble to get to Quade, hollering for others to help. Amid the countless bodies around him, Victor rises to his feet by himself and walks to the street, stepping over the corpses strewn all over the ground. Prime Minister Ari falls before him, breathless. "Messiah!" He reaches for Victor's hand and begins to weep. Others clamor for him, reaching out to touch his clothes, while others burst into tears, unable to control their emotions.

Prime Minister Ari rises to his feet, shouting, "Our Messiah has come!" The prime minister lifts Victor's hand high into the air as the swarm of onlookers grows, pressing in closer, many of them sobbing. Finally, after centuries of waiting, the Jews' Messiah has arrived, and there are no words to express their feelings—only wailing and tears.

"Death could not keep me from saving you!" Victor exclaims over the sobbing and cheers. The sound is deafening as the people roar and celebrate with dancing, shouting, cursing, and crying.

Zerah Adler breaks through the throng waving his arms and yelling. He has been traveling through Israel and spreading the good news of Jesus Christ, who sealed Zerah as one of his 144,000 servants three-and-a-half years earlier, appointing him to preach all over the world. Zerah was present when the two witnesses were shot, lay dead for three-and-a-half days and then came to life again to rise into the heavens. He knew this moment was coming, the great time of deception when his own people would believe that Victor Quade was Messiah, and he has been spreading the word through the nation that the Jews must flee.

"Get out of Israel!" he shouts. "Victor Quade will murder all of you!" Many rush to attack him, but as they do so, they hit an invisible boundary that sends them tumbling onto the debris. "When you worship Victor, you are worshipping Satan! Do not worship darkness," Zerah hollers over the noise of their voices. "Worship Hashem, who raised his son Yeshua from the dead. Choose Yeshua Messiah and live! Get out of Israel now! This resurrection is a work of Satan! Go! Go! Go! Do not be deceived! Quade wants to kill you!"

Victor Quade smooths his hair, which is thick with dried blood, and brushes off his dusty and gore-splattered suit. To a world filled with fear and hopelessness he looks like a savior who has broken the bonds of death, a larger-than-life redeemer who will fearlessly guide them into the future. He walks over the rubble to a man whose arm hangs broken at his side from the earthquake. Victor gently puts his hand under the man's arm and the man cries out in pain, but as Victor lifts the arm higher and higher, it straightens as the bones seem to fuse back together. Victor raises the arm over the man's head and the man waves it, crying as he does. "Messiah," the man whispers, overcome with emotion as the eager mob presses in closer.

A woman with her child in her arms begins to break down as Victor steps closer to them. The mother removes the makeshift bandage on one side of the child's face; it has been mangled in the disaster and it appears that a cavernous hole resides where her eye once was. Victor places his hand over the little girl's face and whispers something that no one can hear. When he removes his hand, the little girl looks out at the crowd with both eyes, and her mother bawls as the throng around them shouts in praise at the miracle that has taken place.

"Do not be deceived by what you're seeing!" Zerah shouts over the roar of the masses. "Hashem warned us about Victor. He is the one who Adonai calls the lawless one. He is going to stop all sacrifices and set himself up inside the temple as Hashem. Hashem told us that his coming is by the activity of Satan with all power, false signs, and lying wonders. You are witnessing lying wonders! Quade's sole purpose is to deceive the world and to destroy every Jew. Listen to me! Get out of Israel!"

Victor touches the arms or faces of those around him as he steps to see Zerah eye to eye. "I know you," Victor sneers, his chest pounding with hatred for Zerah. "I remember the show you put on in Italy, but you don't seem to know who I am or what I will do to you. I will execute you as I killed those two maggots who lay sprawled here for days."

Zerah is small in comparison to Victor and the hoodie he is wearing is much bigger than his small frame can fit. "Unlike most of the world, I know who you are," Zerah says loud enough for those around them to hear. "I know all of your lord's ancient names. I know that he masquerades as an angel of light and you are his puppet. I know that your powers and the signs and the wonders that you do are from Satan to deceive those who will follow you. And I know that you won't touch me or any of Hashem's servants spreading the word of Yeshua around the world. You killed Hashem's two servants only because their time of prophesying was complete according to the work of Hashem. He breathed life into them, and today they live with him."

Victor is fuming, his face is flush as he begins to lift his hand to strike Zerah, but he stops. When being hailed as Messiah, he can't strike anyone just yet. He swears but keeps his voice low and his tone calm. "Get out of my country."

Zerah shakes his head. "This is Hashem's land. He has said of Jerusalem, 'I have put my holy name there.'"

"My holy name is here now," Victor seethes.

Zerah is unmoved. "As it is written, 'And the beast was captured, and with it the false prophet who in its presence had done the signs by which he deceived those who had received the mark of the beast and those who worshipped its image. These two were thrown alive into the lake of fire.'"

Victor's eyes blacken, and he shakes his head, laughing. He steps close to Zerah's ear so only he can hear. "You and all these Jew pigs clamoring around me are dead. You will see who has the real power."

"He is our god!" shouts a man in his mid-to-late forties with dark hair flecked with silver and wearing a white cassock, running up the temple stairs to Victor. He kneels before Victor and takes his hand, kissing it.

"You?" Victor says, looking at the man. "You turned the fountain waters red in Versailles. The E10 watched you perform many miracles. You created gnats from dust just as the two wicked sorcerers from here did. You stopped their curse of frogs from overtaking Berlin." He helps the man to his feet. "Your power is beyond impressive. What is your name?"

"My name is Ubel," he says, bowing low. "I was a misguided priest for many years, a stupid sheep blindly following a weak and powerless shepherd. From east to west and north to south, since the earth purged the hate from among us, I have been proclaiming you as our world's leader. I have been declaring that you alone can save us."

"I have heard you," Victor says, putting his hand on Ubel's shoulder. "You have been a faithful witness to my calling."

Ubel bows low again. "I flew here as soon as I heard that you were in the earthquake. Now that I see that you have defied death, I know that my proclamations have been true. You are our savior and god. You truly are our Victor." Ubel turns to the masses around them. "Our savior lives!" He raises his hand to the sky and flings an imaginary ball to the earth as fire falls from the heavens, leaping off the rubble. The crowd falls back, gasping at the sight.

Victor and Prime Minister Ari laugh in delight and Victor puts his arm around Ubel. "You will be very useful to my work, Ubel," Victor says.

"You are the holy one," Ubel says. "Everyone must know who you are." Victor claps him on the shoulder, and they walk together toward the temple stairs, stopping to heal the broken and wounded bodies lining the street. Frenzied cries and shouts echo in Jerusalem as word spreads throughout Israel and the world about the miraculous power that Victor Quade and his holy prophet possess.

Zerah follows after them, calling out to the pack that is pushing against Victor. "Look up to the sky!" he shouts as they press closer to Victor. He points upward to the swirling red and green auroras over their heads. "Hashem told us there would be wonders in the sky! Hashem wants you to look up to his incredible wonders and power, not to man's false wonders." The people ignore him, calling out to see more of Victor and Ubel's power. "Don't look to them," Zerah pleads. "Hashem tells us they are false and wicked leaders. Hashem says when you see standing in the holy place 'the abomination that causes desolation,' spoken of through the prophet Daniel—flee to the mountains! Victor Quade is that abomination!"

Very few are listening to Zerah as all of Jerusalem follows after their messiah and savior, weeping and wailing as they do. "Do not take anything out of your house," Zerah hollers. "If you are working, do not go back to take what belongs to you. Just run and flee and save your lives!" Some stop following Quade and listen as Zerah implores them to run. "Great sorrow is coming, unequaled from the beginning of the world until now—and never to be equaled again. Get out of Israel and call on Yeshua!" Victor stops and pivots, stepping nose to nose with Zerah. "The time is fulfilled," Zerah says to him without blinking. "And your time is short. Your end is at hand."

Furious, but aware of the throng pressing in on him, Victor nods at Ubel, and together they run up the temple stairs, waving at the watching world. As they approach the temple, the doors fling open by the power of their presence and the multitude shrieks in amazement. Victor leaps onto the wall and springboards to the roof of the temple, and the entire globe staggers in wonder at this miraculous phenomenon. He truly is god! Atop the temple, Victor raises his hands over his head in victory. There can be no delay; his plan must be set into motion at once, and Ubel will be his greatest asset.

CHAPTER 3

New Jersey

Twenty-eight-year-old Emma Perez stands outside the farmhouse assessing its damage with her husband Lerenzo and her friends Brandon and Kennisha, along with the children and adults who had fled New York with them. From reading Revelation, they know that the two witnesses would finally be killed in Jerusalem, and when God raised them from the dead, that the universe would come unhinged—and it did. The entire globe trembled, shifting mountains and islands and rolling the skies back like a scroll. Stars fell, the sun turned black, and the moon turned blood-red. They had read the Bible passages many times, but still weren't prepared for the terror of what had transpired the last two days. Though the sun is still shrouded as in dark gauze, Emma watches the clouds move rapidly overhead, racing from one spot to the next as God continues to use the wonders of the sky to keep people looking up.

Following her mother's disappearance and that of millions or billions of others on the planet three-and-a-half years earlier, Emma went on a desperate search for truth to discover what had happened. When her favorite physical therapy patient, Mrs. Ramos, vanished right in front of her, Emma had the sense to grab Mrs. Ramos's bag and run for her apartment. It was in that bag that Emma found a Bible and began her quest. She simply couldn't believe the TV pundits who were saying that aliens had abducted all those people or that the universe magically expelled them. There had to be something more, and when she began to dig through the pages of the Bible, she discovered the answer. Jesus had stepped into the air and called for all of those who were in Christ to come to him. The dead rose first (gaping holes in cemeteries around the world still prove that the dead were snatched away), and then the living were caught up with them to meet Jesus in the air.

It didn't take long for Russia and Iran to realize that the United States had been hobbled by the vanishings, and they bombed not only New York City but other cities across the United States. Along with China, they decimated the power grid throughout much of the nation, something these countries had longed to do for decades, leaving the United States crippled and gasping for breath.

Besides the initial call from Emma's sister, Sarah, in Indiana, saying that their mother had disappeared, Emma has no idea what has happened to her sister, who at the time was planning her wedding. Though much of Emma's and her friends' lives were spent on social media, online streaming, games, texting, and surfing the Internet prior to the vanishings, none of them carry a cell phone anymore. When many of the country's power grids were struck, electricity and cell and Internet service in most major cities were devastated. Emma has not been able to contact her sister since that great and awful day. She prays that Sarah, like she herself, has remembered their mother's faith in Jesus and has gone on a search for him and has learned that he is the one who snatched away all those who had placed their faith in him alone.

But Emma's search for truth following the disappearances and attack on New York drove an irreparable wedge between her and Matt, her fiancé. When Emma heard Elliott, one of Christ's 144,000 sealed servants speak of salvation in Jesus, she knew she had found the truth, and her relationship with Matt ended. He couldn't tolerate it anymore, but Brandon, her longtime friend, left with her. He, too, had found the truth of Jesus and left his boyfriend, Rick, who refused to believe. When they met Kennisha, whose sister and niece had been snatched away, they knew they had discovered family. They were a ragtag group of new believers, but their search of God's truth fueled their efforts to tell others about Jesus.

Micah was nine years old and alone on the street outside Emma and Matt's apartment window when Emma saw him. Despite her fear, she opened her door for the first time since the disappearances and took him in when his father gave him to her. That heartbreaking encounter inside that same apartment building led to her meeting Lerenzo Perez, the man who would become her husband. Together, they had gone on to live in a former church building in New York and used it as a harbor for kids who were being prostituted, trafficked, or simply left to fend for themselves. They renamed the building Salus, meaning "safety" and "salvation" in Latin, and with the help of countless believers rescued thousands of children off the streets. It was only when life at Salus and in New York had become too dangerous that the group fled for New Jersey. Many of their group were murdered as they were preparing to leave, and the horror of that memory still wakes Emma up in the middle of the night. In spite of losing so many of their team, Emma and the others continue to make daily trips into New York City to rescue any children or teens who are on the streets. They will do this until it is no longer possible.

Emma groans at the sight of the farmhouse that is folding in on itself. The second floor had nearly collapsed, and the earth around the home is pocked by craters from meteors that had fallen like stardust. Many of the trees look like charred matchsticks. It's only a matter of time before the second floor crumbles altogether, and Emma hates the thought of what this means. When they lived in New York, this New Jersey home had been used to plant a garden to help feed all those they were caring for in the city, and when the team fled New York, all 18 moved in here together. No one says a word as they take it all in.

Kennisha pulls two of the children close to her and looks upward into the sky at the dashing and darting clouds. "If only people would look up," she says, sounding as if she's muttering to herself instead of to the group. A scarf holds Kennisha's black hair back, making the lines on her dark almond skin more visible. Although only 32, the last few years have taken their toll. Prior to Jesus snatching away his true followers,

Kennisha was the first to spend a night out in search of a quick hookup, but since the mass vanishings, she has given every aspect of her life to being more like him.

"The air feels different," Emma says, stepping closer to Lerenzo.

"Satan's horde from the abyss have been let loose," Kennisha says, remembering what they've read from the Bible countless times.

Lerenzo realizes they need to do something, and says, "We can't stay here long. We all know what's going to happen. Soon, Victor Quade is going to make his mark a global policy. We won't be able to buy or sell anything without that mark. We'll have to keep moving in order to survive. And we may not survive. Not here on earth, anyway. You understand, right?" He looks at several of the children and they nod.

"We know," Micah says. "You and Mom have taught us that from the beginning." Emma turns quickly to look at Micah when he calls her Mom. Since she met Micah three-and-a-half years ago, his life has been upended. She never realized that this nearly 13-year-old boy thought of her as his mom until now, and she feels a catch in her throat.

"We're going to pray and ask for help and wisdom, and then we're going to get busy," Lerenzo says, reaching his arms out to pull them into a circle. They look at one another, and Emma feels like crying. She knows their time on earth is short, but Satan's is even shorter. God's kingdom is coming. This gives her comfort and courage, and she raises her voice with the others in prayer.

CHAPTER 4

Jerusalem
That Evening

Victor Quade makes the final adjustment on his tie inside the poshest hotel suite in all of Israel not affected by the earthquake. Prime Minister Ari had made sure this suit and everything in the hotel was the best in the land, and Victor smiles, looking at himself. Three generals with the Global Union Forces are inside the room as he finishes dressing. "The Global Union Forces will headquarter in Israel, and your main military facility will be here," Victor says, looking at the generals in the mirror and putting a gun in a holster strapped to him. "Israel built up the finest arsenal in this part of the world, and we will use it for our good. I want Israel surrounded. No one gets in or out."

"The Israelis cannot leave the country?" General Schmidt asks.

Victor sneers at him. "This is not *the* country, General. It is *my* country. And you seem to be under the impression that I don't want them to *leave* my country? Leaving is not the issue." He steps closer to the general. "I don't want them *living* in my country. Is that clearer to you, General?"

General Schmidt nods, understanding exactly what Victor means. "Yes, Sir!"

"The Jews are responsible for the earth's shaking that killed me. Their vile, wicked lives made the entire universe writhe in distress and I died because of them. How many of my citizens died amidst the rubble worldwide?" The generals don't have an answer. "Millions," Victor says, smoothing his hair as he looks again in the mirror. "Millions cannot worship me and live the life that I rose from the dead to give to them because the Jews killed them. So, because their wickedness killed my followers, we will kill them." He steps toward them and every drawer inside the room flings open and the walls move as if alive and breathing, making the generals uneasy and fearful as they become more aware of Victor's power. "I will play the role of their messiah for several days. They will be comfortable and complacent, and in time, you will begin annihilation."

The generals exchange glances. "Of the entire population?" General Lazenby says, unsure of what's being asked of them.

"Yes, General," Victor says. "Every swine in this country must die. They have terrorized my world long enough."

General Lazenby stammers, trying to find the words. "You want us to kill women and children and…"

Victor pulls his gun from its holster and shoots General Lazenby in the head, and he falls at the feet of Generals Bernard and Schmidt. "Yes, General. I want all of them dead. Any further questions?"

Victor puts the gun back in its holster, slips on his suit jacket, and walks to the door. Soldiers with the Global Union Forces have been waiting to escort him to the temple, and as they walk down the hotel hallway, doors sling open as Victor passes. The entire hotel buzzes with the voices of the masses waiting downstairs in the lobby and outside the doors, eager to get a glimpse at what they believe is their long-awaited messiah. Despite the fact that one-tenth of Jerusalem fell during the earthquake and that thousands are dead, even the wounded have dragged themselves here to glance at their savior. The elevator doors open, and the weary throng pushes in on Victor, blubbering and shouting at the sight of him. "Hosanna in the highest!" "Our Messiah!" "Holy one!" "Our redeemer lives!" Soldiers hold the crowd back as Victor smiles and waves, walking to the car waiting for him.

The temple priests have not been able to stop praising Adonai for what he has done, and they have set up the messiah's seat at the altar, awaiting his arrival. This seat has been prepared and ready since the temple was completed, and he has finally come! The sound of voices screaming outside the temple doors causes the priests to rush to see if messiah has arrived. Two of them throw open the doors to find Zerah standing atop the temple stairs and pushing back the massive assembly.

"Get out of Israel!" Zerah cries. "Leave your homes and flee! Victor Quade is going to slaughter you!" The clouds have disappeared from the skies and the sun bores down on the streets of Jerusalem, making tempers flare with greater intensity against him. The temple priests and many among the multitude attempt to charge at Zerah and remove him, but they can't get near him. "As it is written in Hashem's holy word, 'If anyone worships the beast and its image and receives a mark on his forehead or on his hand, he also will drink the wine of God's wrath, poured full strength into the cup of his anger, and he will be tormented with fire and sulfur in the presence of the holy angels and in the presence of the Lamb. And the smoke of their torment goes up forever and ever, and they have no rest, day or night, these worshippers of the beast and its image, and whoever receives the mark of its name.'" Zerah physically blocks the way through the temple doors, making it impossible for people to push past him—the supernatural seal and power of God on his life is too powerful. "If you receive the mark of Victor Quade, there is no turning back for you. There is no salvation. You are eternally damned! Do not enter through these doors and worship him. You will be worshipping Satan!"

The temple priests' animosity erupts against Zerah and the mob of worshippers turns violent, even fighting one another, but some begin to cry, listening to Zerah and running away in fear. The enormous throng curses and rails at Zerah. "You will not speak against our messiah," one of the priests says, his face twisted in anger. "You will be killed, just as those two false prophets were on these very steps."

Zerah looks at the priest, a man in his fifties who still bears wounds on his face and head from the earthquake. "You survived the earthquake," Zerah says. "But that was child's play compared to what is coming. The harvest of the earth is near, and if you worship Victor Quade, you worship the evil one, that ancient serpent, and you will be thrown into the winepress of God's wrath." Zerah's heart pounds with tenderness for this priest and the countless people in front of him. "Hashem's word says, 'Blessed are the dead who die in Hashem from now on.'" He raises his arm and points to the temple doors. "Do not enter this temple and worship Satan. You will die and be eternally separated from Hashem. Call on the name of Yeshua, and even though you die, you will live."

The waiting flock suddenly parts, opening a path for Victor Quade and Ubel, who have arrived. Zerah watches as Victor and Ubel approach. They are not walking up the stairs but levitating over them, and the throng of onlookers becomes excited at the sight. "Do not be deceived! What they are doing and will do are false signs and wonders! Listen to the word of Hashem," Zerah cries out. "When you see the abomination of desolation as spoken of by the prophet Daniel, set up inside the temple, flee to the mountains. He is here now! Just as Daniel prophesied. Get out! Get out!" Zerah can hear his heart pounding in his ears as many more turn and run away from the temple, while others aggressively push to get closer to Victor.

Stepping away from the temple doors so Victor and Ubel can enter, Zerah watches sadly as the priests direct Victor to his seat inside the temple. Young and old, rich and poor, wounded and healthy shove their way into the temple and fall to their knees as Victor is seated. Zerah feels a shiver down his spine as demons rush their way past him and through the temple doors to join them.

CHAPTER 5

New York City
One Week Later

T he man of lawlessness, who the apostle John called the Antichrist, has taken his seat in the temple in Jerusalem, proclaiming himself to be God!" cries out Elliott Hirsch to anyone who will listen as he pedals his way through New York City. Many residents are crying, others look gaunt, while still others curse and scream at the destruction around them from the recent shaking of the earth. Uprooted again from their burrows and nests, rats, foxes, and other animals scurry through the streets looking for food and new places to live.

"This is the time of great tribulation," Elliott shouts. "There has never been a time like this in history and never will be again! Jesus said that if these days weren't cut short that not even the elect would survive! Listen to me and live!" He stops pedaling as he reaches a group of 20 or so people.

Elliott has been doing this for three-and-a-half years as one of the 144,000 servants of Jesus who have been supernaturally sealed from every danger and evil as they proclaim the gospel of Christ. "Victor Quade has set himself up as God inside the temple in Jerusalem," he exclaims, looking at the weary and frightened faces around him. "The power that he has, the false signs and wonders that he and Ubel his prophet do, are by the power of Satan to deceive you. Look up to the sky." He points upward, then says, "Do you see those incredible colors? Do you see the planets hanging close enough for us to see them with our naked eye? The all-powerful creator of the universe is revealing himself to you, trying to get you to look up to him. Time is short. Jesus is coming back. Choose him and live, or choose Victor Quade and die. If you worship Quade, you worship Satan. Very soon, Quade is going to give you a choice. Take his mark on your forehead or right hand so that you can buy or sell anything during his reign." A man at the back of the crowd begins to use profanities and tries to talk over Elliott, but Elliott raises his voice to be heard. "If you take that mark, you are eternally damned. If you don't take the mark, you will live forever with Christ in his kingdom."

"There is no Christ!" the man yells. He appears to be around 30 years old and of South American descent, with thick, black hair and intense, dark eyes. "There is no kingdom!"

Elliott feels great sympathy for the man; he was an unbeliever just like him a few short years ago. "The fool says in his heart there is no Christ. That was me three-and-a-half years ago. I was a fool. I said Jesus was nothing but a man, a prophet. I did not believe he was Messiah and Lord, but then I met him, and I believe. I follow him wherever he leads me. It was Christ who warned us that these days would come. It was Christ who told us to call unto him for salvation. It was Christ who told us not to be deceived during this time. Do not be deceived," he says to the man. "Your life is over if you take that mark. You will be eternally separated from God, and the Bible says the smoke of your torment will go up forever." The man keeps his mouth shut and ponders Elliott's words. "Repent of your sins that separate you from God and declare that Jesus is Lord and live," Elliott says to the small crowd.

A few come forward, wanting to call upon Christ. Elliott leads them in a prayer of salvation, then pedals away.

He had said that same prayer with Jamie's children. On the same day that Emma and the others were leaving New York, Jamie had died at the hands of murderers inside Salus. It was Jamie's church building that Emma and her friends renamed Salus and had been using as a shelter to save and rescue children. Jamie's wife had left him shortly after the disappearances and taken the children to live with another man. They wanted nothing to do with Jamie, and Jamie's final wish—before he was killed—was for Elliott to tell them about Jesus, and Elliott had done as his friend asked. He smiles as he continues to pedal through the streets because one day soon, Jamie will see his kids again—this time, in the kingdom.

Jerusalem, Two Weeks Later

When Victor set himself up as god inside the temple, he stopped the daily sacrifices at once. "Your messiah has arrived," he said, his words broadcast throughout Israel, "and there is no longer any need to make these daily sacrifices. I have sacrificed myself for you once and for all." The Jews gladly gave up the sacrifices; their messiah was here!

The line of people from all around the globe who have made pilgrimage to here stretches down the temple stairs and through the broken streets of Jerusalem. The immigration of Jews from around the planet into Israel stands at an all-time high, with more pouring in daily. Shattered buildings lie in heaps and block the roadways, and although the sun beats down on the people, the queue continues to make its way around the rubble. These worshippers—comprised of Jews and non-Jews alike—are long-suffering because their savior sits inside the temple! No amount of heat or discomfort could stop them from seeing and worshipping him.

Inside the temple, a young Jewish father carries his wounded five-year-old son up to Victor and Ubel. The young boy's legs were broken in the earthquake, and his father and mother have brought him here to see their messiah for healing. With tears streaming down his cheeks, the father falls to the floor with the young boy on his lap. "Please," he says, as his young wife crumples to her knees beside him. "The hospitals are too crowded. Please heal him."

As Victor stands, the walls and ceiling of the temple move as demons shift in their places to watch. The mother and father shrink back for a moment as the walls appear to be alive, but they attribute the movement to Victor's power, and the father lifts his son toward him. Victor waves his hand over the boy, and his small body floats into the air for a moment, shocking the mesmerized bystanders inside the temple. The boy's mother begins to cry as she watches her son's body and legs, which had been dangling lifeless while in his father's arms, shoot straight out in front of him before the boy tumbles to the floor, where he stands on his feet. The walls and ceiling move as if panting; the demons are delighted at what has transpired.

The father and mother weep together. "Praise you!" she shouts, wrapping her arms around Victor. "Praise you! Praise you!"

Victor looks at Ubel, and Ubel steps to the mother, removing her arms from around Victor. "Please," Ubel says to the parents. "There are so many who want to see our lord." The mother and father continue to bawl, lifting their hands in worship as they exit the temple with their son.

"I can't sit among these leeches all day," Victor whispers to Ubel when he turns back to his seat.

"They want to worship you, Glorious One," Ubel says.

"As my global forces get into place, we must continue to prepare for annihilation, and I cannot do it while sitting here." Victor sits down and indicates with his finger for Ubel to bend down to hear him. "Put my image here as all gods have," he says. "Am I not the god of all gods?"

"You are, my lord," Ubel says. "There is no other god but you."

"Then create my image of perfection and place it here and before my people everywhere."

Ubel is giddy with joy. "Yes, my lord and king!"

Victor cringes as more of the Jews approach him. "Create my image, and we will call for a massive celebration," he whispers to Ubel. "Bring the Jews into the city from all over the world in vast multitudes to worship for a few days. The streets will swell with millions anxious to see their messiah. Like sheep led to the slaughter."

Ubel smiles. They are of like mind and spirit. "This will be my highest honor," Ubel says.

"Once the Global Union Forces are completely in place here, they will surround Israel, and the Final Solution will at last be carried out."

Energized by what he's heard, Ubel says, "You alone are god. You alone are the savior of this world, and we are nothing without you. If global citizens do not worship your image, they are not worshipping you and should not be afforded to live." Victor smiles at the thought. Ubel observes the line of worshippers. "I must get these pigs out of here and bring in all the news cameras to capture you performing your powers as you are worshipped."

Ubel runs to the temple doors and calls for the news outlets that have been waiting their turn to be ushered inside. He then urges the Jews standing inside the temple to move outside the doors so the entire temple can be filled with cameras and reporters. Then, one by one, Ubel brings in those who need healing or a sign or wonder to be performed. The cameras capture the lame walking and the blind seeing, and as Ubel calls down fire to surround Victor's throne, the Internet is set ablaze as the world sees their god in all his wonder, majesty, and glory.

CHAPTER 6

Rome, Italy
One Week Later

Adrien Moreau, George Albrecht, Maria Willems, and the remaining four members of the world's governing body, the European 10, and their aides sit at a table inside the garden loggia of the beautiful sixteenth-century Villa Madama, which overlooks the Vatican precinct. The E10's former offices located inside the Palace of Justice were destroyed when the universe shook and toppled much of the building. Adrien, the former president of France, was lucky to be pulled from the rubble alive. He has a broken arm and the wounds on his head are wrapped. Though he still felt weak, he was anxious to come back to his work with the E10. According to the global news networks, three members of the E10—President Banes of the United States, Sophia Clattenberg of Great Britain, and Bruno Neri of Italy—had all tragically died from food poisoning just a few weeks earlier. But the truth is that Victor had poisoned them so he could ascend to power without their interference.

The E10 members rise and applaud wildly when Victor and Ubel enter the room. The walls and furniture shake and the faces on the fresco on the ceiling shift and change, jolting the members as they watch the painting move above them at the presence of Victor. "So good to see you, Victor!" exclaims George Albrecht, the former chancellor of Germany. "We all…"

Victor ignores George and walks past him, slinging obscenities. "Who moved us to this location?"

"Most of the city center has been reduced to rubble," Maria says. Her weary voice betrays that she has been exhausted by the terror of the last few days. At 40, she is the youngest member of the E10, but the last three-and-a-half years have taken their toll, and she looks years older. "There was so much destruction within the city. This building sustained only minor damage, so the generals with the Global Union Forces thought this was a secure location for meetings."

Victor looks around the room and up at the stunning painted ceilings before marching back outside. The others follow him and stop as he looks at the view before them. The moon is clearly visible in the midday sky and the winds are high today. Since the mass vanishings, the weather has been unpredictable and impossible to forecast. Many of the trees and much of the vegetation have been scorched as with fire. The trees' trunks and limbs are charred black, having been burned by meteors that fell during the tempestuous shaking of the earth.

"What is that?" Victor asks, pointing to buildings seen in the distance.

"That's part of Vatican City," Adrien answers.

Victor is infuriated and turns on all of them. "Why aren't we there!"

An aide, a young man in his twenties, stumbles for an answer. "It's the Vatican, Sir."

"Where is a throne found in Rome?" Victor fumes. "In this dump?"

"No one meant any disrespect, Victor," George says. Now 71, George is the oldest member of the E10. He's overweight, and the stress over all that has been happening wears on his face.

Victor steps up to George and stares at him. "Why do you call me Victor, George? Are we friends?" George opens his mouth to answer, but Victor talks over him. "We are not friends, George. I am your sovereign." George's heart feels as if it is throbbing through his chest as he nods at Victor. "And where does an emperor sit?" Victor asks.

"On a throne," Adrien says.

Victor dips his head in agreement. "I ask you again: Where is a throne found in Rome?"

"In the throne room at the Vatican," Ubel says, answering for everyone. "The only place suitable for you, my lord and emperor."

Victor addresses the aide beside him. "Make it happen."

The Pope had died weeks before the mass vanishing, and several cardinals had gone missing during the mass disappearance, but many still remained inside Vatican City. Knowing this, the aide stammers, "But Sir, there are still cardinals and priests and…"

"And who do they worship?" Victor snaps. The aide does not answer quickly enough. "Are they still down there worshipping their pathetic Christ?"

"I don't know, Sir," the aide says haltingly.

"Remove them all. They will no longer occupy the thrones they've grown accustomed to in their fat, lazy religion. The days of their land grab are over. Their riches will end."

The aide's voice is shaking, and he clears his throat to calm it. "There are some very elderly priests and cardinals who…"

Ubel raises his hand and the aide cowers to the ground, held there by an unseen power. "They may stay if they worship our emperor and savior. Otherwise, they must die," Ubel says, stepping up to the whimpering aide. Members of the E10 stare at the aide, who is unable to stand, and realize it is this power that has enabled Ubel to take on such a position of authority.

"Tell them that I am not the Christ of their miserable faith," Victor says. "I am not weak. I do not let people string me up on a cross. I am not a sniveling failure. I am nothing like him. I am against everything he was. I am anti-Christ in every way. And tell them that if they continue to worship their Christ, they will be exterminated like the rodents they are." The aide stands to his feet and nods. Victor shouts at him, "Now! Move!"

Victor then ushers Ubel and the members of the E10 back inside the villa to watch the world news. Three rows of four screens are stretched across the loggia, and members take their seats as aides begin to highlight certain news stories from across the planet. Victor's attention is directed to a screen filled with images of war, and he can hardly believe what he's seeing. "What is happening? Where is that?"

"That is in Indonesia," says General Sarpara. The general directs

Victor's attention to other screens. "These wars have broken out in Pakistan, India, Singapore, and Myanmar."

"All military commands come from me," Victor says, watching the screens. "And I have commanded peace throughout the universe. Why are they at war?"

"For most of their histories, these nations, as well as some in Africa, were under European rule, and according to our intelligence, they have no intention of coming under foreign rule again," says General Sarpara.

Victor's anger bursts and he stands to his feet, cursing. "Are they waging war against me?"

"No declaration has been made," the general replies.

"But your intelligence proves they are conspiring against my reign?" Victor hisses. General Sarpara nods, and Victor is incredulous. "They are at *war* against my Global Union Forces?"

"This is what we believe, Sir," says the general.

Victor's furor explodes. "Annihilate them," he says, working hard to control his voice.

"Sir?" asks the general.

Victor sits back down. "Nuke them, general!"

"That would mean devastation on those lands and people," the general says. "It would mean a global war."

"It would not be a war," Ubel says. "A war means that there are nations fighting against one another, but our news sources would not tell such lies. Our news sources would only tell the truth. Do you understand?" General Sarpara nods as Ubel continues. "The universe wills out those who are most loyal, pure, and true and eliminates those who are traitors to our lord. So, if anyone dies, it will be made known through our global news services that the universe is once again purging the wicked from among us. That will be the reason for their demise. Not rumors of war. Understood?"

"Yes sir," General Sarpara and members of the E10 say in unison.

To discover more about the biblical facts behind the story, read Where in the Word? *on page 225, or continue reading the novel.*

CHAPTER 7

Rome, Italy

Victor points to a screen filled with at least 100,000 Muslims inside the Istiqlal Mosque in Indonesia, who are bowing on prayer rugs. "Would someone like to explain what they are doing?" he asks, keeping his voice low.

"The Muslims have been establishing their caliphate since the mass cleansing of the earth three-and-a-half years ago," Maria says. "As you are aware, we have been keeping an eye on the caliphate's spread, but their ideology is not dangerous like that of Christianity."

Victor watches the screen without replying to Maria before shifting his gaze to another screen filled with thousands of people inside a stadium in Brazil. He exhales with force, "Is that another Jew who is speaking against me?"

A lone man is on a stage at the center of the stadium, holding a Bible and talking to the crowd. "Jesus said, 'I am the way and the truth and the life. No one comes to the Father except through me.' Jesus is the only way to life with the Father. You will die if you worship Victor Quade. Call on the name of Jesus today and be saved!"

Another screen features a Jew in Istanbul who is inside the Hagia Sophia preaching to Muslims, and another screen shows a Jew in Baltimore, Maryland, preaching in what's left of Oriole Park at Camden Yards. Victor listens as the man speaks. "My name is Elliott. I am a Jew and a follower of Jesus Christ, who said that now there will be great tribulation. The Bible says woe unto us because Satan has come down to us in great wrath because he knows his time is short. Do not be deceived by Victor Quade. You have a choice. Call on the name of Jesus and live, or follow and worship Victor Quade and die."

Victor's facial muscles tense up hard as flint as he listens to Elliott.

"Why are those Jews still out there and speaking against me! Why aren't they all dead, General?" He directs his comments to General Locke. "Why isn't that cockroach in Israel dead?" he asks, referring to Zerah. "Every time I turn around, he's there!"

"We continue all efforts to eradicate these men without success, Sir," General Locke replies.

Pointing to the screen filled with thousands of Brazilians crying out the name of Jesus, Ubel speaks up. "What do you have in your arsenal that can destroy that stadium, General?"

General Locke is not certain of what Ubel has asked. "Sir?"

"Execute those people," Ubel says.

The general hesitates, and Victor smiles in delight. "Now," he says calmly.

The general makes a telephone call, and they all wait, watching the screens in grueling silence for several long minutes before the entire stadium is struck and collapses on itself; plumes of ash rise silently to the sky. No one seems to be breathing among the E10 as they watch the mushroom cloud expand.

"They will no longer worship their false god," Ubel says with great satisfaction.

But the pleasure is short-lived. "What is that?" Maria asks, pointing to the screen. "There! Right there!" They all watch in fascination as the man who was telling everyone about Jesus walks out from amidst the dust and ash. "He's not dead," Maria says. "He's not even limping or covered in dust." She glances at the others around the room. "It's impossible."

Victor is incensed and shaking as the man walks away from the bombing site. He jumps from his seat, watching as the plume above the stadium continues to rise. "I have put up with them long enough! They will not speak against me any longer. They will not worship another savior. There is no other savior! I alone am god! I want those Jews who are preaching against me and every Jew in the world dead." He looks to the generals. "It is now time to wipe every Jew off the planet. I've put up with their whining and thievery and condescension for centuries."

The members of the E10 assume Victor is exaggerating when he uses the word *centuries*. After all, the Jews who had been preaching the name of Jesus and warning against the E10 had been doing so for only the past three-and-a-half years.

Victor points to the Jew on the screen from Brazil. "They are destroying my planet and turning my followers against me. Those animals are stinking up my world and must be exterminated. Israel belongs to me! Not them. Everything they have belongs to me and must be taken." The members of the E10 heartily agree. They have had far too many meetings about the problem of Israel, and now was the time for action.

"These meetings where the Jews are preaching against our lord will no longer take place," Ubel says, rising from his seat, his voice controlled and full of strength. "The emperor and I have had many meetings, and no one will set foot in any public arena without bearing our lord and savior's name on their bodies. The spread of Christianity will stop. The spread of Islam will stop. We will bring a swift and sudden end to the caliphate." He walks around the room, looking each member in the eye. "Our lord is the only one to be worshipped and praised." He addresses the five generals with the Global Union Forces. "No one will buy anything without having our emperor's name or mark. That will determine who is true to our lord and who is true to the other false teachers and prophets."

"Yes, Sir!" the generals say in unison.

Ubel walks behind Victor, who is seated at the head of the table. "Victor is lord and emperor. He is god. No mortal man rises from death as he did. No mortal man brings peace as he does. He is no mortal man. He is not their insipid Christ," he says, referring to the screen of the bombed-out stadium in Brazil. "They *died* worshipping him. Those who worship our emperor, lord, and savior of the world will *live*." He pauses, letting the words sink in for the team of scientists and researchers who are standing along the wall behind Maria and George. "I know great strides have been made in hybrid intelligence in recent years. Is it capable of incorporating some of our emperor's DNA for the mark?"

The team of researchers nods. "More than capable," says a scientist with thick black hair and an Indian accent.

Victor smiles at the thought as Ubel steps up to General Sarpara. "I will work with our emperor's researchers in developing the mark, and then the Global Union Forces will work with my office and administer Emperor Victor's name or mark to every human being on the planet."

"Yes, Sir!" General Sarpara says.

"Does this please you, my lord?" Ubel asks, his head bowed before Victor.

Victor seems drunk with delight. "It is beautiful and as it should be. We cannot be united in one world if I am not somehow inside each person. My consciousness will be theirs. It will no longer be I…but we. We will be one. Brilliant, Ubel!" He opens his arms to members of the E10. "Look around you. Look around the world. God is dead. But I am alive and worthy of all worship."

Ubel kneels before him. "That is why we praise you, our emperor and lord." He stands and speaks to all those in the room. "We will make the proclamation to the earth's citizens, and they will watch as we become the first to receive our savior's mark. We must lead the way to unity."

Victor raises his hand, and they all look to him. "And the world will no longer refer to you as the E10. Each Roman emperor in history had a court, and you are mine. My kingdom, Victor's Empire, has come, and this will be our finest hour. I am no longer leader of the E10; I am your sovereign and lord." The demons are beside themselves at Victor's words, and the walls tremble and the faces on the ceiling fresco shriek in pleasure.

There is a moment of terrifying silence before George rises from his seat and walks to Victor, kneeling down before him and kissing his hand. Adrien, Maria, and the rest of Victor's court and the generals and scientists all kneel before Victor and praise him as emperor and lord.

The members of the court gather their computers and miscellaneous files and belongings and head for their vehicles. Victor and Ubel exit the building as well and step into the back seat of an armored Maserati Quattroporte, and Victor smiles. His image will be worshipped as god inside the temple in Jerusalem, and he will reign as emperor of the world from his throne in Rome.

CHAPTER 8

Jerusalem
Two Weeks Later

U bel works with a team of 22 scientists and researchers from
Israel and around the world to test advanced 3-D telepresence
and other technology that has been utilized to create a human-like
image of Victor Quade inside the temple. The men have been without
cell phones and closely monitored by soldiers with the Global Union
Forces to make sure that no one communicates with anyone outside of
the temple walls. If this works as they hope, the image will look, move,
and sound like Victor, bringing complete awe for every person who
comes here on pilgrimage.

"No screen!" Ubel told them on the day of their arrival. "I know
these 3-D images need a screen, but I will not allow it."

"New technology has been developed in recent years," said a scientist from the United States. "You'll be amazed…"

"It's not about me being amazed," Ubel said. "I don't want any
smoke and mirrors. When people enter those doors to worship our
emperor and lord, they must *believe* they are worshipping him."

Ubel watches the team work today as one of the scientists spear-
heading the hybrid intelligence marking system approaches him.
"What is it, Doctor?"

"We have exciting developments to share with you, my prophet.
When you are able to come to the lab, we can demonstrate."

Ubel smiles. "Has it been tested?"

The doctor nods. "With positive results, my prophet. The test subjects can feel our emperor and lord's presence within them."

This news is spellbinding to Ubel. "To have our lord and emperor inside our mortal bodies! Imagine the power, the strength, and the wisdom each of us will attain." He pats the doctor's shoulder. "I will be there soon." The doctor hurries out the door, and Ubel claps his hands in victory. Everything is turning out more beautifully than he imagined. He is fascinated by the work being accomplished inside the temple.

Nearly 300 projectors have been hidden to achieve a 3-D effect from any angle, and a see-through screen using technology that has been perfected in recent years hangs from floor to ceiling and wall to wall. Unable to understand the full science behind the system the researchers have created, Ubel stands in amazement, anxious for the first test to be run. He stops pacing when the lights get brighter and a 3-D image of Victor Quade appears in front of his throne.

"It can't be," Ubel whispers, stepping closer to the image and gasping as the image's eyes lock onto his. "How did you do this?" he asks, breathless as he studies the image. "This looks just like our king. It is incredible in every way. Truly unbelievable!" He claps again in wonder, and the team of researchers cheer and laugh together at what they've accomplished. "Weary pilgrims will come inside and take our lord's mark, which will fill them with his presence and enable them to live." He reaches out to touch the lifelike image and laughs at the beautiful magic of it all. "And then this image will bring them to a place of complete rapture."

"We are perfecting the system for movement and for our king's voice," one of the scientists says. "That should be completed by…"

Ubel waves his hand in the air to dismiss the rest of what he's saying. "Come!" Ubel says, spreading his arms over his head and summoning demons. "Come and fill our lord's image with power and strength!"

The team of scientists and researchers are shocked into silence as the image of Victor wakes to life and sits down on the throne like a human being. It curses, and the team explodes in cheers and laughter. It sounds just like Emperor Victor.

"How?" one of the scientists asks as they gasp at what they're seeing.

"It is the power of our lord," Ubel says, smiling.

CHAPTER 9

New Jersey

Emma, Lerenzo, Brandon, and Kennisha sit at the table inside the kitchen of an abandoned home. It is less than a mile from the collapsing farmhouse, and it is far too small to hold 18 people. The shortwave radio sits on the table and they listen to news that is coming from somewhere in Africa. The connection is broken and hard to understand, and they all lean closer to the radio to make out what the announcer is saying. "Men, women, and children are sold daily as slaves throughout the globe. Vicious sexual attacks against women and children are common in the streets."

What they had seen during the last three-and-a-half years was already unthinkable, but with the demonic forces released from the abyss, the plague of sexual immorality is on a scale the world has never known. Children and teens who have been abandoned or separated from their family are often seen for sale on street corners or in store windows. Believers like Emma and her group put their lives on the line when they walk into nearby towns or back into New York City to attempt a rescue. While some rescuers have died, many children have been saved and placed into the care of believers who are running here and there to survive. In addition to violence against children and teens, women are attacked and violated openly in the streets. Emma became sick one day as they passed a store window displaying images from around the world.

Global Union Forces members were shown violating women, laughing and bellowing at what they were doing. Nothing is restraining evil anymore, goodness is gone, and wickedness is celebrated.

"Global Union Forces continue to fire nuclear weapons on India, Pakistan, Indonesia, Singapore, Kenya, Nigeria, Myanmar, and Uganda in order to force universal recognition of Victor Quade as emperor and serve him as sovereign," the announcer says. "After centuries of oppression at the hand of European rule, these countries will not bow again to foreign power. The death toll mounts in cities and villages, and lands are devastated. Earthquakes shake our world daily, and hurricanes, typhoons, cyclones, tsunamis, and tornadoes destroy property and lives across the…"

The signal goes dead, and Lerenzo knows what has happened. "Victor's government stopped the transmission," he says. "His global news media won't report any of these things. Quade doesn't want the world to know there are wars against him."

"Global Forces are dropping nukes," Kennisha says. "Much of those countries will look like New York City." Her face is grim as she pictures what is happening to countless lives inside those countries.

A signal begins to return to the shortwave radio, and Brandon adjusts the dial to pick it up better. "Victor Quade would not let death keep him from helping you, all you citizens of the earth." Emma and the others don't recognize this voice.

Ubel is standing on the temple stairs in Jerusalem and talking to anxious Jews who have lined up to worship their messiah inside the temple. Many Jews have already left Israel, leaving behind their belongings and family members when Victor Quade set himself up as god inside the temple, but the majority have stayed to worship their risen messiah. News reporters from across the world swarm around Ubel, broadcasting his words throughout the globe.

"I am Ubel, our lord's holy prophet."

"The false prophet," Brandon says, looking at Emma and the others around the table.

"Our lord was the only one able to end the lives of the two abominable parasites who brought curses on the entire world from here," Ubel says, referring to God's two witnesses who had preached from Jerusalem for three-and-a-half years before Victor had them killed. Ubel speaks with a passion that strikes awe in many who hear him. "Our lord then defied the grave in the devastating earthquake that struck Jerusalem and rose up from the darkness of death so that each one of us could be saved! He is our victor and lord! Let it be known on this day that when you step into the temple to see him, you fall in worship, for there is no one like him on the face of the earth. Each home is required to have a photo on the wall of our lord to worship. Images of our redeemer will be placed throughout the world. If you live on the streets, you are commanded to find such an image each day so that you may worship and live. Worship of our beautiful savior brings life and hope to our dying spirits and the world."

Emma glances at the others. "Worship of Quade brings life. We know where this is headed." Lerenzo squeezes her hand as they listen.

Ubel waves his hand in the air, and a powerful breeze blows over those all around him who are listening. The crowd mutters in astonishment at his power. "When you do not worship our emperor and lord," Ubel says, "you bring darkness upon yourself." He moves his hand again, and clouds cover the sun. Once more, the people are amazed at his supernatural abilities. "The worship of Christ and Mohammed and all other false prophets has ended," Ubel continues. "They have proven themselves to be liars and charlatans and darkness cannot dwell with light. Their dark and wicked deeds will be purged from the earth as the reign of our savior of light shines forth. Our spirits need life, and worship of our god brings that life and light." He waves his hand again, and this time, fire lashes down around those surrounding the temple. Many applaud at the greatness of his remarkable power, making Ubel smile. "Choose that light and live today. You will lose your life when you do not."

Brandon exhales as he listens to Ubel. "We're dead men walking," he says.

"We're dead men living," Kennisha says, correcting him. "Even in death, we're the ones who will live."

CHAPTER 10

Victor City, Italy
Two Days Later

Built on top of what once was the gardens of Emperor Nero, Vatican City sits on about 110 acres and includes renowned buildings like the Sistine Chapel and St. Peter's Basilica, built in the fifteenth and seventeenth centuries, and has been home to the Roman Catholic Church since the building of a basilica in the fourth century over what was thought to be St. Peter's grave. The entire city was given over to Victor Quade without a whimper, and along with the city of Rome, it is where he reigns as emperor and rules the world that is desperate for a savior.

Some cardinals were killed when they refused to worship Victor as God, but most of them remain on the grounds, proclaiming Victor as their new lord. Victor renamed the city after himself, and inspired by Amsterdam, Bangkok, Tijuana, New Orleans, and other cities celebrated for their debauchery, the city is being refurbished or rebuilt throughout. The best of the world's engineers, architects, carpenters, and designers are working around the clock to create the preeminent city on the planet. Only the finest restaurants and retail stores will be allowed, and posh hotels are being designed for the world's elite and celebrities who will consider it their greatest honor to be invited to Victor City. Erotic theaters, casinos, and bars that will sell the hardest of liquor and drugs will be alongside elegant retail stores with adult and child sex workers in the windows. Only the most attractive people in the world will be allowed to work inside Victor City, even in the windows.

The members of Victor's court and their aides live in the finest homes in Rome and have the best of the world brought to them through the city's port, which is being enlarged in order to conduct all the world's trade from Victor's seat of government. The slave trade is being routed through the port as well, making it the hub for this all-important business. Men, women, and children are bought and sold here for servitude or sex and shipped all over the globe. The world's economy will be controlled from Rome, and only the most brilliant minds in banking, trade, agriculture, goods and services, transportation, and industry will live and have their offices here.

Since Victor's rise from death and arrival, the entire city of Rome has had its own resurrection as the city hums with life again. Thousands upon thousands of workers have transformed it, and theaters, restaurants, bars, sports arenas, sex entertainment venues, the finest retail and grocery stores, and television and movie studios are up and running again. The globe's rich and famous are flocking here to purchase or build their dream home and be closer to Emperor Victor, who is often photographed with the world's most beautiful and influential. There is no greater honor than to have your picture taken and seen with Victor Quade's arm around your waist or shoulder.

Victor has chosen to live inside Rome's largest mansion, complete with 16 bedrooms and 21 bathrooms. The home was taken from a billionaire and his wife who stood aside as Global Union Forces stormed in and forced them to leave. It is also being refurbished with several more rooms added at Victor's command, but he doesn't conduct the affairs of the world from here. He makes his orders and proclamations from what was once the Pope's throne room in what is now Victor City. Hundreds of workers labored nonstop to quickly overhaul the throne room to his specifications. They had worked tirelessly to eradicate all symbols or names relating to Christianity—within this room, throughout Victor City, and over all of Rome. All crosses, religious paintings, and Bibles have been burned.

As Victor took his throne for the first time in a ceremony broadcast everywhere, he quoted in part from what King Nebuchadnezzar had said when he ascended the throne in ancient Babylon. "This house that I have built will endure forever," Victor said to deafening applause. "I will be satiated with its splendor and live forever therein, and receive tribute of my subjects of all regions, from all mankind." The six days of celebration and raunchy debauchery following his announcement were livestreamed around the world for all his subjects.

Victor stands at his throne and admires the entire room, which has been transformed to represent the kingdom of his lord, Satan. Several of the demonic forces unleashed from the abyss perch on the walls or hang from the ceiling, ready at Victor's beck and call. He waves his arms in the air, and the walls roll and ripple at the sound of his voice. In a room that was once filled with the presence of the Pope and his cardinals, hundreds of Victor's global reporters stand with their equipment and cameras and marvel that the walls are alive in the presence of Victor.

"Welcome once more to my throne room!" Victor says, smiling. "You are always welcome here!" He motions for everyone to be silent. "Please. Please quiet down." Looking at Ubel, he nods, ushering him forward. "You have heard him, but I have failed to properly introduce to you my prophet, Ubel. I know you are familiar with his extraordinary powers; you have seen him turning waters to blood, healing the sick, causing the wind to blow, or calling down fire, but you have not met him." Victor puts his arm around Ubel. "Ubel lived a life of deception for decades, but he has been healed. His brain is now whole. He knows who the true savior of the world is."

The reporters cheer for Ubel's great awakening, and he waits for them to stop before addressing them. "I was deceived for so many years as I followed the Christ of my misguided faith," he says, looking into the cameras. "I thought he had power—healing power, saving power, but he had none. He was weak. He did not come down from the cross. He died there in his weakness.

"Prior to King Victor's resurrection, I had been traveling throughout our sovereign's world and proclaiming his strength and might, and now it my greatest honor to join him personally as he leads us all. Our emperor is the anointed one and the savior who will redeem this earth. Our allegiance is to him." The reporters whoop and holler, and the mouths of the goat heads hanging on wall mounts twist and elongate as if screeching in agreement. "Today, our great king Victor and I declare that the false worship that has generated from this city for centuries is destroyed and cleansed from the earth. It will no longer use our emperor and lord for its purposes, and it will no longer flourish." The reporters cheer again. "In the same way, the Islamic caliphate has ended by order of our supreme one. There is only one who is worthy of worship, and that is our glorious and beautiful one. The one risen from the dead so that we may live."

"All praise to King Victor!" a reporter shouts from the back of the crowd as the others join in the glorification of Victor.

"All praise to our great king!" the reporters shout in adoration.

"This governing body decrees that anyone caught worshipping any god other than our glorious one will be executed," Ubel says. He turns to look at the screen at his side, which shows footage being broadcast worldwide of Christians being killed. Images follow of Muslims tearing down their mosques and removing their hijabs, ghutrahs, and other such clothing. Victor appears in several videos as Muslims in Indonesia and Pakistan now bow to worship Victor with looks of joy on their faces. Ubel grins as he watches. "Such beauty!" He turns back to the reporters and cameras. "Do you see what happens when we are of one mind and spirit? Look at the joy on their faces." He points to the screens featuring the ecstatic and jubilant crowds that follow Victor and worship him. "Only our lord and savior Victor can do that. Only our king can bring us together in one true religion. There is no one good but him. All praise to our great god and king!"

Noisy chatter and applause fill the room, and Victor stands straight and proud as the hundreds of reporters bow before him.

"Emperor Victor," says a reporter near the front. "O great king…," he stammers, looking down at the notes in his hand and trying to find the right words. "The entire globe is still reeling from the massive earthquake that shook your great world and from the meteors that caused irreparable damage. There is word now that wars have broken out against you in India…"

Victor puts up his hand to quiet the man. "We cannot be filled with such fear." His voice is calm, and his eyes beam as he answers the reporter. "How will we be one world if you speak these words?" The man nods, realizing his error. "There are no wars. You are hearing lies. All those in my kingdom—everyone on my court—will only tell you the truth. The shaking of the universe did some damage, yes, but look at us. We are all here and healthy. And those who perished did so only because they were not strong enough to survive. All this is as it should be. We are the strong ones. We are the chosen who are thriving here."

He steps down from the throne and walks to the man. "Did you know that…" he pauses to read the reporter's nametag and puts his hand on the man's shoulder. "Darius? Do you realize that you are a chosen one?" Victor says as his eyes change from blue to black and his face changes shape. Taken aback, Darius doesn't respond, and Victor squeezes his shoulder. "The universe shook out the weak, the liars, the hatemongers, the vile, and the wicked. Remember, the universe spoke to us after the mass vanishings a few years ago. Do you remember that, Darius? The universe told us that we were the chosen ones and was pleased with us. And the universe is pleased once more with us." He pats Darius on the shoulder. "With *you*, Darius. The chosen." Victor walks back to his throne to think for a moment, then extends his hands toward the reporters. "I give all of you chosen ones my peace. All who call upon me will be saved."

A delicious idea comes to Victor, and he motions for the reporters to step over the line behind which they were to stand, to come ever closer to him and his throne. "This is strictly off the record," he says, leaning close to those in the front. "And for your ears only—my most trusted communicators." He rubs his hands together, then holds them open to the reporters. "In your hands, you hold my power of information.

The entire planet looks to you to share my hope, my peace, my plans for our amazing world. My truth can come only through you. The evil, the lies, the fraud, and corruption must be blocked in any way. Only my truth that comes from my kingdom and as reported by you can be placed on the Internet or aired on television or radio. You are my most important truth givers, and today I bless your work.

"Now, this next part is on the record and needs to be spread far and wide. Everyone throughout the globe must deny, suppress, block, and completely censure any news or information that is not from me or this kingdom. We cannot tolerate such thoughts, as they will divide us and not unify us. We must be guided by one thought only." Victor's eyes twinkle and the massive group hangs on his every word. "My government is already pulling down Internet sites that promoted the heretic Jesus and all other false religions, and we need all of you to stop, condemn, and tear down any that we miss. Those who do not comply will be severely punished. We all must work together to ensure that our thoughts are one. There is no other way that we will have true peace and security." Pondering once more the reporter's question about war, he adds, "Now let's stop spreading fear and proclaim the hope of salvation that comes to our world through me."

When the reporters cheer in unison that Victor is lord and fill the throne room with raucous noise, the demonic spirits seize their opportunity to enter in and possess each one of them.

Ubel raises his hand to say something and bows before Victor before doing so. "Our god lives! Salvation comes through our great lord and king! And that salvation begins today." More whoops and hollers swell inside the throne room and Ubel lifts both his hands in the air to quiet them. "For far too long, our world has been divided by different government and economic systems working in competition with one another. For the benefit of our world, our emperor's citizens must be able to do all their buying and selling with ease and in a manner that promotes peace and unity. We have the finest economic minds from around the globe, along with the most brilliant in advanced technology, and we are ready to implement our economic system to keep the planet running efficiently. Our emperor's government is already making the planet a better place; this will further put the burden of peace and security on our lord's shoulders and take it off yours."

Ubel steps forward so the reporters can see what's in his hand. It is a small device that looks something like a pen, and he's holding it as if it were something precious and holy. "These are already available in some parts of the world and will be more widely distributed in the days to come." He holds it up for all the reporters to see. "This is hybrid intelligence. It is the wonder of nanotechnology and biotechnology combined. Our emperor and lord's own DNA is in each of these. When you take his name or mark, it will be visible on your forehead or on your right hand. Why the forehead? Because it reveals to others that you have the mind of our lord and that you are wise. Why the right hand? Because that is always equated with power, and when you take our lord's mark, you will have the power to do whatever you want. Freedom is yours. Our sovereign's mark will be visibly seen on your body, and he will also be coursing through your veins. He will breathe life into your spirit and fill your heart. He is the head, and we will make up his body. When you take his name or mark, we will all be made up of one another. We will complete each other. Through this oneness, we will achieve great and impossible things for our world. Our spirits, our consciousnesses will be able to interact at any time. This mark will not only enable you to buy and sell, but will make all humanity of one mind and one spirit!"

The reporters are enthralled by what they're hearing, and Ubel's words ring as they are broadcast throughout the earth. Ubel nods at Maria, and she steps forward. "Again, each citizen will take our lord's name or mark on their forehead or right hand. It's your choice. And then you will be one with our Victor and lord."

Ubel demonstrates the use of the device on Maria's right hand, which leaves Victor's name permanently branded on the back of her hand. Her head and back jolt backward in a moment of ecstasy as the mark seems to take possession of her, and she turns her hand and proudly displays it for reporters to snap a picture or film video. She is now one with her lord.

All the members of Victor's court receive his mark, and together they stand in unity, holding up their hands or pointing to their foreheads and smiling as pictures are snapped and uploaded all over the world.

CHAPTER 11

Jerusalem
Five Days Later

An estimated two million Jews flood the streets of Jerusalem as they wait to see what they believe to be their messiah inside the temple for the grand celebration. Each Jew who comes out of the temple is in tears after having worshipped and praised their long-awaited redeemer. During the last few weeks, millions of Jews from around the world have been immigrating to Israel, and it seems that every Jew in the country is in the streets today.

The atmosphere is noisy and brimming with life; music, songs, and laughter bathe the formerly earthquake-stricken streets with joy. It took around-the-clock efforts, but all the rubble was removed in time for this dreamed-about day. Coordinated celebrations are also happening in Tel Aviv, Haifa, Rishon LeZion, and Petah Tikva, with enormous street parties in honor of the messiah who has come at last for his people! The clouds overhead look like fluffy purple and pink cotton balls, and the moon hangs opposite the mid-morning sun, begging people to look up at the wonderment above them. Soldiers with the Global Union Forces are passing out water, popsicles, or ice cream to every person.

Prime Minister Ari sits inside his office with several cabinet members as a news conference from Rome begins to air on the TV in the background. The prime minister and his cabinet have been exhausting themselves, working hard to clean up and bring relief to Israel following the earthquake in preparation for this day. The prime minister's face reflects the strain and exuberance they have all experienced in recent days. All talk in the room ceases when the prime minister raises his hand upon hearing the voice of Victor Quade.

"Israel has proven to be a whore," Victor says.

Prime Minister Ari and his cabinet look at each other with alarm. "That is not our messiah," the prime minister says. "It is artificial intelligence. Our messiah is inside the temple right now for the celebration. Find another channel," he directs one of the aides. The channel is switched to the same news conference out of Rome, with Victor sitting on his throne.

"It can't be. He is inside the temple!" Ari says, trying to piece together what he's seeing and hearing.

"The Jews are a blight on my world," Victor states plainly. "We have received proven intelligence that these predators not only caused the earthquake that killed me in Jerusalem but have started an uprising and incited violence against me, my forces, and citizens all over my planet." The prime minister and his cabinet members look stricken, and a few can't catch their breath. "You have seen some of these Jew dogs preaching against me and citing the false prophet Jesus," Victor says. "Wherever you hear them preaching, they must be stopped by any means possible. Their propaganda of lies and hate must be dismantled at once.

"As for the whore Israel and the Jews within my country there, I know what they have done and what they are planning. They are instigating terrorism against my peaceful reign and have already killed more than one-hundred thousand unity-loving citizens." The prime minister, becoming pale and feeling lightheaded, grasps the arm of his chair so he doesn't fall over. "They are extremely dangerous, and their deadly rampage must be destroyed before more of us, the innocent ones, are murdered. It is now our goal to rid the world of Jews altogether in order to usher in real peace." The prime minister realizes that Jerusalem is filled with massive crowds of Jews who are surrounded by Global Union Forces soldiers. They are all trapped, with no way to escape.

"Before my kingdom was established," Victor says. "Roman emperors and world leaders through the ages worked tirelessly to scourge the known world of the problem of the Jews. They all failed. I will not. Because the Jews have declared war against us, the peace deal that I confirmed with Prime Minister Ari and Israel three-and-a-half years ago is now void, and everyone is free to end the plague against us by killing a Jew."

The prime minister suddenly recalls Zerah's urgent pleas for the Jews to flee Israel. He jumps to his feet. "Get out!" he shouts to his cabinet. "We must get out of Israel now!" Lunging for the door, he flings it open and is seized by a soldier with the Global Union Forces. Several other soldiers run into the room and grab the cabinet members. The soldiers drag them screaming down the stairs and into the street, where their executions are livestreamed onto the Internet.

When word reaches Zerah on the other side of Jerusalem, he runs through the streets, yelling, "Get out of the country! Go to the mountains!" He then sees a large truck filled with soldiers approaching the temple, and he races after it. As it pulls to a stop in front of the temple, soldiers carrying rifles pour out the back and run up the temple stairs. "They're going to kill you!" Zerah shouts, waving his arms and breaking through the throng. "They have executed the prime minister and his cabinet! They are going to slaughter all of you! Get out of the country!"

Fear seizes many in the bloated streets and they panic as they realize what is happening. But soldiers, who are stationed everywhere, step forward to grab and stop Jews who are trying to escape. Women and men scream in horror as they are dragged up the temple stairs and forced to their knees. Those who are Jewish are shocked and horrified at what is transpiring, but many of the pilgrims from around the world who are here to worship Victor are spellbound and step forward to get a better look.

Soldiers pull all the priests from the temple and thrust them to their knees. "By order of our Sovereign, Emperor Victor," one of the soldiers says, loud enough for the enormous throng to hear, "all Jewish vermin must be purged from his land."

Zerah falls to the ground at the top of the temple stairs and pleads to his fellow Jews who are on their knees. "Call on the name of Yeshua," he shouts above the noise. "Call on Yeshua!" The soldiers then fire and shoot all their victims in the head, and many in the crowd scream in terror. But many others cheer, whooping and shouting at what they've seen.

Chaos grips the city as the Jews realize what is happening, and everyone stampedes through the streets. But their attempt to escape is impeded by something darker and more sinister. One by one, the Jews fall to their knees, then sprawl out on the ground, foaming at the mouth. Terror seizes Zerah as he realizes everyone has been poisoned through the water, popsicles, and ice cream that the soldiers had handed out. He stumbles down the temple stairs, shouting. "You are dying! Call on the name of Yeshua for eternal life!" Many drop dead where they had been standing, while others linger, the poison slowly stopping their hearts. This scene is repeated in Tel Aviv and the other cities, with people succumbing to the venomous toxin, their bodies falling to the confetti-strewn pavement.

"If any Jews survive, bring them to us!" a soldier atop the temple stairs yells to the mob of onlookers.

Zerah watches in horror as the pilgrims who had been waiting in line to get inside the temple begin to run through the streets of Jerusalem, looking for Jews who had managed to survive the poison. They are giddy, eager to drag anyone they can to the firing squad. Jewish merchants are dragged from their shops and their store shelves emptied as people rush in to loot the goods. Jew after Jew is pulled forcefully to the temple, kicking and screaming for their lives.

Helicopters then fill the skies over Jerusalem, Tel Aviv, and the other cities. Machine-gun fire rips through the crowds, killing Jews and travelers alike. In Jerusalem, Zerah shouts at the top of his lungs for every Jew to escape. And all over Israel, the sound of wailing is heard as Emperor Victor's dream of a world without Jews is carried out.

CHAPTER 12

Singapore

The transmitter is powering up and a thin, wiry young man plugs in the microphone before sitting down in front of it. The room is stark and only a small crack of light makes its way in beneath the dark curtains. He will begin his broadcast as soon as the transmitter comes to full power, and as usual, he will call himself "John," but that is not his name. Prior to the mass vanishings, he worked in cybersecurity intelligence. When thousands of architects, engineers, construction workers, designers, and security experts from around the world flew to Italy to transform the Vatican grounds into Victor City and to rebuild Rome, many of them had become awakened to who the Bible says Victor is and what he was going to do to the world.

Victor had demanded that a massive number of surveillance bugs and cameras be installed throughout Victor City, at his palace, and in the buildings and streets of Rome. Security experts like John had worked countless hours making this area the most heavily secured on earth. But at the same time that the bugs, cameras, miniature drones, and other means of surveillance were installed for Victor, hundreds more were secretly hidden inside the walls and furnishing of the throne room and Victor's palace by Christ followers. These rogue bugs and cameras relayed information to a secret hub in Rome, where someone resent it to others throughout the planet—others like John—who would then relay that information under the cover of darkness.

The transmitter is ready, and John speaks in code, knowing that only followers of Christ will understand. "The Revelator says Dragon is spewing water out of his mouth like a flood against the apple of his eye. The fig tree is breaking under the weight. Loser has made war with the saints, and doves are taking flight to the skies by the thousands each day." His words are carried around the earth to those eager to hear what is really happening in the world. "For life beyond the pale, say no to Mark. He's a killer. Keep watch. Things are looking up."

John unplugs the microphone from the transmitter and puts them inside his backpack before leaving the empty room. He will not use this location again.

New Jersey

Emma looks ashen as she, Lerenzo, Brandon, Kennisha, and the other adults in their group finish listening to John's transmission. "Loser has to be Victor, right? Doves are taking flight," she says, her voice trailing.

"Doves represent the Holy Spirit," Kennisha says. "He must mean believers. They're taking flight. They're being killed all over the world."

"A flood coming against the apple of his eye," Brandon says, looking at each of them. "The Jews are being murdered by the masses."

Victor's global news services never report what is really happening. All they do is spread Victor's propaganda, and Lerenzo looks as troubled as the others as they realize what is taking place elsewhere. "Victor must have broken the peace deal with Israel and is now wiping out the Jewish people."

"And everyone agrees with him," Emma says. "The entire world will come against Israel. Just as it's written."

"But Victor's reign is short," Kennisha says. "His time is running out."

Brandon turns the dial on the transmitter and stops when he hears Victor's voice. "My intelligence directors from around the world have assured me that there are no longer followers of Islam, but there continues to be followers of the false prophet Jesus. I reiterate that, in addition to the Jews, all those who follow this false god must be killed. Our world cannot tolerate the hate generated by the Jews or the fraudulent religion of Christianity. I have warned you about their lawlessness before and warn you again: Watch out for those Jews who go from place to place preaching about this wicked Jesus. Find these cockroaches wherever they may be, and slay them and all those listening to them."

"It's true," Emma says, her voice shaking. "He's broken the peace covenant with Israel and is directing that all Jews and Christians be killed."

"Don't, Emma," Kennisha says, looking at her across the table. "Don't dwell on any of us being killed. We should dwell on those who don't know Jesus. We know where we're going. We will be with Jesus. They are doomed without him. We can't focus on ourselves."

Emma nods. "I know. But the Bible says this will continue for three-and-a-half years before Jesus sets foot on the Mount of Olives." Her voice lowers. "That's a long time."

Lerenzo puts his arm around Emma and kisses her forehead. "We've said it before and will continue in faith to say it. When we die, we will see the face of Jesus instantly. Elliott always says, 'I'll see you soon.' We know that. If one of us dies, we'll see him or her soon." They are quiet for a moment. Of course they all know that, but the terror of the coming days weighs on all of them.

"Lerenzo and I have looked through our supplies and food and believe we have enough to last a month, maybe six weeks," Brandon says, changing the subject. "And that's if we eat only one small meal a day every couple of days."

Emma looks at everyone around the table and is as concerned as each one of them. "Then we need to find more food and supplies."

Brandon tries to smile at his old friend. He had worked for years in the publicity department of a publishing house in New York City and had never imagined he would find himself in what he would have considered a science fiction plotline. He has been hungry, fought off assailants, buried friends, and helped rescue abandoned or trafficked kids for the last three-and-a-half years, a far cry from his former life. "It was difficult to find food and supplies before, but now it's going to be next to impossible," he says. "If we live with Christ eternally, we don't take Quade's name or mark. Without that mark, we can't buy groceries or supplies. We can't fill the car with gas, get a job, rent a house or apartment, buy medicine, clothes, or anything else. We have to get more food and supplies in here without actually buying anything."

"And local authorities or someone with the Global Union Forces will be coming by at some point to give us the mark," Kennisha says, verbalizing what everyone is thinking.

"We need to keep moving," says Lerenzo. "We can't stay in one place too long. With whatever time we have left, we have to continue to get out into the streets and tell people to worship Jesus, not Quade. We have to keep rescuing children, and in order to do that, we need to split up into smaller groups. We've got eighteen of us. That's too many people to move quickly."

The thought of breaking into smaller groups is heartbreaking to Emma. They have known and worked with one another for most of the time since the vanishings. But they know it's impossible for a group of 18 to stay together in Victor Quade's world.

Kennisha opens her Bible and turns to John chapter 16. "This is what Jesus said. 'I am not alone, for the Father is with me. I have said these things to you, that in me you may have peace. In the world you will have tribulation. But take heart; I have overcome the world.'" She pats the Bible in her hand. "No matter how far apart we may be in the coming days, Jesus has overcome this world, and we can too. Revelation 12 says, 'They have conquered him by the blood of the Lamb and by the word of their testimony, for they loved not their lives even unto death.'" Her eyes fill with tears. "I will keep telling others about Jesus because that is my testimony. I have life only through him. We keep telling and telling and telling people because that's how we overcome—even unto death."

Emma knows that Kennisha is right, and a sad smile crosses her face. They will keep telling people about Christ and they will keep rescuing children from the street—even unto death.

> *To discover more about the biblical facts behind the story, read* Where in the Word? *on page 233, or continue reading the novel.*

CHAPTER 13

Modiin, Israel
Three Days Later

Zerah travels throughout the country, screaming for Jews who have gone into hiding to leave, and there is nothing the Global Union Forces can do to stop him. It is physically impossible for anything to kill him. Since Emperor Victor broke the peace covenant with Israel, nearly four million Jews have been killed. Thousands more have been rounded up and thrown together into packed cages in the sun so they will starve, and others have been put into overcrowded semitruck trailers. Once the doors are closed, poisonous gas is leaked into the truck's trailer to kill them, and then the bodies are discarded in mass graves. Many Jews have fled Israel, but there are countless numbers still left inside the country, hiding and waiting for an opportunity to escape.

As a hailstorm rages, Zerah flings open the car door and bolts for the front porch of his mom and dad's home. The door is locked, and he pounds on it before digging in his pocket for a spare key his mother gave him years ago. He places the key in the lock and turns it, opening the door and bursting into the home. He flicks on the lights in each room as he stumbles through the house. He has prayed countless times that they have escaped, and shouts as he rushes down the hall. "It's Zerah! Are you home?" He looks into each bedroom before running to the door for the bomb shelter and flings it open. "It's Zerah," he hollers, running down the stairs. The room is empty, and Zerah races back upstairs. He steps onto the landing and notices a large piece of bright-green paper taped to the refrigerator. Zerah approaches the refrigerator and quickly reads the words:

> Zerah, we hear the mountains are particularly nice this time of year. Headed there with your dad, Rada, and the grands! We will see you soon! Matt 2416

He yanks the paper off the refrigerator and his eyes fill as he reads the words again. It's his mother's handwriting, and she references Matthew 24:16: "then let those who are in Judea flee to the mountains." They have heeded the words of Jesus and fled, even his father. The last time Zerah saw his dad, he had stormed out of the house in unbelief. Zerah doesn't know whether his father believes that Yeshua is Messiah, but he has left Israel and will be safe in the mountains. He prays that his dad will come to know Yeshua just as his mom, sister Rada, and her children know him. Zerah reads the note again before folding it and putting it in the back pocket of his jeans. How many have fled Israel? How many are still here?

He heads out the front door, not bothering to lock it, and despite the falling hail, stands in the middle of the dark road. "Leave Israel now!" Zerah yells, his voice echoing over the sound of hail drumming on cars and rooftops throughout the neighborhood. "I know that some of you must be hiding inside your homes. The locks on your doors will not keep you from being killed. The Global Union Forces have surrounded the country to murder you."

By the street's light, Zerah notices the curtain trembling at a window in the home across from his parent's house. A man's face appears, and Zerah recognizes him as the young father who moved in only a short time ago. "Don't pack anything," Zerah shouts. "Don't wait for this hail to end! Go to the mountains." He knows that every Jew understands this means to run to the mountains of Jordan, because the mountains of Israel crumbled at God's command when Russia, Iran, and Turkey carried out their massive invasion attempt several years ago.

"Don't stop for anything! Just run." A look of fright crosses the man's face, and he disappears from the window. "Don't take your cars," Zerah continues. "Victor's forces are stopping anything that moves. Whoever is left here, I know that you can hear me! Come out of your homes and flee Israel right now. I know it's dark, but you must do it. Victor Quade wants all of you dead. Come out and go to the mountains!"

One door opens down the street, and Zerah watches as an older man peers out into the darkness. It is old man Cohen, who has lived on this street since Zerah was a boy. "I am an old man, Zerah," he calls over the noise of the hail.

Zerah rushes toward him. "But you are alive, and you will continue to live if you flee to the mountains of Jordan. Don't take anything with you. You will be taken care of. Leave right now." The old man's eyes appear anxious as he looks at the hail pounding onto his driveway and Zerah knows what he is thinking. "You can't wait! My parents are there, Mr. Cohen. My sister Rada and her children. Please go!"

The old man's hands shake as he grips Zerah's hands in his. "I have always liked you, Zerah. I will see you soon, yes?"

Zerah smiles. "Yes. Very soon!" He watches as the young man and his wife and children from across the street quietly leave their home. As they do so, the father nods at Mr. Cohen. They will make this journey together through the hail and rain. "There are people who will help as you get close to the border of Jordan, but you must be very careful. Global Union soldiers are everywhere." The young family and old man sneak away into the night, and Zerah continues to shout as he walks along the street, banging on doors for the people he's known most of his life to leave the country they all love.

CHAPTER 14

Victor City, Italy
Two Months Later

Emperor Victor has returned from a triumphant two-month world tour that was unlike any in history. Millions upon millions lined the streets around the planet to catch a glimpse of and raise their hand in the symbol of victory to their emperor as his motorcade passed. Pictures were plastered all over the Internet and on the global news of Victor with the best of society proudly showing off their mark from inside boardrooms, plush homes, yachts, theaters, and businesses in France, Spain, Japan, India, and Hong Kong, proving to the world that food, pleasure, peace, and riches are still in abundance under his reign and with his mark. Videos show Victor praising his followers and commending how they have been unified as one world as they continue to rid the planet of Jews and Jesus followers.

Surrounded by Ubel and his court inside his throne room, Victor sits on his throne and watches with great pleasure the images replayed from his victorious tour. As usual, many of the demonic throng from the abyss cling to the ceiling and walls, ready for any command from their lord.

While Victor was away for two months, throngs of workers had descended upon Victor City to transform it. The Sistine Chapel had been painted and converted into a restaurant with live entertainment and mediums who conjure the dead. St. Peter's Basilica had been refurbished into a casino and strip joint, and St. Peter's Square was renamed Victor Square and now features an enormous statue of Victor seated on a throne with horns protruding from his head. The statue's goat-like arms reach out in a welcoming manner so passersby can lay themselves in his arms or put their children in his arms, as if sacrificing themselves or their children to him. Many claim to "feel" Victor indwelling them after doing this and can be seen twisting or wriggling on the ground in a state of vile euphoria, which attracts others to sacrifice their lives in the same way.

All of Rome bustles with depraved energy. Statues of Victor are set up throughout the city and often move as if alive, and the demonic horde can be seen on rooftops, crawling along the sides of buildings, and roaming the streets. Demons loosed from the bottomless pit look to possess those who follow Victor, giving those people greater power and strength. Extravagant shops litter the street selling all sorts of sensuous depravity as well as hard liquor and drugs to customers from all over the world. And the planet's most renowned flock to this celebrated yet wicked city, anxious to indulge in the evils now rampant in the empire.

While on his tour, only the most famous and wealthy of the glitterati were photographed with Victor. They stand in stark contrast to the impoverished inhabitants of desolate villages and neighborhoods all across the globe. Many forests and hills have been scorched by fire, blackened and utterly destroyed, but there are still areas in which many trees are strong and vibrant. Every patch of grass around the globe is dead, including here in Victor City. In many countries, people are desperately trying to protect their property from thieves, or rushing here and there and fighting for survival. "We would not see these images if people weren't burdened with property of their own," Victor says. "Ownership causes a great burden and puts enormous strain on my planet."

Ubel heartily agrees. "What we are witnessing is the idolization of things and of property instead of a pure and holy worship of our lord." He stands to get closer to the screens. "Without the burden of ownership, the people of your kingdom would finally be able to truly live unencumbered."

"The earth and all that is in it belongs to you, O lord," Maria says to Victor, smiling. "We should willingly give all that we have to you." Maria sits on the governing board of the entire world and holds more authority than any other woman on the planet, but it isn't enough for her. She has tried many times to seduce Victor, but to no avail. He constantly dismisses her, and his blatant rejection of her is an ongoing embarrassment. His time and effort are dedicated to building his global power and dominance; he has no desire to take time for her or anyone else.

Victor waves his hand toward the screens. "All this fighting over property ends today. For the good of the universe, there must be no more private ownership. We shall tie this in with my mark. Citizens who bear my mark and will put their trust and faith solely in me. Their lives, property, belongings, children, everything will belong to me and this will bring them tremendous happiness." Victor's eyes gleam. This is a wonderful idea.

"It is our greatest pleasure to serve you, my lord," Ubel says.

Victor and Ubel are lost in this marvelous revelation when George says, "Why is all the grass dead?" He leans forward in his chair, confused by the images he's seeing. "And what killed some trees but not others?"

"Obviously it was a beetle of some sort," Adrien says. "Or some other pest."

George scoffs. "The same pest all over the world?"

"What happened to them?" Victor asks, looking at a small team of scientists who have been brought in to advise.

A Japanese man who looks to be in his sixties with short-cropped salt-and-pepper hair and glasses speaks for the assembled scientists. "We believe that in certain countries and those surrounding them that one possibility is from nuclear fallout from the war that is..."

"There is no war, Doctor," the emperor says, correcting him. "There is no nuclear fallout. No countries have been using nuclear weapons. Isn't that right, General?" Victor looks at General Abar.

The general is put in an impossible situation. Victor has already killed two generals since coming to power; the first was General Lazenby in Jerusalem, and just three days ago, he had killed General Locke, who had dared to talk about the war Egypt and other countries were raging against the Global Union Forces. General Abar knew this war was still going on—just this morning, Pakistan had dropped a bomb on Global Union Forces stationed in the United Arab Emirates. But to save his own life and those of the other generals in the room, he nods in agreement. "All nuclear weapons have been disabled since your reign began, my lord," the general says.

Emperor Victor stares at the doctor until the doctor looks down at the papers he's holding. "So, we know that nuclear fallout is not even a remote possibility, Doctor. Now, what is your explanation for the dead trees and grass?"

The scientist's hands tremble as he studies his notes. "Our findings indicate that the burning was most likely caused by super flares," he says, his mind racing for something to say that sounds plausible.

"From the sun," the emperor says, his voice rising in excitement.

"From stars larger than the sun," the scientist says, recalling data from previous solar flares. "With much stronger magnetic fields. There have been some stars that have unleashed 10,000 times the power of the strongest solar flare ever detected."

Victor looks at the images of burnt trees and grass on the screens. "And these stars that did this had 10,000 times the power?"

The doctor fumbles for the right words and shakes his head. "We have not yet been able to calculate the power from these super flares, but we will. From what we have observed," he says, thinking quickly on his feet, "these super flares have not only burned the trees but their entire root systems as well."

"And I assume there is no root system to the grass," Adrien says.

"None," the doctor says.

"And without grass, the livestock will not be able to…" George begins to say.

"We know what a lack of grass means," the emperor says, interrupting him. "Get this information out to my media right away," he says to the generals. "My world must know that it is super flares from stars that has destroyed so many of the trees and all the grass. I don't want anyone to succumb to deception. Everyone must know my truth. For it is my truth that sets them free."

CHAPTER 15

New York City

Emma, Lerenzo, Brandon, and Kennisha canvas the streets of New York City in the hopes of finding any children who have been abandoned or are being prostituted or trafficked. Child trafficking was already a scourge in the time prior to the mass disappearances, but in the years since, the problem has festered into an ever-worsening plague. On top of that, women have been taken captive in growing numbers and are being sold as if they were little more than cattle.

Since leaving New York City for the farmhouse in New Jersey, the streets have become far more desperate. Fear and constant panic have a chokehold on the city. Walking through the Bronx, their eyes search all alleyways for children and teens who may be hiding and storefronts that may be used to sell them. Brandon and Kennisha agree to take one street as Emma and Lerenzo search up and down another.

When Emma and Lerenzo discover a boy around 11 or so cowering in an alley, they run up to him. "Hi," she says to the boy, who reminds her of a young Lerenzo. He is huddled among boxes and bags of garbage. "I'm Emma, and this is my husband, Lerenzo. We help kids on the street find a place to live where you can be safe. Are you alone?"

The boy shifts his eyes from Emma to Lerenzo and doesn't respond. "Are you hungry?" Lerenzo asks. The boy nods, and Lerenzo reaches into his backpack for a few crackers with peanut butter on them and hands them to him. "Are you alone out here?" The boy gobbles the crackers, then looks down.

"What's your name?" Emma asks, crouching down in front of him.

"Antonio," the boy says, wary of her and Lerenzo.

"Are you thirsty, Antonio?" He nods, and Emma opens her backpack, but doesn't find any water. She looks up at Lerenzo. "Do you have the water?"

Lerenzo checks his backpack, then shakes his head. "We must have left all of it with Brandon and Kennisha."

Emma sighs. She can see that Antonio is starving. "When is the last time you've eaten or had anything to drink?" He shrugs, and Emma stands up. "There's a market around the corner," she says, hesitating at the thought.

Lerenzo shakes his head. "No, Emma. What if they're checking for the mark?"

"I don't think they're doing that here yet. I haven't heard a word about it. None of us have. We drove into the city without any problems."

Lerenzo thinks for a moment, then says, "Let me go. You stay here."

Emma steps close to him, keeping her voice low. "I can't protect him like you could. I can buy a couple of waters."

Lerenzo hates this idea but nods. They could all use some water out in this sun. "If anything looks suspicious, get out of there right away." She nods, and he kisses her forehead.

"I'll be right back," she says to Antonio.

Emma passes retail shops and restaurants that have long since been looted and gutted. A block later, she turns the corner, and a market stands on the other side of the road. The street is busy with cars and pedestrians, and she scans it for any Global Union Forces soldiers or anyone else who might be administering Victor Quade's mark. Everything looks clear, and she prays for protection as she crosses the road.

Entering the market, Emma is alert for anyone who looks suspicious, and heads to the back, searching for bottled water. Ahead of her, Emma sees a man reaching for a bottle of water from what used to be a refrigerated cooler. With the exception of a few stores with generators, refrigeration hasn't been possible since the attack on the city. As the man turns around, Emma gasps.

"Matt!" she cries out. She hadn't seen her former fiancé since the vanishings. After she became a follower of Christ, Matt could no longer tolerate her or the name of Jesus.

"Emma," he says, surprised. His once-toned frame is thin and scrawny. "How are you?" he stammers, hardly believing he is seeing her again.

"As good as anybody can be right now," she says. "I'm married. I met Lerenzo in Micah's apartment building. You remember Micah. He's thirteen now."

Matt nods. He had wanted Emma to get rid of Micah because he was somebody else's problem, not theirs. "Wow," he says. "You're married and you have a teenager. That's great, Emma."

"We've had hundreds of children over the last few years," she says, talking fast; she feels so nervous to be around him again. "We help rescue them from the street, tell them about Jesus, and find homes for them. I came in here for some water because Lerenzo and I found a boy around the corner." She pauses, feeling awkward and knowing she needs to get back to Lerenzo and Antonio. "What have you been doing since all of this…" She finds herself at a loss for words, unable to describe the nightmare that their city and world have become.

"Well, you know that law school ended with the bombing," he says. "I go from job to job, and…" He trails off, and Emma knows he feels as strange as she does. "I didn't treat you well, Emma." His eyes are filled with kindness; Emma remembers the gentleness that had attracted her to Matt all those years ago but that ended when Jesus snatched up all those who were his own. Matt's heart had become like stone against her and anything pertaining to God's Word. "I shoved you away, and I've wondered so many times about what happened to you…about whether you were even alive. I'm sorry for everything that I…"

The smell of sulfur floods the store, and harsh words spoken at the front cause Emma and Matt to stop and listen. Matt peeks around the end of a display and can see two large beings who appear to be humanlike but aren't. His blood runs cold when he sees them, and he puts his finger to his lips, indicating for Emma to stay silent.

"Yes…yes, I own…I own store," the cashier says in broken English.

"You need our sovereign's mark to stay in business," one of the creatures says, his voice a heart-stopping combination of human and beast.

"Yes, yes! I know," the man replies, holding out his right hand. "I need my store. I own, I own." He nods toward his right hand, and one of the beings holds up a device that will brand Victor's mark onto the store owner's hand.

Matt turns quickly to look at Emma. "You need to get out of here," he whispers. "They're giving the mark."

Her eyes are large in fright. "You need to get out too. Don't take that mark, Matt! I tried to tell you about this before. Remember? You can live if you claim Jesus, but that mark means eternal death! You'll live if you claim Jesus, Matt, but if you don't…"

He shushes her and grabs her by the shoulders. "I'll go this way and knock over a display. You'll need to run."

"No, Matt…"

"Run back to your husband, Emma!" he whispers, cutting her off and running up the far aisle. He pushes over a display toward the wall while screaming, and the beings turn their attention to the noise. Matt continues to scream, and Emma runs for the door when the creatures approach Matt. She races out of the store and dashes around the corner, stopping against a wall and breathing hard. As people hurry past her on the street, she glances around in search of Matt and is filled with terror when she sees the beings, who she realizes are fallen angels from the abyss, drag him into the street. They are big and powerful; their faces are twisted in agony and the smell of decomposing flesh emits from them. Cars and pedestrians all come to a stop, and Emma is unable to take a breath as they force Matt to his knees.

"Is Victor Quade your Sovereign?" one of the dark angels asks, holding Matt's arm behind his back.

"No," Matt groans in pain.

"Will you take his mark?"

"No! I claim Jesus Christ as my Lord!" Matt yells, loud enough for everyone around him to hear. "Jesus is life and Victor Quade is death! Jesus is my Lord!"

The dark creature twists Matt's head, breaking his neck, and his body falls to the pavement as many people scream in fright. Emma covers her mouth in shock and feels like she'll pass out, but she can't take her eyes off Matt's body and the demonic beings beside him. Some people flee after witnessing what had just happened, but many line up to take Victor's mark.

Emma stumbles toward the alleyway where Lerenzo and Antonio are waiting. She is gasping and feels as though she will collapse when she sees Brandon and Kennisha approaching. "Brandon!" she yells, falling to her knees. Brandon and Kennisha head toward her, but Emma rises to her feet and runs toward them, shouting and pointing, "Run that way to the next alley!"

They dart into the alley together and Emma bends over, on the verge of throwing up. Lerenzo rushes to Emma's side. "What happened?"

"We have to get out now," she says, her breath coming out in ragged gasps. She looks at Lerenzo. "I just saw two fallen angels kill Matt, the man I was engaged to."

"What?" Brandon cries out, feeling sick over the news of his murdered friend.

"Matt was in the market," Emma says. "We talked for a few seconds, then smelled this rotten, sulfur smell. It was from them. They came into the store checking to see if people had Victor's mark. Matt made sure that I got away from them, but they killed him in the street." Her voice shakes, and Lerenzo wraps his arms around her. "I saw them do it."

"Could you hear anything, Em?" Brandon asked. "From Matt? Or from them?"

"They asked if he would take the mark, and he said no. He claimed Jesus as Lord."

Emma's eyes fill along with Brandon's, and he smiles. "Then we shouldn't cry, Em. He didn't take the mark. Matt is with Jesus now."

She had been so traumatized by Matt's death that she hadn't yet processed what had happened. "He claimed Jesus," she says, her voice soft and full of emotion. "I never thought he would believe. He was so hard and against anything I said about Jesus."

"Maybe it happened at that moment, when he realized that two demonic beings had hold of him," Lerenzo says. "Or maybe he was already a believer because you and Brandon had planted the seeds. Whatever the case, he's safe now, Emma."

Kennisha extends her hand toward Antonio, who looks frightened. "Come on! Come with us. We have to get out of here." The boy nods and jumps to his feet.

Tears would come every time Emma thought about what had happened to Matt, but comfort would follow when she remembered Brandon and Lerenzo's words: Matt was with Jesus and was safe now.

CHAPTER 16

Victor City, Italy
Three Months Later

The doors fling open for Victor as he enters his throne room. The members of his court, who are seated upon thrones, drift into the air, and the walls move in waves as Victor sits on his throne. Court members love the surge of power they feel when they levitate into the air, feeling as though they are highly exalted above the rest of Victor's kingdom. Demonic creatures cling to the ceiling and the walls, and hover throughout the room. As the court floats back down to their seats, they turn their attention to the screens around them, which feature videos from Victor's second world tour. He is more popular than any other leader in human history, as evidenced by the millions who wait hours in the streets to worship him as he and his soldiers parade by. Women weep upon seeing him and men and children cheer, lifting their hands in the symbol of victory to pay tribute and honor to Victor, their king.

At each rally, thousands who could not squeeze their way into the arenas stood outside, with all in attendance hanging on to Victor's every word about peace, safety, unity, and the cleansing of the earth. The adoring masses were able to witness and feel firsthand Victor's remarkable powers of strength and healing. Many times, he made his entrance from atop an arena roof, and would crawl down the walls, or he would leap from wall to wall or to the ceiling, leaving every mouth agape. With one wave of his hand, a person could fall to the floor healed or fly across the room swiftly. No one on earth has ever possessed this type of supernatural ability. The masses adore and worship him as the one true god, the savior who is breathing life into a broken world. And at each rally, they open themselves for the demonic spirits to take full possession of each of them.

As the video ends, Victor says to his court, "They are my sheep," and his voice drips with pleasure and pride. "They know they are nothing without me." He looks to one of the aides. "Show me the purification that is taking place."

The aide clicks the remote in his hand, and images from Israel reveal the ongoing roundup of Jews. They are brought before firing squads throughout the country, gassed with poison inside truck trailers or prisons, dying in cages, strung up as human torches along city streets, or packed into a home that is then set on fire. "How many so far?" he asks, looking at General Nygard.

"More than one-hundred thousand this month alone," the general says.

"Is that all?" the emperor says sharply. "Why isn't this more expedient? You do have soldiers throughout my land, don't you?"

"Yes, Sir!"

Victor studies the footage of Jews being dragged into lines of 20 or more before a firing squad. "What are you doing with their carcasses?" he asks, looking at General Schmidt and waiting for a response.

"We have mass graves throughout the country, my lord," General Schmidt says.

Victor explodes at this revelation. "You are burying them in my land! Their rotting poison will seep into my waterways and damage precious oil reserves!" He stands and walks to the generals. "What about the weapons that are being burned from the invasion several years ago? Are we still burning them?"

"We are, sir," General Bernard says. "We are burning them to create fuel."

The emperor smiles, thinking out loud. "Those fires are exceedingly hot to burn tanks and fallen aircraft, correct?" General Bernard nods, agreeing. "I seem to recall a time in history when a leader bungled his ability to burn the Jew cockroaches from the face of the earth. I will not make that same mistake. These incinerators for the weapons—how big are they?"

General Bernard thinks for a moment. "They are large enough to fit two tanks."

"So they could hold a lot of filthy rats?" Victor asks. The general nods. "The firing squads, poisoning them…all that takes too much time and resources. Too many mass graves. Let's utilize the incinerators. Load the Jews onto trucks, then throw them into the incinerators. How many could fit into one incinerator, General?"

"Hundreds, at least," the general says.

The emperor smiles. "Well, there's our answer for expediency. Dig up their bodies and burn them at once. My land must be purified and made holy before me."

"And the weapons, my lord?" General Schmidt asks.

Victor returns to his throne. "Keep burning them, of course. They do provide the energy needed to keep the incinerators operating." He addresses his court. "How are the Jews and followers of the false god Jesus being extinguished throughout my earth?"

An aide points to a screen that shows some 50 or more people in a village somewhere in Africa being slaughtered by machetes. On another screen, a large group of people in China are led into a field and beheaded at the hands of their former friends and neighbors. Another screen features several Jews who are being torn apart by lions in an arena. "Excellent!" the king says, his eyes gleaming. Victor stands at his throne and smiles. "Bring the reporters to Victor Square so I can make a global announcement commending everyone for this earth-cleansing work."

North Carolina, Two Months Later

Elliott has been riding his bicycle along the coastline of Maryland and preaching as he pedals his way through towns. Since Victor

Quade's order to massacre all Jews and Christians, Elliott can no longer draw crowds in theaters, bars, or even on street corners. He shouts the gospel message of Christ as he walks or pedals through the streets so people can hear, although most pretend not to listen.

Even though it is still morning, stars are dancing against a violet sky, as if pirouetting on a magnificent stage. "Jesus died for our sins," Elliott cries as he pedals slowly along a street crawling with dogs, foxes, and coyotes that are looking for food. Although some passersby try to shut him up or to knock him off the bicycle, they realize there's nothing they can do to stop him. "According to the Bible, he was buried and rose again on the third day. There are many who say there is no resurrection. If there is no resurrection, then Christ is not risen. If there is no resurrection, then your loved ones who disappeared from their graves are not risen."

Elliott turns the bicycle around and pedals back down the same street so all those pretending not to listen can continue to hear him. "Your loved ones have risen and are alive today with Jesus," he says to a husband and wife who barely catch his eye as they hurry past him. "He is returning to earth, and your time is running out. If you take Victor Quade's name or mark, you will die and be eternally condemned. If you want to live, if you want to see your loved ones again who were snatched from their graves or taken from this world, you need to claim Jesus as Lord of your life. Even if you lose your life here, you will live eternally!" He stops pedaling in the middle of the road, which forces traffic to stop. "Call on Jesus today! Forsake your sins and turn to him!"

Shouts from behind him cause Elliott to jump, and he is puzzled as he sees what appears to be ash falling from the violet sky and masking the sun. Elliott quickly pedals his bike and heads for the ocean, jumping off the bike when he gets to the beach. The air around him is thick with cinder and ash as he races toward the ocean. Upon reaching the water, he stops and hears frantic voices from the pier. He can barely see through the thick haze but runs to the pier, helping people as they feel their way off.

On the pier, a woman is frightened and pointing to something.

Elliott rushes to her and can see that her hands are bloody. "Are you okay?" he shouts.

"Look!" she says, her voice edged with panic. Her fishing pole is resting on the pier with a large, dead fish at the end of the line. The fish is covered with blood. "We've been fishing all morning, and I just pulled this one out." She is shaking, and her boyfriend or husband comes to make sure that she isn't hurt as Elliott kneels to examine the fish. It is whole and coated with blood. He lays down and looks over the edge of the pier, struggling to see the water. It appears that several fish are floating on the surface of the ocean.

Elliott turns and looks up at the woman and man. "Do you have a rag or something that I can put on the end of your fishing line?" he asks, standing back up. The man hurries and reaches for a rag near their tackle box and secures it to the hook at the end of his fishing pole. "Cast it in, and bring it back up when it's good and wet," Elliott says, watching as the man does so. The man reels the rag back in, and Elliott reaches for it. It is dripping with blood.

"It's Revelation 8," Elliott says, almost to himself. The man and woman look at him dumbfounded. "A huge mountain, all ablaze, was thrown into the sea. A third of the sea turned into blood, a third of the living creatures in the sea died, and a third of the ships were destroyed."

The woman's eyes are wide and anxious. "A mountain burning with fire?" she asks, trying to grasp it all. "You mean a volcano erupted and killed the fish?"

"Scientists have said for years that there are super volcanoes that are time bombs," the man says, piecing it together.

Elliott nods. "In the Bible, God told us this would happen. From the very beginning, he told us everything that is to come. Rivers will be next."

The woman turns angry. "You say there's a God? Why would *God* take our food from us? We need these fish! There are so few food trucks that we count on these fish to survive!"

"There are still fish," Elliott says. "Even in wrath, God is merciful. In his mercy, he told us everything that will take place in the days ahead. In his mercy, he's leaving two-thirds of the sea creatures alive. He's not sending his wrath all at once. He continues to give time for people to call on Jesus as Savior, not Victor Quade. If you take Quade's mark, you will absolutely die. You must claim Jesus as Lord, but time is running out."

Elliott can hear distraught voices on the beach below and begins to preach to the crowd from Revelation 8, telling them about what is to come. For the first time in weeks, a crowd of more than 20 people listen as he shares the gospel of Christ—and ash continues to fall around them.

CHAPTER 17

Rome, Italy
Five Days Later

All of Rome is veiled with chalky dust following the volcanic eruptions that took place in Indonesia and the United States, the largest on the volcanic explosivity index in the history of the world. Many have perished and much of the planet is blanketed with ash, making the air too thick to see through. Within days of the explosions, the earth's atmosphere grew darker and cooler. Scientists were quick to identify these volcanoes as super volcanoes and describe the drop of the earth's temperature as a *volcanic winter*. The volcanic ash and droplets of sulfuric acid and water filled the air to the point of obscuring the sun and creating long-term cooling effects.

Some people recalled that the 1991 eruption of Mount Pinatubo in the Philippines had cooled global temperatures for nearly three years. Would that happen again? In 1815, the eruption of Mount Tambora, also in Indonesia, had led to worldwide crop failures and no summer in 1816. The crop failures led to food shortages, riots, and hundreds of thousands of deaths. Today's citizens are desperate, wondering if this is what they will face following these recent and deadly eruptions.

Victor speaks to his citizens from the living room of his palace and assures them that all is well. "Very few have perished," he claims. Information continues to pour in from around the planet of people who have died, of sea creatures bobbing upon the ocean's surface, and of ships and barges that have been destroyed, and the numbers are devastating. The eruptions *did* stop the war that had been raging against Victor and the Global Union Forces, which has killed hundreds of thousands, but his propaganda machine had covered up that war from the beginning, so he doesn't mention that in his announcement.

"The massive shaking of the planet many months ago awakened these volcanoes," he says with confidence. "But those who lost their lives were the weakest among us. The strong not only survived the earth's shaking but continue to survive and prosper following these eruptions." He smiles into the cameras. "I sit in my home today, just as you sit among your family and friends because you have survived. You are brave and victorious, like the name of your emperor. You are thriving because you have taken my name or my mark as life. You have survived because you are warriors and champions, and my world continues to cleanse the weakest from among us. It is my will that the ash will settle, the sun will burst through and shine once more, and lives will be restored.

"It is at this time once again that I know you are comforted without the burden of property and ownership. What each of us has, we gladly give to our neighbor. What is yours, is mine. And what is mine, is yours. If your property has been destroyed or damaged from the volcanic ash, today is your day to receive my mark so help can come to you. Save your home. Save your business. Save your health, your life, and the lives of your family today by taking my name or mark." He smiles wider into the cameras, his eyes shining. Who wouldn't want to take his mark and live? "We will get through this as we have gotten through so many other adverse circumstances. We are a united world, and we will have peace in my name. We will continue to rid the globe of hatred from the Jews and Christians, and peace will once again prevail throughout my world. With me as your king and savior, we will flourish together."

*

Negev, Israel, Two Weeks Later

Victor and Ubel have come to the Negev Desert region accompanied by General Bernard and some soldiers from the Global Union Forces. After their vehicles come to a stop, they step out and walk up a viewing platform that has been built specifically for Victor. The skies are still dark and the air remains dusky with cinder and ash from the volcanic eruptions, coloring the world a lifeless gray. The air is chilly, as if the sun is straining to shine through the haze and warm the earth. A row of massive buildings is visible from atop the platform. "I thought there were more incinerators?" Victor says, annoyed that he has to strain to see through the bothersome powder.

"There are seven here, my lord," General Bernard says. "But we discovered that with seven burning at once no man working in this area could withstand the heat. Six can be managed. There are six more over there further into the desert," he says pointing. "Six more that way, and six more over there." At least 50 or more soldiers stand in front of each incinerator.

Ubel looks pleased. "And these are all operational now?"

"They are, my lord," General Bernard says. He nods at a commander on the ground and, at his direction, a line of box trucks drive up. Two or three trucks park in front of each incinerator, and the soldiers at each one spring into action. When the back doors are opened, it's clear that the trucks are packed full. These Jews had been caught hiding throughout Israel, found by soldiers who had systematically searched every single home and business, and any other place a person might attempt to hide. Jews had been discovered cowering behind walls, inside boxes, in warehouses, deep in caves, in hollowed-out trees, or wherever they thought they could hole up.

Dark creatures are seen flying victoriously over the trucks and incinerators, and many hover above Victor and Ubel. Shrieks are heard as Jews topple out of the backs of the trucks like dominos and are forced at gunpoint into the incinerators. Victor smiles as many fight back and scream as they are thrown into the flames. "Are my global reporters and cameras here?" Victor asks, his eyes fixated on the scene in front of him.

"They are, glorious one," Ubel says, looking over at other platforms that have been erected for the hundreds of reporters who were all clamoring for the best angle.

Victor smiles as the wind strokes his face. "When the swine are ashes, I will make a statement. Citizens will be so pleased at the purification that is happening here." Ubel nods, sending word with an aide to the swarms of waiting reporters. Victor sighs happily. "The best day is when a Jew dies. Look at all of them down there. *This* is an incredible day."

CHAPTER 18

New Jersey

With soldiers, local officials, volunteers, and fallen angels canvassing towns, neighborhoods, and businesses in order to force residents to take Victor's mark, Emma, Lerenzo, and the others in the abandoned home knew it was time for them to break into two smaller groups. She and Lerenzo, along with Brandon, Kennisha, Micah, Antonio, and two other children—ten-year-old Habib and nine-year-old Esther—packed their share of supplies and food into backpacks and tote bags before setting out on foot. They carried blankets around their necks and wore as many extra pairs of clothing as they could. They knew that their days of hiding in an abandoned home were over; from now on, they would be on the run.

They left their van behind because soldiers were stopping vehicles to make sure everyone inside had Victor's mark. The days were long and terrifying as they searched for a safe place to sleep at night. Neighborhoods were off limits because they would be too easily seen. Voltaire's words "Those who can make you believe absurdities can make you commit audacities" ring true as once-affable neighbors commit heinous acts against those who don't bear Victor's name or mark. Deserted homes in the open countryside were preferable for hiding because of the distances between homes, but even then, it was too dangerous for them to linger inside any one vacant building for long.

Sometimes all they could do was scavenge through a home in search of food, clean clothing, and supplies that had been left behind by the former residents.

When a home wasn't available, they would sleep in barns or sheds to help shield them from rain, wind, cold, and wild animals. Sleeping in a vacated building without electricity was hard enough, but sleeping on the ground in what was little more than a shelter was another thing altogether.

Both the earth and sky remain a gloomy slate color in the wake of the volcanic eruptions, and much of the vegetation around them is burnt or gone. The presence of wild animals and, even more frightening, the demonic hordes of the abyss makes everything far worse than any scenario depicted in a science fiction movie. The unimaginable state of the world, the constant hunger, and life on the run weigh heavy on Emma and the others, but they remain together, knowing that as a group, they're stronger. They keep each other going and remind one another that Christ is coming again to set everything right and make all things new.

After days of traveling, they had stumbled upon miles of woods, which now serve as their temporary home. They know it has to be temporary because of the risk of being in one place too long. They soon discover that other believers have taken shelter here as well, and thankfully, many among them are hunters and have killed any predators that have drawn near. The hunters have even shown Emma and others how to bow hunt, since a rifle would be too noisy and draw attention to their whereabouts. Hunting is completely foreign to Emma and her group, who have lived most or all of their lives in a city. "I don't think I'd ever be able to kill an animal," she tells Scott, a 60-something-year-old man who taught her how to hold a recurve bow, load an arrow, and then aim and release it.

"If a predator is near the people you love, what are you going to do?" Scott asks, showing her and Lerenzo and the others how to make their own arrows using a straight stick, a piece of sharp bone or rock, string, and feathers. "If you haven't eaten in days, what are you going to do?" Emma and her group know that their lives are going to depend on their newfound skill, and they each take their daily turn at practice shooting with the bow and arrows that Scott generously gives them, and they make as many arrows as possible to keep in the quiver.

This larger group of Jesus followers have spread throughout the woods; staying together would create too much noise and make them easier to spot. When someone kills a deer, turkey, rabbits, squirrels, or birds, the sound of an owl is simulated so each group can send a person from their part of the woods to gather some meat.

Emma and her group are so grateful for the taste of meat again; besides a chicken here or there, they haven't eaten meat since the mass vanishings. Emma had brought along a skillet and a pot from the abandoned home, and when meat is available, a small fire is built so the meat can be boiled or fried, and then the fire is put out so no one can track them. With the provisions they brought with them from New York gone, Lerenzo and Brandon often wait for nightfall to gather beans, tomatoes, cabbage, or whatever they can find growing in nearby gardens to help feed their group, but that can be risky and frightening, as guard dogs are often keeping watch, and many times, traps are set within the gardens.

Some of the believers sleep in tents that they have camouflaged with branches, while others have built a small fort against an embankment using tarps and other coverings, like Emma and her family does. On colder nights, they sleep with as many clothes on as possible and bundle up close together. A stream that winds through the woods is used for bathing and washing clothes.

The groups have developed a system of communication by leaving messages in trees, in a hole in the side of an embankment, and even in earthquake debris. These messages alert everyone to a child in need, or to food or supplies that have been discovered. Often, they leave a word of encouragement to stand strong, or a sad note about who died from sickness or hunger. Death is now a part of their everyday existence as viruses continue to spread or because doctor visits aren't possible without Victor's mark and medicine can't be purchased for diabetes, high blood pressure, heart conditions, arthritis, cancer, or any other ailments. Six owl hoots means that someone has died, and whenever

Emma and her group hear the sound, they all say together, "Praise God. Someone's new life begins today."

On the occasions that these believers walk into nearby towns, they watch for children or teens who are alone on the streets or rescue them from a prostitution or trafficking ring. Sadly, many parents in desperate need of money continue to sell their children. Before the mass disappearances, the legality of murdering a baby born alive during a botched abortion was oftentimes battled in the chambers of Congress, but the heinous slaughter of babies and children is now legal in Victor Quade's world as a means of population control.

Today, the sky looks corrugated in a rainbow of colors. No artist has ever painted such a stunning scene. Following their morning Bible reading and prayers, Emma and her group walk the perimeter of a pasture in search of food and can hear a farm tractor in the distance. It has been three days since any of them have eaten anything more than wild onions, onion grass, wild bergamot, dandelion, and bittercress, and they are all weary and weak. They haven't eaten anything hot in days, since their last meal of boiled squirrel and rabbit, and there are days when Emma's stomach groans for something warm and comforting like soup or one of her mother's casseroles. Although he's lost considerable weight and is fatigued today, Brandon crouches down so Habib can climb onto his back.

"There's a corn crop over there," Kennisha says, straining to see through the pervasive gray air. "Maybe we can wait until the farmer is done with his work, and we can each get a few ears of corn."

The thought of eating raw corn makes Emma's stomach queasy, but they are all beyond being picky about what they eat. She pauses when she hears raised voices in the distance. "Shh!" she says, crouching down. "Does anyone hear that?" They turn their attention to the sounds, and Emma inhales sharply when she sees a woman and what were evidently her two teenage sons held at gunpoint by two men who are not soldiers, but there is something unusual and frightening about them. Emma is too far away, and the ash remains too thick to see their faces, but the men move with inhuman swiftness and power.

"Supernatural strength," Brandon says, observing the men. "More fallen angels."

Lerenzo nods grimly. He pulls Esther close to him and urges everyone, "Stay down."

The sound of the tractor can be heard again, and Emma, Lerenzo, Brandon, and Kennisha crane their necks to see the farmer driving it toward his family. "No! Jesus is my Lord," the woman screams, making Micah and the other children jump.

Emma frantically prays for the family. "Give them strength and courage, Lord!" she says out loud, her voice shaking.

One of the dark angels grabs the woman, and the teen boys jump on him, attempting to beat him off their mother. The second fallen being quickly slits the throat of one son, and then the other. As the mother screams, the first dark creature kills her. The suddenness and brutality of the attack stops Emma's breath, and her blood runs cold. Trembling, she watches the farmer jump from the tractor and run toward the bodies of his wife and sons. He falls beside them and shouts, "Jesus is King! Jesus is Savior!" as one of the fallen angels twists his neck, killing him. They then go into the farmer's home, and Emma collapses to the ground, shaking. She reaches for Micah and wraps her arms around him. They are all too traumatized and stricken to move. Several minutes later, the two beings leave the house, walking past the dead bodies and carrying away some of the family's treasures.

Emma and the others sit amidst the corn in shocked silence as hot tears fill their eyes. They know this gruesome scene is being played out all over the world, not just on a country farm in New Jersey. People are losing their lives for refusing to accept Victor's mark.

They don't know why the farmer and his family were still working their farm. Maybe the farmer thought they had time to harvest their crop and use the money to find a safe place to live. Maybe he and his wife assumed that Victor's henchmen hadn't brought his mark to the countryside yet. Or maybe they knew that if they died, their lives were secure with Christ and they wanted to provide this corn crop for others to live on after their deaths.

Emma and the others discuss what they should do before reluctantly deciding to search for food inside the home. They enter through the back and thank God for the courage and unwavering faith of the farmer and his family. Using sacks and backpacks they find within the home, they take only the food, clothing, and supplies they can carry, along with many ears of corn from the crop. They pray over the crop and ask God to bless it for those who are hungry and in search of food. As they head back into the woods, they leave messages in hiding places along the way to inform other believers about the crop. For several miles, they don't say a word to one another. They feel so overwhelmed by what they had just experienced that they were all moved to stay silent.

To discover more about the biblical facts behind the story, read Where in the Word? *on page 239, or continue reading the novel.*

CHAPTER 19

Israel
Two Months Later

Zerah clears away some scrub brush and small tree limbs before removing a wooden lid over a small hole in the ground. Going down stairs cut out of the earth, he enters an underground bunker near the Jordan border. It is dark and quiet, but Zerah knows they are here. The stench is unbearable, and he pulls his sweatshirt up to cover his mouth and nose. "It's all right," he says into the blackness. "It's Zerah," he whispers. He can hear them begin to breathe along with the sound of a woman's muffled crying. "How long have you been in here?"

"Three days," a man replies raggedly.

"How many of you are here?"

"Twenty-one," the same man says.

"We must move quickly," Zerah says. "Zev was found and killed yesterday." Zev Jacobs was one of the many Jews responsible for hiding and helping other Jews cross the border into Jordan, where someone there would then smuggle them the rest of the way to the mountains. "The Global Union Forces were too close to your location and he distracted them, leading them away from you."

More soft crying can be heard, and Zerah says, "Don't weep for Zev. He is with Messiah Yeshua. Listen to me. Listen!" He waits until he's certain they are all quiet. "At the border, there is a row of trees that was partly decimated during the enemy coalition invasion a few years ago. You can identify the row in the moonlight because all the trees except one have been cut in half. Only one tree remains at its full height. Get to that row of trees and fall down on your stomachs, covering yourselves with the scrub brush that has been placed there. You will wait for Khaled, who will help you into Jordan. Then run for Petra."

"How long will we wait?" a voice in the dark asks.

"I don't know," Zerah says. "If Khaled cannot do it safely tonight, you must remain still and hidden. Hashem is with you, and I pray he will protect you from every evil. Come. Quietly, quietly." The sound of soft rustling fills the small space, and Zerah climbs back up the stairs into the night air. It is eerily silent as one by one, he helps the weary Jews climb out of the pit. He knows they haven't eaten for at least three days, probably more, as they've been moving from one hiding spot to the next as they made their way to this bunker.

"Here are a few figs and bread loaves," he whispers, handing a woman a pillowcase filled with the few food items. "Move quietly but quickly."

Because of the darkness, Zerah cannot see much more than shadowy faces, but he can feel their fear as each man, woman, and child squeezes his hand as they begin their journey to the border.

Washington, DC

Elliott stands preaching by the Potomac River in front of where the US Capitol once stood. This area has been turned into a street market where food or supplies are bought or traded. People often fight to the death for commodities and food as simple as toilet paper or eggs. Global Union soldiers and Victor's followers are always nearby to make sure that anyone who enters the market area bears his name or mark, and Elliott warns everyone about the mark before they enter. He knows that the desperate and starving are lurking at the perimeter, sometimes crouched among the Capitol ruins, waiting for the opportunity to steal something. They are hiding because they don't want to take the mark, but Elliott realizes that hunger and desperation can change a person's mind to do the unthinkable. If he can urge them to salvation in Christ, they will live eternally, and he uses a bullhorn to carry his message to the lost and hidden.

"Today is the day of salvation! Jesus Christ is the author of eternal salvation. Victor Quade is a liar and fraud. He is what the Bible calls the Antichrist, and if you take his mark, you will be separated from God and eternal salvation forever!"

A pungent odor like that of rotten eggs wafts through the air, and Elliott scans the Capitol ruins for the source. He turns around and sees that several human-like creatures are looming nearby and recognizes them as demonic lords from the abyss. They are powerful and fleet-footed as they lunge for him, yet they are unable to make contact. Momentarily, men and women look on in alarm at the scuffle, then turn back to haggling over water, bread, and milk.

"You can't touch me," Elliott says to the hellish fiends raging in front of him. "The Lord Jesus Christ has sealed my life." The name of Jesus invokes shrieks and howls from the infernal ones, who, like their master, are murderous, and they slay several people shopping at the market. "Go away in the name of Jesus," Elliott says as he walks after them. The savage devils shrink back at the name, and Elliott steps over the bodies of the slain and shouts, "Jesus Christ be glorified! There is no other name under heaven by which we are saved! Jesus Christ lives today and will return to redeem the earth from Satan." Hell's goblins take flight, leaving the smell of sulfur behind as Elliott lifts up his bullhorn to preach again.

"To those with ears to hear!" he says to those who are lurking and hiding. "Call on the name of the Lord Jesus Christ while you can still be saved. He is returning soon and wants you to live with him forever. If you take Victor's name or mark, you will die. Do you understand that there will be no more life for you? I know you're tired. I know you're hungry, but listen to the voice of Jesus, who is the way, the truth, and the life. Your life can be in him if you call on his name!"

A loud roar is heard overhead, and Elliott stops preaching and looks up. Fiery rocks are hurtling from the sky and into the Potomac for as far as the eye can see. People in the marketplace scream as they watch the fiery rocks fall, which stay ablaze on the water's surface until they sink. Running to the river's edge, they peer over the bank to see what is happening. Bloated fish rise to the surface, covering all the water.

"This is Wormwood!" Elliott yells over the raucous noise. "A great falling star has broken apart and will contaminate rivers and fountains all over the world, as it is written in God's Word! One-third of the waters will be affected, and many people will die because the waters have been poisoned." He runs toward the Capitol ruins again and hollers for all those in hiding to hear him. "God's judgments will continue to fall until Jesus returns. Call on his name and live while you still can!"

CHAPTER 20

Singapore
One Week Later

Scurrying into the dark and empty room, John's slender fingers tremble as he plugs in the microphone and waits for the transmitter to power up. He sits on the floor and when the transmitter is ready, holds the microphone to his lips.

"The Revelator says there is death in the cup as many waters are Wormwood now," he whispers as the receiver crackles. His voice is heard across the world to those with ears to hear. "Famine sweeping the world, but the elite have their cake and eat it too. Upwards of one million piles of ashes in the desert now and millions more doves lose their heads. Mark is far deadlier, so save your soul. Everything now in place for more doves to soar. More than one hundred volcanoes around ring of fire erupting, the earth is shaking in Venezuela, Chile, Colombia, New Zealand, and countless other locations. Hurricanes, typhoons, tornadoes chewing up land. Loser says no but famine is increasing. Birth pangs closer together. Cleopatra is baring her teeth with Loser in sight."

A noise outside the window makes him jump. Shoving the transmitter and microphone into a backpack, he hurries out the door and into the black of night.

Jerusalem

Ubel stands atop the temple stairs addressing the many pilgrims who have traveled from across the earth to worship Emperor Victor. Several planets hang low in the sky like ornaments, but very few look up to see their beauty. "Welcome! Welcome into the king of kings' presence!" Ubel says, ignoring the magnificence above him. "All who enter here will find rest for your weary souls. Our king has come that you might have life and have it in abundance," he says, walking down the stairs amidst the waiting masses. He puts his hands on top of a small Palestinian girl's head, smiling. "You do not have our savior's mark. Is that why you're waiting today? Do you want everyone to see that you are sealed with our savior's mark and for our great lord to reside within you so that you may have life?" The little girl looks up at her mother, whose hands are trembling and eyes are wide with fright. She nods at her daughter, and the little girl looks at Ubel, smiling. He puts his hands on each side of her face. "Yes, yes! What is your name, sweet one?"

"Ayah," she says.

"And your name?" Ubel asks the mother.

"Garda," she says, her voice barely a whisper.

"Beautiful names for beautiful citizens of our savior's kingdom." He points to the temple. "Abundant life is just a few steps away when you receive the mark of our king."

The mother feels sick to her stomach. With the escalation of murder and violence against women and children, Garda has kept Ayah locked away inside their small home in Gaza. In recent months they have been able to survive on the few fruits and vegetables at their home and the food that was in their cupboards, but now those cupboards are empty, and Garda needs to feed her daughter. She can't do that without the mark. As Ubel makes his way down the line, Garda puts her hand on her forehead, feeling faint, and wonders if her weakness is from hunger or something else.

"Do not take Victor's name or mark!"

Garda jumps at the voice, and she and Ayah turn to see a Jew shouting at those waiting in line. Ubel quickly moves to the man and begins cursing in his face. "Get out of our lord's holy city! This is where he resides to bring comfort and peace and life to those who love him."

"God rebukes you!" Zerah says, using the names of God that Gentiles would recognize. He is inches from Ubel's face and can see his eyes flashing with rage. "You are a liar and follow the father of lies, and your doom is sealed. As a reminder, the Lord God has said that you and Victor Quade will be bound and thrown alive into the lake of fire."

Garda's heart throbs and she pulls Ayah closer to her, squeezing her shoulders. Ubel begins to laugh and opens his arms to all those waiting in line. "Do you hear this babble? This man is deranged, and all those who listen to him are losing their lives around our great lord's world. He is a murderer!"

Zerah looks at the long line of weary travelers and his chest swells with empathy; he was once as lost as each one of them. "God's holy word says that if you take Victor Quade's mark you will not live. You will die. That mark will enable you to buy and sell for the next three years. That's it. You will gain life for just a few more months on earth, but then you will die and be eternally separated from life and from God. If you do not take Victor's name or mark, you will live forever with Jesus, who has gone to prepare a place for you in heaven."

Ubel's voice rises in anger. "You will stop these lies!" He lifts his hand and appears to throw something in front of Zerah, and a fireball lights up the ground.

The fire does not touch Zerah, and he continues to talk to the pilgrims. "Jesus said, 'Let not your hearts be troubled. Believe in God; believe also in me. In my Father's house are many rooms. If it were not so, would I have told you that I go to prepare a place for you? And if I go and prepare a place for you, I will come again and will take you to myself, that where I am you may be also. And you know the way to where I am going.' Thomas said to him, 'Lord, we do not know where you are going. How can we know the way?' Jesus said to him, 'I am the way, and the truth, and the life. No one comes to the Father except through me.'" Garda's heart feels like it's jumping inside her chest as she listens to the words.

"Jesus did as he said," Zerah says, imploring the crowd. "They were snatched away quicker than that." He snaps his fingers and Garda gasps, remembering that terrible day when people across the globe disappeared. "He is coming back with all those he took with him and he will step foot on the Mount of Olives. There will be no more chances to follow him after that. Call on Jesus right now. Repent and call on Jesus! There is no other name that can save you!"

Four people in line begin to cry and murmur the name of Jesus beneath their breath, and Ubel rises into the air, raises his hand, and flings fire down upon them. The flames devour the four and they fall to the ground, screaming in agony as they perish in front of the terrified line. Garda and Ayah's eyes fill with tears at the sight, and Ayah buries her head in her mother's abdomen. "This man is a liar and Jesus is the father of lies!" Ubel shouts for all to hear as he floats down to the street. "This man is a deceiver and must be killed." Several men in line rush to attack Zerah, but they are unable to touch him. Ubel throws another fireball at Zerah, hitting the men instead. They scream and roll in the street to put out the flames.

"No weapon formed against me can prosper," Zerah shouts above the cries of suffering. "I am a servant of the Holy One of Israel, Jesus Christ of Nazareth. Only in him is life in abundance." He looks to the sky and says, "Look up! Only our creator God could display those planets for us to see. Only God could hold them in place. Look up at his beauty. Look up at his power. Look up at his great love for us."

Ubel steps forward to an elderly man standing in line and leaning on a cane. He reaches for the cane and throws it on the ground near Zerah and the cane turns into a viper, which bares its fangs and slithers toward Zerah. Garda, Ayah, and others around them jump back in fear of this poisonous serpent capable of inflicting death with a single bite. The snake strikes at Zerah, but inexplicably, its head flings backward. It attempts to strike over and over but keeps hitting an invisible barrier. Zerah leans over and picks up the deadly creature, twisting its neck before throwing it to the ground and crushing its head beneath his foot.

Garda begins to weep at what she's witnessed and bends over, picking up Ayah. "Jesus is Lord," she whispers into Ayah's ear, tears streaming down her face and mingling with Ayah's hair. "Do you hear me, my

precious one? Jesus is Lord!" Ayah nods and Garda pulls back, looking at her. "Jesus is Lord!"

"Jesus is Lord," Ayah says, looking into her mother's eyes. "Jesus is life." Ayah puts her hands on her mother's face and Garda kisses her as a shot rings out. The little girl's body goes limp in her mother's arms and the crowd around them shrieks, many of them running away from the Global Union Forces who have killed the little girl. A second shot strikes Garda, bringing her to her knees as she clutches Ayah. Zerah runs to Garda and holds onto her as she takes her final breaths.

"I have you," he says, putting Garda's hands on top of Ayah's.

"Jesus has me," Garda says, gasping. "Jesus...Jesus..." Her breath leaves her and Zerah looks on her face, then Ayah's.

"They are with Jesus," Zerah says, looking at the pilgrims who are nearby.

"They are simpletons who were deceived," Ubel says. "They are now forever separated from our lord and king. Do not be deceived as they were! Go to the house of our lord and worship him today. Receive his mark. Receive life eternal in him."

The line begins to reform, making its way around Zerah, who is clinging to Garda and Ayah's bodies. He raises his voice once again to preach to these who are just moments away from eternal death.

CHAPTER 21

The Negev, Israel
One Month Later

W hy aren't three of the incinerators operating?" Victor says atop
the platform, with Ubel at his side.

"We have men working on these and the others and will get them
all operational in rapid order," General Durand says.

Ubel turns to look at the general. "The others? How many?"

"There are seven total, my prophet."

Victor comes unhinged and curses at the general and the soldiers
surrounding him. "Can you smell that, General? That is the smell of
the swine that you are *not* killing each day that are stinking up my land!"
Victor looks out at a truck pulling up to an incinerator with a load of
Jews and begins yelling. "Get them off the truck. Get them into the
fires now! Now! Now! Now!" His face is red, and his body is shaking
when he turns back to General Durand. "Why aren't there more truck-
loads of vermin? Why just one truck?"

"We are scouring the land, my king," General Durand says. "But
they are…"

"You have still not found them in their hiding places!" Victor shouts
as he fires off obscenities at the very thought of Jews still hiding in his
land. He puts a hand on the general's neck and lifts him off his feet as
the general struggles to breathe.

Ubel raises his hand in a peaceful gesture. "It will be dealt with, my lord," Ubel says, reassuring Victor. He puts his hand on Victor's arm and lowers it so the general can stand again on the ground and breathe. "Your forces have gone through homes, but you must do a more thorough sweep," he says to the general. The general nods as he pants for breath.

"Go through cities and towns and take all that is valuable and then torch the homes and businesses," Victor says. "Burn them down. Raze them so nothing is left. We must cleanse the land of every trace of Jew stench."

"The tech and business sectors?" General Durand asks.

"Leave them, of course," Victor snaps. "I need them. But get rid of every lasting memory of life of the Jew in my land."

Screams of terror from the direction of the incinerators lead Victor and Ubel to glance out over the platform again. They look elated as they see a hundred or so Jews with their arms bound behind their backs forced out of the truck by soldiers. Hundreds of demonic creatures fly overhead, and Victor's chest puffs up with satisfaction at the sight. The Jews are pleading for their lives, and Victor curses in glee at the sound of what he calls "the swine squealing."

"Call on Yeshua and be saved!" yells Zerah, who suddenly appears nearby as the Jews are pushed into the incinerator.

"Burn him!" Victor bellows. The dark throng of demonic creatures swoop around Zerah but can't get close to him. The general and his soldiers, along with Ubel, run down the stairs of the platform, and the general can be heard barking orders to the soldiers near Zerah.

"Claim Yeshua as Lord and your soul will be saved!" Zerah pleads with the Jews as soldiers, many of whom are clearly possessed with demonic spirits, push and beat the Jews with clubs.

General Durand and his men run to Zerah, and three of the soldiers try to shoot him without success. They then try to tackle him, but fall on one another. Ubel lifts his hand for a fireball from the skies and directs it at Zerah but it misses, scorching three soldiers instead, who fall to the ground, rolling and shouting as the fire sears through to their skin.

Zerah cries louder for all to hear. "Call now on the name of Yeshua Messiah so you will be saved and be with him today!" Three more soldiers attempt to grab Zerah and they manage to secure his arms, pulling him into the incinerator. Zerah notices that Ubel is smiling at his apparent demise. Ubel orders the door closed before the soldiers can exit, and they scream for the doors to be opened, banging on them with their guns and fists, hysteria rising in their voices. As the fires blaze, Zerah roars over the wails of his beloved countrymen. "Cry out to Yeshua Messiah that you may be with him today! I believe Yeshua is Lord! I believe Yeshua is Lord!"

From the platform, Victor pumps his fist into the air and black clouds roil above him as the platform sways back and forth in Victor's pleasure. More Jews are dying, including the pig Zerah, who has antagonized him since he killed the two scum witnesses in Jerusalem. "Go, General!" Victor yells to General Durand who is near the incinerator. "Go through all this land and burn it down. Purify it for me! Slay every Jew!"

Victor stops shouting as General Durand appears to shrink back in fear. Victor turns to where the general is looking and is outraged to see that the incinerator doors have opened, the heat from the blaze killing several soldiers standing outside. Zerah steps out of the incinerator, unharmed; his clothes aren't even scorched. He walks to General Durand, whose knees have buckled at Zerah's appearance. Zerah reaches for the general's hand and taps on Victor's mark. "The fire of that incinerator is nothing compared to what this has done to you."

"Noooo!" Victor's voice is full of rage as he runs down the stairs of the platform to Zerah.

"We will rid our great planet of all of you!" Ubel shouts as he approaches Zerah.

Zerah steps up to Ubel and shakes his head. "No you won't. You've known that from the beginning. Jesus is returning, and you both are going to your eternal destruction."

Victor looks upward and screams into the air before looking at General Durand, who is rising to his feet again. "Kill him! Slaughter them all! Go now!" The general rushes to a truck to command his soldiers to sweep the towns and cities more thoroughly. Victor raises his hands to the sky and shouts, "Come, my beauties! Come!" A black cloud of demonic creatures can be seen moving swiftly through the desert as Victor points to the general and soldiers who are jumping into the trucks. "Go and destroy!" Piercing shrieks permeate the atmosphere as the dark horde surround the caravan of destruction.

Zerah steps in front of Victor, and several soldiers rush to keep him from harming Victor but are held back by an unseen power. He and Victor watch as the perverted beings from the bottomless pit surround and lead the trucks that will go throughout Israel to massacre the Jews who have evaded capture. "A staggering and beautiful sight," Victor says, sneering.

Zerah's voice is strong and calm. "As it is written, 'He will say to those on his left, "Depart from me, you cursed, into the eternal fire prepared for the devil and his angels."'"

"No one will touch me!" Victor seethes, his body shaking with rage. He curses at Zerah and replies, "Your God cannot touch me."

"As it is also written, 'You have come to a dreadful end and shall be no more forever,'" Zerah says, walking after the line of trucks that are leaving the incinerators.

CHAPTER 22

New Jersey
Three Months Later

Emma, Lerenzo, Brandon, Kennisha, and the children sit outside a pickup truck with a camper top they found sitting abandoned at the back of a farm in Pennsylvania two weeks ago. A search inside the cab revealed the keys inside the glovebox, and Lerenzo's years of driving and doing minor repairs on the box truck he used for his job in New York came in handy as he and Brandon worked to get the truck running again. With black paint they discovered in the barn, they all worked together to camouflage the tan truck and the white camper top. Knowing they couldn't buy gas because they don't bear the mark, Lerenzo was relieved to see there was just enough fuel in the tank—along with a few gas cans with fuel inside the barn—to get the truck through pastureland and to a clump of woods at the base of rolling hillsides. Using branches from charred trees, they covered the truck as best they could so it wasn't easily seen.

They were heartbroken to leave the woods of New Jersey, but when a nearby resident spotted several people living in the woods, he brought back a dozen or so Victor followers who set the woods ablaze and opened fire on all those running for their lives. Besides Scott, the man who taught them how to use a bow and arrow and was shouting for all the people hiding in the woods to flee, Emma doesn't know how many were killed that day. She and her group gathered what they could of their bedding and belongings before escaping.

There is one bed inside the camper top that Emma and Lerenzo sleep in, and the tabletop is turned into a bed, on which Kennisha and Esther sleep. The rest of the camper is filled with supplies, food items, and clothing they have collected from abandoned buildings along the way. Emma and the others sit on the ground outside the truck and turn on the shortwave radio, keeping the volume low so no one who might happen to be walking nearby can hear.

"Our king is so pleased to bear your burden of ownership for you." They cringe at the sound of Ubel's voice. "It is his greatest joy to watch as you unsaddle the weight of property that you have carried on your backs for far too long. Owning nothing and giving it to our lord releases you from slavery and bondage, and together we breathe easier without the albatross of debt around our necks. It is so wonderful to know how we can save each other and our lord's planet: We simply give the hardship of ownership to our god and king, and he uses it for our good. We are one world living one life together and worshipping our one true god together."

Brandon grunts and shakes his head. "It's hard to imagine how deceived you have to be to believe what he's saying."

"Our glorious one is also pleased with all your efforts to restore peace to our earth!" Ubel says. "Your work cleansing our globe of the fascists and terrorists is changing our lives for the better. The atmosphere is being filled with our lord's energy and light as you shut the mouths of the lions. Everywhere from New Delhi to Ecuador, it is his great joy to learn that the false witnesses and teachers of Christ are dying because they do not bear our sovereign's mark, and their deaths are freeing our universe of their toxic spirits.

"You may be aware that ammunition and firearms are scarce—we believe that many of these predators of Christ are stockpiling them, which makes them dangerous. You must be ready to protect yourselves, using whatever weapons you can. I have also signed into production the manufacturing of more guillotines to be used all over the planet. Thousands are already being used to kill these Christ-following rodents, and thousands more will be in production this week. They are simple to operate and more cost-effective than firearms. Our emperor is thrilled at the progress being made across his magnificent world, and I am glad to announce that the eradication of Jews is enabling the universe to pulsate with victory. Take all that belongs to these vile creatures, for it does not belong to them. These Jew dogs have stolen it from our lord!"

"I can't listen anymore," Emma says.

Kennisha turns the dial to search for news outside of Victor's propaganda, which has infiltrated all the known radio channels. The few who have had the courage to broadcast what is really happening around the world continue to be removed from the air, most likely murdered by Victor's soldiers. Kennisha continues to turn the dial and stops when she hears the voice that they recognize as John.

"Ashes piling higher in the desert," John says. Emma and the others look at one another, sickened and frightened by what they're hearing. "The more than six million ashes have been collected since the day of celebration are the crowning achievement of Loser. Ash collecting will not stop."

"More than six million Jews," Emma says, her blood racing. "And that's just in Israel. How many have been killed worldwide? O God, open their eyes to believe in Jesus Messiah," she whispers.

"Cleopatra's nails are sharpened and she's ready to strike," John says.

Lerenzo nods soberly. "Egypt is ready to attack Victor."

"More than twenty thousand doves soared to new heights in Chad today," John continues. "And in Yugoslavia, another three thousand doves flew the coop, along with eighteen hundred in Bulgaria, nearly a thousand in Mongolia, well over four thousand in Spain, and thirteen thousand doves in Saudi Arabia…"

As John continues to rattle off numbers, Emma buries her face in her hands. "Christians are being martyred all over the world."

"Nearly eight thousand doves took flight in Argentina, forty-one thousand in Niger, nearly three thousand soared in the United States…"

Brandon looks to the sky as he listens. "I've lost count. How many is that?"

Lerenzo shakes his head. "I have no idea. Thousands and thousands. Martyred for Christ."

The transmission ends, and Emma realizes John has stopped broadcasting. "With the help of Satan's army from the abyss, there will be more people killed than at any other time in history. What do we do?" she asks, her voice sounding small and afraid.

"We keep finding kids and telling them about Jesus and we keep praying," Micah says, putting his hand on top of Emma's. "We continue what you've done since the very beginning."

CHAPTER 23

Victor City, Italy

Victor, Ubel, and Victor's court all sit upon their thrones as they watch the screens filled with images from around the world feature people carrying dead loved ones from homes, hospitals, or through the streets. "These are more deaths from the poisoned rivers, springs, and wells," an aide informs them.

"Do we know how many rivers have been affected?" George asks.

Dr. Ito, who heads the World Department of Health, steps forward. "We don't have an exact number, but we know at least one-third of the earth's waters have been poisoned from the meteor."

"And how many have died because of the waters?" Adrien asks.

Dr. Ito shakes his head. "We don't have a number. Countless millions, along with fish, and various livestock."

"What are you doing about the waters?" Victor says, looking directly at Dr. Ito. "How close are you to restoring them?"

"We…" Dr. Ito stammers. "We don't fully comprehend how the meteor poisoned the waters."

"It broke apart and fell into the waters, Doctor," Ubel says, stating the obvious.

"Yes, yes, my prophet," Dr. Ito says, bowing. "But we haven't identified the chemical…"

Victor directs his gaze at the doctor. "Are you fixing the waters?"

Dr. Ito does not answer quickly enough, and he rises into the air, desperately using his hands to remove something invisible from around his neck that is choking him.

Dr. Ito attempts to nod, knowing his life is on the line. "Yes, we are, my lord," he says, straining for breath.

"Good," Victor says as Dr. Ito falls to the floor. "I will assure my citizens that you are working diligently to purify our waters. In the meantime, we will broadcast the news that this is proof that my world continues to eliminate the weak and wicked among us."

Maria looks at screens with people lined up in Finland and Belarus waiting to receive Victor's mark. Upon receiving the mark, they are rewarded a loaf of bread with some cheese. "I would like to point out that the distribution of our sovereign's mark is going better than expected," she says, smiling in a way that she hopes will attract Victor's attention. "We have discovered that an award of some sort of food item is great incentive to receive the mark, as you can see here in Belarus. I fully believe that the mark will eradicate famine altogether."

"There is no famine, Maria," Victor says, correcting her. "If someone is hungry, it is only because he is too foolish to receive my mark. My mark is life. If I have marked you, if I am inside you, you can never be hungry or thirsty again, can you?"

"No, my lord," Maria says in a desirous and dreamy way.

Ubel points to a screen with a couple dozen people being thrust to the ground, each of them behind an enormous guillotine. "This is in Bangkok," Ubel says with excitement. Young and old alike are thrust into place by Victor's followers, many of them possessing the demoniacal strength and speed that has become characteristic of them. "For some reason," Ubel says, "there has been an increase in false religion in Thailand, many parts of Africa, Iran, Iraq, and other Middle Eastern countries. The untrue narrative of the false prophet Christ continues to spread despite our exterminating well over three million of his followers in Iran alone. Our beloved's image appears everywhere in the land, but too many people refuse to bow or worship or make holy pilgrimage to Israel to bless your image there."

Videos play of tanks moving across a desert and of soldiers jumping into military aircraft, as if preparing for war. Victor scowls. "Where is that, General?" he asks, looking at General Abar.

"That is in Egypt, and this," the general says, pointing to another screen, "is in Syria."

"What are they doing?" Victor asks. "Is this being directed by the Global Union Forces?"

General Abar shakes his head. "Global Union Forces have not issued any commands."

Victor stands and walks to the screens to examine them more closely. "Then what is happening here, General?"

"From the intelligence we've gathered, it appears Syria and Egypt are declaring war against your kingdom."

Victor and his court erupt at this news, swearing and shouting. "How is this happening, General Abar?" Victor yells.

"Intelligence reveals that these nations believe your kingdom has an obsession with destroying the Jews and Christ followers and not in leading the world."

Victor strings together a slew of profanities. "Another war against my kingdom! Destroy them all! No weapon aimed against my kingdom will succeed. I will thwart every plot, plan, and scheme against me. Issue the command to attack, General!"

"Yes, my lord!" the general says, bowing and exiting the room.

"They will be swiftly defeated," Adrien says.

"Your forces are too great," George adds. "This will end as abruptly as it starts."

Victor nods, soothed by their words. He watches as more people lose their heads when a colossal guillotine blade falls in Bangkok. Deep within, he's irritated by the general's words about Egypt and Syria believing he is obsessed with destroying Jews and Christians. "This seems a rather slow process for execution," Victor says, pointing to the guillotine. "How many of these do we have?"

"Thousands," Ubel says, proudly. "We have been working at warp speed and are able to eliminate hundreds of thousands of cockroaches every day all over your world."

"Hmm," Victor murmurs, watching another 20 or so people kneel behind a guillotine in Shanghai. "Put forth an order for thousands more immediately!" He pauses for a moment as the blade comes down and more radicals lose their heads. "What other methods are you utilizing to scour my earth?"

"The contaminated rivers and springs are, of course, cleansing your world, and we have been apprised that there is a new virus, my king," Ubel says. "It is far deadlier than any previous plague. We don't know where it came from, but millions of the feeble and faint should be gone in just a matter of weeks, furthering our efforts at population control."

"What about us?" Maria asks. "How will the king's court survive?"

Ubel smiles. "The emperor's scientists have assured me there are enough vaccines and medicines for the elite, but never forget, our lord's own blood is inside of you giving life to your mortal bodies. The strong will survive, and our emperor's earth will continue to dispose the weak from us, along with the lying, bigoted, rebel-hearted Christ terrorists who are running like scared rabbits from one hole to another."

Victor watches as another 20-some people are thrown behind a guillotine in Mumbai. "But still, before the virus takes effect, there must be faster ways to rid my world of this particular pollution."

An aide clicks a button on a remote and the screens change to scenes of machete-wielding attackers in Africa killing large crowds of Christians in a field, swords being used on a beach in Japan, and axes being swung in Norway to decapitate Christ followers. Victor is outraged as he hears cries of praises being lifted up to Jesus by those who are being slaughtered, and each time Jesus's name is shouted, Victor curses, covering his ears.

Ubel raises his hand to soothe Victor. "It is all right. They are all dead cockroaches now," he says, indicating the corpses on the screens. "They cannot say that vile name anymore. You are lord and savior here, my god and king."

Ubel and Victor's court all bow before him, and Victor begins to laugh. "Of course! I am lord and savior! We need a celebration, Ubel! Livestream these remarkable images and those from the Negev with the Jews being torched." He stands, excited, clapping his hands together.

"Organize these guillotines all over the world tonight and open Victor City. I will address my planet, and we'll have a massive celebration as we watch. Bring in whatever you want—the sorcerers and whores, the finest drugs and celebrities, and the most extravagant food and drink as we watch all through the night!"

CHAPTER 24

Lambertville, New Jersey

E mma, Lerenzo, Kennisha, and Brandon leave the bow and arrows with Micah, Habib, and Esther at the camper truck before they make their trip into the closest town. They continue their efforts to rescue children and teens, and today, they walk into Lambertville, a town that was once considered one of America's prettiest with its picturesque streets and Victorian homes. But the mass vanishings, meteors, earthquakes, volcanic eruptions, and poisoning of the Delaware River have left it fighting for life.

The winds are high today, lifting dirt from the streets and forming mini-cyclones. The four adults are careful as they maneuver through the streets, staying close together and watching for fallen angels or anyone who is giving or looking for Victor's mark. As usual, there are long food lines throughout the streets as people with Victor's mark wait to get inside a market with limited and overpriced groceries and goods. Emma and the others have been unsuccessful in killing any rabbits or squirrels lately, and their last meal, made up of apples, nuts, and chickweed, was two days ago. Emma is looking behind them to make certain that no one with the mark is approaching them when the sickening odor of sulfur overwhelms the air. She hears Kennisha yell and turns forward as Kennisha races across the street.

"Let her go!" Kennisha shouts.

Emma, Lerenzo and Brandon chase after her as they see what is happening. A young woman is being attacked in plain sight by one of the malignant hell-breathers smelling of death, who is easily overpowering her. The woman begins to scream, and Kennisha jumps onto the foul angel's back and punches the dark lord in the head, yelling as she does. With one swift motion, he reaches over his head and grabs hold of Kennisha, flinging her off and throwing her to the ground like a rag doll. When she jumps back up, his fist lands hard on her face, making her stumble back to the ground. Passersby ignore what is happening and choose to cross the street, hurrying to get in line for food.

Lerenzo pummels the hellion, and Emma picks up a brick from the nearby debris to strike the beast as Brandon jumps into the fray. The power of the abyss dweller—coupled with the strong winds—is beyond the three of them, and even though Emma struck him in the head with the brick, he is landing one punch after another against Lerenzo's face. "Go away in Jesus's name!" Emma shouts. The creature stumbles a bit but continues to batter Lerenzo.

"Stop in the name of Jesus!" Lerenzo shouts.

"Jesus is King!" Kennisha cries as the beast uses Brandon as a punching bag. "Jesus is King of kings. Jesus is Lord of lords!"

All four of them shout the name of Jesus louder and louder, and Satan's minion staggers away, leaving them all shaking. Lerenzo and Brandon both have bloodied faces, and blood trickling from one of Kennisha's eyes is beginning to stream down her face. They all turn to look at the young woman who had been attacked and her face is battered; she is shaking and frightened. Kennisha checks her forehead and right hand and notices she hasn't taken Victor's mark. The woman is still terrified, and Kennisha helps to straighten her clothes. "Are you hurt?" Kennisha asks, still breathless.

"I don't know," she says, trembling, her voice barely audible above the gusts. "Just bruised and sore, I think." Tears form in her eyes and she covers her mouth. "Frightened." Her hands shake as she tries to keep her hair from blowing in her face.

"What's your name?" Emma asks. Brandon and Lerenzo are keeping an eye out for the menacing dark angel or for anyone who may be giving or checking for Victor's mark.

"Marissa," the young woman says.

"Do you have family or friends you live with, Marissa?" Kennisha asks with urgency. She knows they have to keep moving.

Marissa nods. "My mom and several relatives."

Kennisha uses a piece of cloth that she always keeps in her back pocket to wipe the blood from Marissa's mouth and eye. "Do you know what that humanlike beast was?" Kennisha asks. Marissa shakes her head. "A satanic angel that has been let loose from the abyss. Do you know why it ran away?" Marissa doesn't reply. "Because of the name of Jesus. They can't bear the name of Jesus. The name of Jesus is more powerful than Satan and his entire realm of demonic creatures."

Marissa's eyes are full of concern, or maybe it's astonishment. Kennisha puts her hand on Marissa's shoulder. "Did you come into town for food?" Marissa nods. "Victor Quade is making people take his mark, telling them that they'll live if they do," Kennisha says, talking fast. "But the only one who can truly give you life is Jesus. His name was strong enough to send your demonic rapist running. The name of Victor Quade can't stop anything. His fate is sealed. He's a dead man. There is no life in him. Only in Jesus." She then takes hold of Marissa's hand. "Do you understand what I'm saying?" Marissa looks down. "If you proclaim that Jesus is Lord, even though you will die here on earth, you will live forever. If you and your family take Victor's name or mark, you are doomed for eternity. Your life is over."

"I claim Jesus as my Lord," Marissa says, her voice quivering.

"Get home and tell your family right now," Emma says, speaking rapidly. "Tell them not to take the mark. Tell them to proclaim Jesus as Lord and Savior, and they will live. Tell them that Jesus is returning soon. He tells us that in the Bible. Read the book of Revelation, which is at the very end of the Bible. It will tell you what is happening on earth and in heaven right now."

Marissa quickly hugs Emma and Kennisha before running away, her hair caught up in the wind and blowing behind her.

Emma uses the piece of cloth in Kennisha's hand to wipe the blood coming from Kennisha's eye. "You're the bravest woman I know, Kennisha. You didn't even think before trying to save Marissa. You just did it."

"The name of Jesus did it," Kennisha says.

The four of them resume their walk through the town, looking down every side street for any children or teens working as prostitutes. Besides the food line, there seems to be no one else in sight and they hurry to leave, anxious to get back to Micah and the other children. Movement in an alleyway catches Kennisha's attention and she calls out for the others to slow down, but she's not sure if they heard her in these high winds. Kennisha enters the alley and approaches a teenage girl around 17 years of age, sitting crouched against the wall.

"Are you alone?" Kennisha asks, stepping around garbage and debris to get to her. The girl looks frightened and doesn't answer. Kennisha kneels down in front of her. "When's the last time you've eaten?"

"I don't know. Can you help me?"

The girl lifts her hand to swipe it across her nose, and Kennisha feels blood rush from her head. Victor's mark is on the girl's right hand. Kennisha realizes this is a trap, and she spins around to warn Emma, Lerenzo, and Brandon. They have turned the corner into the alley in time to see the fallen angel who had attacked Marissa crawl down the side of the building like a demoniac spider and jump onto Kennisha. Emma screams as Kennisha looks at them and shouts, "I'll see you soon!"

CHAPTER 25

Israel
Two Weeks Later

Smoke has blackened the skies of Israel over the past two weeks as the Global Union Forces pillage and burn towns and cities. First, they go into homes and take anything of value that can benefit Victor's government or their own pockets. It has been a dizzying and delightful work for the soldiers; countless Jews have been found hiding in freshly dug holes, fake walls, beneath trap doors, in underground bunkers, and any other place they can tuck themselves away. Upon discovering these Jews, the soldiers are thrilled to either kill them immediately or torture them, making them scream and beg for their lives. Some Jews are hung from cranes or street poles and lit on fire as human torches. Others are gassed or poisoned so the soldiers can witness and mock their slow, gruesome deaths. Women and teen girls are often violated in front of their families and the horror is recorded on the soldiers' phones and uploaded for the world to see.

Zerah, who is on a bicycle, follows the slow-moving tanks filled with soldiers who use flamethrowers to torch homes along the way. Zerah speeds in front of the tanks, shouting through a bullhorn for all sheltering Jews to hear him. He canvasses one neighborhood after another, as he has been doing for months, but now with Israel going up in flames, his warnings are more dire. "The soldiers are here to burn your homes and kill you. You cannot hide this out. Run for the mountains! Call on the name of Messiah Yeshua to save you!"

Over and over, Zerah witnesses Jews trying to sneak out of their homes only to be shot or captured, but there are some who are able to get away. "Yeshua said to flee to the mountains!" he yells as they run for their lives. There are thousands of Global Union soldiers working on this mission, and Victor has told them to continue night and day in their attempt to obliterate all the Jews. Time and again the soldiers try to kill Zerah, an irritating pest that buzzes around them, but to no avail. He cannot be stopped.

Zerah is weary with exhaustion tonight as he shouts through the dark, quiet streets of Haifa. "We will help you, my brother," says someone behind him. Zerah jumps and turns to see a man who looks to be twentysomething wearing glasses, jeans, and a hoodie. He is surrounded by 50 or more other men who have appeared with him. "My name is Elliott. Adonai brought all of us here to help."

Zerah reaches out to Elliott and embraces him, then stands back to look at the others as tears fill his eyes. Adonai has translated some of the 144,000 to Israel to help him. "I'm Zerah. Praise Hashem that you are here!"

"We don't know for how long," Elliott says.

"Okay," Zerah says, understanding that Adonai could translate these men to another location as quickly as they had come here. He notices many of them have bullhorns, and he smiles. "You all know what to do. The forces will be coming through here soon, so do whatever you must to sound the warning. As Yeshua said, people can't take anything with them when they flee. There is no time. Just get them out the door and running to the mountains before soldiers come." That is all the plan that is needed. Zerah quickly prays over them, and within seconds of meeting each other, Zerah and the men separate and begin shouting for people to escape to the mountains.

To discover more about the biblical facts behind the story, read Where in the Word? *on page 245, or continue reading the novel.*

CHAPTER 26

Victor City
Five Months Later

Victor stands proudly in Victor Square as he is about to address the world. The square is packed with his global news journalists and reporters and, as usual, they are jockeying for the best and closest positions to the emperor. Hundreds of netherworld dwellers can be seen atop the buildings, crawling along the sides of them, or hovering above their master, awaiting any need he may have.

Ubel walks to the podium and smiles at the reporters. "Millions continue to make pilgrimage to Israel to worship our lord inside his temple." He points to several large screens that are placed throughout the square for viewing. All show video of a line that runs through the streets of Jerusalem as people wait to worship Victor inside the temple. Individuals are shown taking the mark before stepping inside, and as they do so, their bodies react in euphoria. Victor's eyes fill with elation as he watches them. Once the mark is administered, his DNA is deeply embedded within them, making them one with him.

The screens change to show a woman going into the temple in a wheelchair, and then once inside, levitating out of it. Weary pilgrims fall to the floor upon witnessing the miracle taking place before them. When the woman's feet touch the floor, she jumps high into the air, proving that she can walk again and leaving everyone amazed.

"Worshippers continue to be healed," Ubel says. "And their faith in our lord and his power is strengthened. Let it be proclaimed that there is no other god but our god, Victor. He alone is worthy to be praised. In him is the truth that sets all mankind free! In him is healing for our bodies and for our world!"

"I need to be healed!" A reporter with dark skin and a Pakistani accent steps forward. The skin on his face and arms is peeling away as if rotting. "This is the result of nuclear fallout," he says, stepping toward Ubel. Months ago, the Global Union Forces had dropped a nuclear bomb on a city 50 miles from the man's home, and now, residents there and in surrounding towns and villages are breaking out in oozing sores and skin that is blistering and coming off.

Ubel stretches out his arms. "There has been no nuclear fallout, my son," he says, propagating the lie that there have been no wars in Victor's kingdom of peace. "Let me see." Ubel examines the man's face and arms. "You have a skin condition. That is all." He puts one hand over the man's face and the other on his arm, and says, "I plead the blood of our emperor and savior, Victor, over you. It is by his blood that is inside of you that you are healed." To the astonishment of the man and the reporters crowding around him, his skin miraculously heals over. The video is instantly dispersed all over the planet, making believers of many who had been skeptical.

Ubel turns his attention back to the screens and points out a recently produced commercial featuring the smiling, happy faces of those who have taken Victor's mark.

"With the mark, we're happier than we've ever been," says a young couple in Sweden.

"We are able to do anything we want with the mark," a group of friends shout while partying on a boat in the Mediterranean.

"You'll never go hungry with the mark," says a man in front of a market in Bulgaria.

"With the mark, you'll never sleep on the streets," says a woman inside her home in Malaysia.

"With the mark, you'll never lose the business you've worked your whole life for," says a couple inside their retail store in the United States.

"You won't have to give up your lifestyle with the mark," a family says before boarding an airplane in France.

"With the mark, you don't have to give up your future," says a group of college students inside a university classroom in England.

"You'll never lose your livelihood with the mark," says a farmer standing in the middle of his crop in Guatemala.

"You'll never lose your healthcare," says a woman with her children in Berlin while getting medicine from a local pharmacy.

"Or your peace of mind," says an elderly couple from Japan.

Individual pictures of thousands of people from around the world flash on the screens. "Don't give up your life," they say together in unison. "Take the mark and live!"

"This is the most successful effort in the history of the world!" Ubel declares at the conclusion of the commercial, raising his hand in victory. The screens suddenly show people from around the globe literally running to stand in line at marking stations, packing in together like cattle. "It is safe and easy to receive the mark, and global citizens are eagerly getting it so that they and their friends and families can continue to live and succeed and have peace of mind. Marking units are set up at retail and business establishments everywhere and are ready to serve you. There is no life without our sovereign's mark, and everyone is quickly realizing that it really is a matter of life and death."

Ubel waits for the cheers of the global network reporters to die down before continuing. "All praise and worship go to our savior, Victor, because without him, we would not be thriving as we are. His world is being cleansed of the reprobates, extremists, terrorists, radicals, and fanatics who openly refuse to worship our king and continue to spread lies and hate. And our land is increasingly being purified of Jewish blood. You have helped to find so many creative ways to eradicate this poison from our universe. You are lighting up our streets around the world." Ubel points to the screens, which feature Jews lit up as torches in different cities. "You are taking out the garbage." The images on the screens shift to bodies strewn on top of landfills. "You are going on safari or to an arena near you." The screens show Jews fleeing in different parts of Africa as lions or tigers chase them down, and Jews being attacked and mauled inside arenas. "You are killing the weeds growing among you." A video of Jews in Europe being doused with poison and collapsing causes Victor's eyes to glow as he watches them die.

"As you destroy this filth," Ubel says, "it is your holy act of worship and our lord's delight. You are making our universe beautiful and kind again. You are making it pristine. Religion that is pure and undefiled is this: to remove the Jew and Christ affliction from our world and to keep ourselves unstained from their influence as we worship Victor our lord."

The reporters cheer again, and as the noise fades, an African reporter raises his voice to be heard over the crowd. "We keep hearing rumblings that Egypt and Syria are at war with the emperor. Is that true?"

Victor scoffs and steps forward to address this. "I have just returned from another successful world tour and can assure you that there is no truth whatsoever in that. There is no reason for war. Many of you have been with me on these tours and know that people everywhere revere and worship me. Why would anyone come against a kingdom of peace? A kingdom of life? A kingdom of hope? Look at what I've done. Look at my name or mark on your bodies, which has joined my life together with yours. As my holy prophet stated, look how I have already cleansed and am continuing to cleanse this world of hatred, bigotry, and the evil of false religion. The liars, the frauds, the immoral, the reprobates, the fascists, the racists, the assassins, the extremists, and the wicked of every kind are being eliminated so we can live in harmony. Each day, millions of Jews and Jesus fanatics are being eradicated. All of you are helping with these life-giving methods. My kingdom will now pay for the life of every Jew or Christ follower that you take. Each one that you remove gives life to the rest of us. My world literally feels the release of the poison each time one dies. We are creating a unified, beautiful world. Can you feel it?"

The reporters heartily agree, but an Asian woman rises up on her toes so that she can be seen. "What about the rivers and streams? Many of them are still poisoned."

"Who told you that?" Victor says, smiling at her in a way that makes her blush. "Because that person is a liar, and there is no room for liars in my kingdom. We eliminate liars, don't we?" The reporter nods. "My scientists have assured me that the waters are safe now. We have nothing to fear. Drink freely, my dear."

"We have received word that Dr. Ito, who originally warned about the waters, has taken his life because the waters are still plagued," another reporter states. "Is that true?"

Victor shrugs. "If he took his life, then he is among the weak and should not live. If he's dead, he did the world a favor." Again, the reporters eagerly agree. Victor is tired of this nonsense and he shifts to his final thoughts as the sun's light on the square fades. The earth has never recovered from the ash that has seemingly put the sun on a dimmer, but now the world is darker still. Shadows fall across the faces of the reporters, but Victor ignores what is happening and smiles for the cameras. "We continue to build a better and stronger world and are thriving. Remember, my mark gives life. It means freedom. Do you have it? Do your family members and friends have it? Look out for one another and go to a site today to receive my mark. Then go out and be free to do anything you want!"

The reporters cheer, and Victor's court and the generals follow him back inside the building. As soon as the last aide enters and the door is shut, Victor begins screaming and swearing. The ceiling and walls in the long hallway throb with demonic movement as he rages. "Who lied about Egypt and Syria? Who lied about the waters?"

"We have all been in agreement that the waters are pure," George says, running to keep up with Victor, who is storming toward the throne room.

"Haven't we eliminated all Internet and social media sites that are for the Christ terrorist regime?" Victor says, flopping down on his throne.

An aide nods. "They have all been deleted. There is nothing left of their radical thoughts anywhere online."

"It has to be one of those rogue news announcers," Adrien says, taking his seat. "Because it's not anyone within your global media."

Victor turns on Adrien. "How many of these rogue news announcers are there?"

Maria shrugs. "We don't know for sure. There aren't many. Perhaps five or ten."

Victor is breathing hard, thinking. "How are they getting information? How are they transmitting?" Victor's court and his generals glance at one another. "How are they getting information?" Victor shouts.

"We don't know," an aide replies.

"Then find out and bring an end to all of them," Victor says. He flings his arm toward the screens. "Show me how you're destroying the Egyptian and Syrian troops, General!" General Nygard nods at an aide, and videos appear of the war taking place between Egypt and Syria against the Global Union Forces. The images are vicious and gruesome. Victor is incensed. "How is it possible that they are still fighting?"

"They are determined and skilled," General Nygard says.

"Determined to destroy my world!" Victor shouts. "How many of my forces have been killed?"

General Nygard shakes his head. "The most up-to-date number is just under thirty thousand, but nuclear weapons have been unleashed and we don't..."

"End it today," Victor says calmly, walking to a window that normally is a source of light and heat for the room. "Use whatever force is necessary. I have the finest military capabilities in Israel. They are the only worthy resources the Jew scum left me. I never want to hear another reporter ask me about this so-called war. Do you understand?" He turns and looks at the generals, who nod and bow in reverence. "Get out! All of you!" The generals and Victor's court do as he commands and quickly exit the room.

Victor looks out the window and notices that what should be the bright of day is still muted and overcast. The room feels chilly, and Victor's face darkens. "You will not win," he says, looking up at the dim gray sky. "Can't you see what is happening? They are following and worshipping me. Not you. You have no power here."

CHAPTER 27

Pennsylvania

Emma, Lerenzo, Brandon, Micah, Esther, Antonio, and Habib walk atop the wooded hillsides of Pennsylvania at twilight, keeping their voices low. This time of day is murkier now, and they know from reading Revelation 8 that one-third of the stars, sun, and moon have been darkened, making it difficult to see far into the distance. These woods are like all the others they've traveled: partly gray from the trees plagued many months ago, and now darkness clings like death over these hills.

Emma and the others left the camper in the days following Kennisha's murder when they smelled fallen angels in the woods. They realized it was only a matter of time before they were discovered, so they set out on foot once again in search of a cave or abandoned building of some sort. It has been three days since they last found some wild blueberry bushes and picked them clean. Lerenzo and Micah have tried to kill several rabbits, squirrels, and even a bobcat, but have missed all of them, and although Emma knows they are all getting weak with hunger, no one says a word. Hunger and thirst are a constant part of their lives. "We need to stop and rest," Emma says, noticing that Habib is struggling as they walk up the hillside.

Lerenzo nods, and Emma and the children sit down, each resting against a tree. "This hill and that one over there plunge into a valley," Lerenzo says, looking at Emma. "Maybe there's a stream or waterfall nearby. Stay here with the kids while Brandon and I search a little more."

Emma nods, and encourages Habib to lay down and rest his head on her lap. In the distance she sees five black bears and prays they won't come near them. Despite the presence of the bears, she leans back against the tree and closes her eyes. It seems like days since she last slept.

The sound of rustling awakens Emma, and her eyes flash open to see darkness surrounding them. She wonders how long she's been asleep. "Lerenzo?" she whispers. "Brandon?"

"They aren't back," Micah says, barely audible.

The rustling is getting closer, and Emma wonders if it's the bears. But when she smells the rotten odor of fallen angels, she stops breathing. She stretches in search of Micah's hand and gives it an urgent squeeze. "Don't move," she whispers, praying that the other children will remain asleep. Emma then hears the sound of other hellions in the woods, and she prays that Lerenzo and Brandon are a safe distance from them. Noise that resembles laughter or crying—she can't tell which—echoes through the woods, and she realizes that women are with the dark beasts. The reverberation of heinous shrieks makes Habib jump up from his sleep, and Emma puts her hand over his mouth to keep him quiet. As the noise escalates, Emma tugs on Micah's hand. "Wake the kids," she whispers. "We have to move. Leave everything here. There's no time to gather it."

Her heart races and she is breathing in short spurts as she stands to her feet and lifts Habib into her arms, whispering into his ear. "Stay super quiet." She reaches for Esther's and Antonio's hands and directs them to hold on to her shirt behind her and for Micah to follow them. When the shrieking, laughing, and screaming get louder, Emma takes a step away from the noise. Rustling in the trees above them makes her blood run cold and she stands frozen, wondering if one of hell's angels has found them. Abominable sounds of terror echo throughout the woods, and Habib covers his ears. Emma begins walking again, careful as she takes each step so she doesn't stumble over a fallen tree or trip on an exposed root. They have probably been moving for only a few minutes, but she feels as though they've been taking painstaking steps for hours when the ground beneath Emma ends. She sticks her foot out further to figure out where they are, but can't feel anything. She sets Habib down and sits on the ground, hanging her legs over what feels like an embankment. Getting back up, she reaches behind her to find Micah and directs him to come forward.

"I can't tell if this is an embankment or something deeper," she whispers into his ear. "Can you lower yourself to see if you can touch anything?"

Micah doesn't answer but quietly moves into action. He lays on his stomach and lowers his legs. He keeps sliding further over the edge until one foot touches the ground below. He lets go and then lands, using his foot to make sure this area doesn't take another plunge downward. "It's okay," he whispers. "Hand each of them to me."

Emma directs Habib to get down on his stomach. The unspeakable sounds grow louder in the woods, and Emma can't imagine what sort of hell on earth is taking place behind them. She crouches down so she can help lower Habib, and then Esther and Antonio. She is still on the ground when she hears movement a few feet from her and she flattens out on her stomach. Micah hears it too, and squeezes her hands to come down with him and the kids, but she can't move; it's too dangerous.

Micah sits down in the middle of the children and makes sure they stay tight against the embankment. They barely breathe as the vile creature walks through the woods a few feet from their hiding place. In a narrow stream of moonlight, Emma can just make out the satanic beast as it swings into the top of a tree like a possessed monkey and then slithers down another tree's trunk like its serpent ancestor. Her heart is racing, and she feels faint at the sight and smell of it. It takes a few steps toward her and pauses as if it has heard something. Emma stops breathing, praying for the children to remain hidden from its view. Shrieks from the middle of the woods cause the dark fiend to turn its gruesome head in that direction as it opens its mouth in a horrifying and shrill roar that strikes terror in Emma and takes her breath. Micah and the children cover their ears against the vicious sound coming from just above them, and they each pray silently that the animal from hell won't find Emma.

Emma watches as the monstrosity turns toward the noise coming from the heart of the woods and shrieks again, swinging from one tree to another as it makes his way to hell's hordes that are filling the air with unspeakable evil. Shaking, Emma gets up onto her knees and quickly throws her legs over the embankment, jumping down. The children throw their arms around her, and she feels nauseous and weak. "I'm okay. I'm okay," she whispers. "Praise God, we're all okay," she says, praying for Lerenzo and Brandon.

Jordan

The cloak of night covers the land as the group of Jews, weary from exhaustion and sick with hunger, weep at what they can barely see in the distance. Farouq, their smuggler, puts his finger to his lips to keep them quiet. Over the past few weeks, the size of the groups of Jews fleeing Israel have gotten bigger and bigger, making it more difficult to travel quickly. There are several Jordanians, Egyptians, and Arabs who have pledged their lives to Christ and to helping his people, and they put their own lives on the line several times a week sneaking Jews out of Israel and into Jordan.

Just a few days ago in Israel, Elliott lifted a log of acacia wood and set it aside in the darkness before moving a small panel of wood covered with dirt, leaves, and twigs. Lowering himself into the hole, he could hear the faint breathing of those closest to him. "I'm Elliott," he whispered in the pitch-black darkness. "How many are here?"

"Thirty-three," said a man hoarse with illness.

Thirty-three people were crammed into the makeshift burrow. The air was so hot and stale that Elliott quickly made his way up the earthen stairs into the night air so he could breathe. "Follow me," he whispered. He had lost count of how many times he had been translated to Israel to help Jews out of these holes to send them toward the border. He had also lost count of how many had been killed as they ran for the safety of the mountains. Many in the group were skeletal. A life in hiding without much food for the last several months had reduced most of them to bones.

Tonight, all 33 of them are still together, and Farouq picks up a boy around five years of age who is too tired to continue. "We are almost there," he whispers into the boy's ear. "Just a little further to go and you will be safe." From the border of Israel, the group had walked 15 miles before hiding inside a cave in Jordan. Then at nightfall, they walked another 15 miles. The last five miles of their journey have been tonight, and now, with the rocky silhouette of Petra in sight, the Jews begin to cry.

"I see the mountains!" says a middle-aged woman with a face lined from the burdens and terrors of escaping. Farouq waves his arm toward the woman to silence her. They haven't eaten in seven days and have had very little water. Many fall to their knees and weep silently at the view before Farouq runs to them with the boy in his arms, snatching at their hair or clothing and urging them to stay quiet and keep moving.

When the cool air below the crags is felt, many in the group begin to shake. Can it be that they have outrun the horrors taking place in Israel? Farouq leads them through Petra's mile-long entrance, called the Siq, and into a great open space where even in the darkness the group can feel the lives of others among the rocks. Some 2,000 years ago, tens of thousands of caves had been carved into the miles of walls and canyons at Petra. "You are safe now," a woman says, and then everyone in the group falls to the ground and weeps. "It is all right," the woman says, taking the young boy from Farouq's arms so Farouq can flee back out of the mountains.

"Thank you," says an elderly man, grabbing Farouq's arm as he runs past. "May Adonai bless you and keep you." Farouq's eyes glisten in the moonlight at the words of the old man, but he runs away as quickly as he can. There is still much work to be done.

Footsteps can be heard drawing near, and cups of water are placed in their trembling hands. A chorus of voices say, "You are safe now." "Praise Messiah Yeshua!" "You are home!" "Adonai is powerful to save!"

When daybreak comes, the group will see the faces of those caring for them. But for now, they cry and laugh together among the rocks that will be their home until Messiah returns.

CHAPTER 28

Pennsylvania

As the sun rises, Emma looks over at Micah, who, like her, has been awake all night as snow fell on them. They had left all their blankets with the belongings they had abandoned the day before, and had shivered through the night. Satan's lords had left a few hours ago, but sleep was impossible. Emma is stiff with cold and from sitting straight up for hours and groans as she moves Esther and Antonio from her lap. "We have to get back to where we were," she says as each child wakes up and she brushes snow from them.

"What about Lerenzo and Brandon?" Esther asks.

"That's why we have to get back. They'll look for us there. We need to find a place to get out of this snow," Emma says, unable to think of finding a place to rest right now; all she can think and pray about are Lerenzo and Brandon. She wants to find them and get out of these wretched hills as quickly as possible.

Emma shimmies up the embankment first, and Micah helps each child from below as she pulls them up. When they don't stumble upon their belongings right away, they realize how far they must have walked last night. Just the memory of the terror of what had happened makes the hair on the back of Emma's neck stand up, and she quickens her pace. Voices in the distance make her stop, and she holds up her hand so the kids will stop as well. They crouch down and listen closely.

When Emma recognizes Lerenzo's voice, she pops back up. "Lerenzo," she says, keeping her voice low but hoping it's loud enough for him to hear.

"Emma!"

Emma can hear the sound of running footsteps and she and the children rush forward, falling into Lerenzo's arms, exhausted and relieved. His and Brandon's clothes are soaking wet. "Where were you?" she asks, breathing hard.

"We found a stream running down the hillside and then smelled the sulfur," Lerenzo says. "There was no way to get past the demonic beasts, so we stayed all night at the stream." He and Brandon hug each of the children and can see they've had a harrowing night. "When we found our things, we thought you..."

"We found an embankment," Emma says, feeling weak and unable to tell them the rest. "I can't even imagine what was happening here last night, but I know we heard a little of what hell sounds like."

Nobody wants to talk about what they heard or experienced, and there's a long pause. Finally, Micah breaks the quiet. "We need water."

"The stream is that way," Brandon says, pointing. "And we found a cabin. We can rest while it snows."

"Did you go in?" Emma asks, wondering if there might be food.

"It's abandoned," Lerenzo says. "Looks like maybe it was a hunting cabin. There are some bunk beds in one room and a full-sized bed in the other. The windows have been left opened and birds and squirrels have been inside. We ran through the place so fast. It doesn't look like there's any food, but we didn't open every cabinet. We can rest there for a bit." They put their blankets around their necks and gather their belongings, and Lerenzo notices how tiny Emma has become. Her backpack looks almost as big as her. He reaches for her backpack, taking it from her and smiling, reaching for her hand. It's icy cold, and he wraps her blanket tight around her.

When they find the stream, they each bend down like thirsty

animals and lap up the water. They fill their water bottles and an old gallon milk container they had found over a year ago. After they are all done, they walk to the cabin, which is tucked away in the hillside. "Could we possibly sleep here?" Emma asks, hurrying to keep up.

Lerenzo stops to look at her and realizes again how exhausted they all are. He glances at Brandon, and Brandon nods. "Sure," Lerenzo says. "At least for a night."

Once inside, the children open the cabinets inside the kitchen as if they're raiding it, which is exactly what they're doing. "Crackers!" Micah says, lifting a half-empty box.

"A little cereal!" Esther declares as she kneels in front of one of the lower cupboards.

Emma lifts the handle of the kitchen faucet. "Water!" she says. "We could shower!" She moves out of the kitchen to search for a bathroom, and the hallway is dark. Stepping into a bedroom, she can see the dim light of the moon peering through a window in the bathroom. Emma makes her way across the room and enters the bathroom, where she finds the shower and turns on the knob. Cold water pours over her hand and she groans. They can't take a cold shower in this weather. Besides an occasional dip into a stream, lake, or river, Emma hasn't used shampoo or soap in nearly two years and was hoping she could find some here. But they would have to settle for giving themselves what her mother had called "a bird bath."

Before leaving the bathroom, Emma pokes her head through a door and can feel clothes hanging inside a closet. "Clean clothes," she says, grateful for the possibility that some of these might be useful for her and the others. They've worn the same clothes for months now because it's been that long since they've last found an abandoned home. She moves further into the closet and steps on what she thinks is a shoe. A soft noise makes Emma's heart jump, and she leaps out of the closet. She hears a sound again, but it's not the scurrying of a mouse or squirrel. She feels her way through the bedroom again and into the hall. "Lerenzo! Brandon! There's something in the bedroom closet." She strains her eyes to see all of them scouring the kitchen cabinets. "We have to find a flashlight or a candle. Hurry!"

Each of them pulls open drawers and feels around inside until Habib shouts, "Here's one!"

"Stay in here," Brandon says to the children as he takes the flashlight. He, Lerenzo, and Emma run back into the bathroom, where he shines the dim beam into the closet and into the eyes of a woman in her late fifties or early sixties. She is crumpled on the floor.

"Get her up!" Emma says, taking the flashlight from Brandon.

Lerenzo lifts the woman carefully, and her limbs feel as if they'll snap in his hands. Brandon lifts her legs and they ease her from the closet and onto the bed in the bedroom. "Can you hear us?" Lerenzo asks. Emma keeps the flashlight away from her face, but they can see the woman nod.

Emma shines the light on the woman's right hand and forehead. "No mark."

"No," the woman whispers. "I won't take the mark. Do what you have to do. My soul is with Jesus."

Emma steps closer to the woman and takes hold of her hand. "We're not here to hurt you. Our souls are with Jesus too. We don't have the mark." She sits on the side of the bed and squeezes the woman's hand. Emma can hear Micah, Esther, Antonio, and Habib run just inside the bedroom doorway and stop.

The woman begins to cry and uses her other hand to cover her mouth. "I thought you were here to kill me," she says, struggling for air. "But it didn't matter because I know I don't have long, and I'm so close to being with Jesus and my family."

Emma feels tears forming in her eyes. "How long have you been ill?"

"For months," the woman whispers. "My dad died of heart disease when he was 52. My brother died of the same at 47. I thought I was so lucky all my life because I never had any signs of it until over a year ago, but of course I couldn't go to a doctor or buy medicine. My daughter and I ran from place to place trying to live. She helped me until two weeks ago." Her voice fades and tears cover her cheeks.

"Is your daughter dead?" Emma asks.

The woman nods, crying. "Out there somewhere," she says, gesturing to a window. "She died in the night about two weeks ago and I had no other choice but to leave her there. I found this place a few days later but could barely breathe then." She tries to lift her head off the bed, and Lerenzo moves closer to help her lean up. "Will you stay with me?" Her eyes are pleading with them in the half-glow of the flashlight. "Please."

Emma glances at Lerenzo and Brandon, and they all know that the woman doesn't have long. "Of course we'll stay," Emma says. "What's your name?"

"Natalie," she says, relieved.

"I'm Emma, and this is my husband, Lerenzo, and our friend, Brandon. We have four children who are with us, and I hear them standing over there in the doorway."

"They must be hungry," Natalie says, using her hand to point toward the bathroom. "I took all the food into the closet. I was trying to make it look like there was no food in this place and tried to hide from anyone who would want to break in." She pauses, looking up at Emma. "That plan didn't work too well." Emma, Lerenzo, and Brandon smile. "There's some cans of soup and vegetables, some noodles, cereal, and a few other things that might fill your bellies."

Emma pats her arm. "How long have you been in the closet?"

"Since I got here. When I was hiding the food, I passed out, and when I woke up, I couldn't get back up." She squeezes Emma's hand. "Please, go get the food and feed yourselves."

"Kids, please come and say hello to Natalie," Emma says, speaking in their direction.

Brandon shines the flashlight toward the bedroom door, and more tears cascade down Natalie's face when she sees the children. "I had four grandchildren," she says, reaching out her hand for Micah. He takes hold of it, and Emma smiles. Despite having been abandoned into her care when the world turned upside down in madness, he had grown into a loving and compassionate young man. "My grandchildren all knew Jesus and were snatched away in the blink of an eye. I can't tell you how happy I am to be able to see them very soon because they were my greatest joy. What are your names?" The children each tell her, and Natalie sighs, so happy to hear the voices of children once again.

"Did you live in Pennsylvania?" Brandon asks.

"Born and raised. Married my high school sweetheart and I worked in city transportation for over thirty years. I lived with the love of my life until Jesus snatched him away along with my son, daughter-in-law, and grandchildren. My daughter Claire and I were left." She reaches out her hands to touch Antonio, Esther, and Habib. "I wish I'd had the faith of a child so many years ago. Jesus is coming again, isn't he?" The children nod and she catches her breath. "You are overcomers! Even though you're weak with hunger, you are strong in the Lord. I can see it on your faces!"

"You're an overcomer too," Micah says. "That's what Jesus calls you."

Natalie closes her eyes at the words and a pained smile appears on her face. "Thank you," she says, her breath faint. "Thank you all."

CHAPTER 29

Two Days Later

As the children sleep on the bunks in the bedroom next to them, Emma sits on the bed next to Natalie's body, and Lerenzo and Brandon stand beside her. "I can't imagine your celebration right now, Natalie," Emma says, holding her hand. Natalie lost consciousness a few hours ago, but true to their word, they stayed with her until she died.

"We can try to find a shovel and bury her," Lerenzo says to Brandon, moving the flashlight so he can see Brandon's face. "If there isn't a shovel, I don't know what…"

"I'm so tired," Emma whispers, cutting him off. Lerenzo sits down next to her, pulling her blanket up around her neck and letting her lean her head on his shoulder. "I can't do this again," she whispers, looking at Natalie. "We've already done it so many times. And I'm not over Kennisha."

"You're not supposed to be over Kennisha," Lerenzo says, holding her closer in the chilly room.

"We'll never be over her," Brandon says. Although they've all lost weight and strength, Brandon has lost weight faster than any of them, looking emaciated and frail. "But Kennisha's final words are our comfort, Em. We *will* see her soon. It's what Elliott has always said. It's what we've always said to each other, and she reminded us! She was always reminding us about something, and it was just like her to do it one final time."

Tears form in Emma's eyes, and she blurts out laughing. "That *was* just like her! I'd be so mad or about to cry, and she'd remind me of what God has said. *Every* time!" She rests her head again on Lerenzo's shoulder and lets the laughter take over. "I can hear her now: *We keep trusting God, Emma. We keep praying. We keep saving kids until Jesus comes.*" She shakes her head. "Where'd she get that kind of faith?"

"From you, Mom," Micah says. Emma leans up and, in the first rays of morning light, can see that all four children have walked into the room with blankets wrapped around them. Micah steps over to the bed and looks down at Natalie, and then to Emma. "Kennisha got it from Brandon and Jamie and Elliott and Bella and Dad," Micah says, looking at Lerenzo. "We build each other's faith, right?"

"Right," Emma says. "And you built our faith in the short time we knew you, Natalie," she says, patting Natalie's hand.

A voice outside the home makes all of them stiffen. They can't quite make out what is being said, but the voice is loud and seems to be repeating the same words over and over. They move cautiously to the window, where they can see streaks of daylight piercing the teal-colored sky. Snow has stopped falling and the woods are beautiful, draped in white. The voice sounds as if it is coming from some distance away. Micah leads them as they run to the back door and step outside, straining to hear the voice. The air is still and cold, and they don't move as they listen.

"Woe, woe, woe..."

It turns out the voice isn't at ground level but overhead, and Emma is the first to spot something moving above the trees. "There!" she says, pointing.

The others are unable to see it, but Micah spots something flying toward them. "It's an eagle!" he says, directing them where to see it in the sky.

"Woe, woe, woe to those who dwell on the earth, at the blasts of the other trumpets that the three angels are about to blow!" The eagle's words boom through the sky and send a chill down each of their spines.

"It's talking," Esther says, mystified.

"From Revelation," Emma says. "He's warning everyone about what's coming."

"Woe, woe, woe to those who dwell on the earth…" the eagle cries again as it flies away.

CHAPTER 30

Victor City, Italy

Victor, his court, their aides, Ubel, and several generals are inside the throne room watching the latest videos of parades for Victor from around the world when strange flying insects buzz their way beneath the doors and through the windows and wing their way into the room. Maria is the first to fall from her chair, yelping as they attack her. She shrieks, using her hands to bat the pests from her arms, legs, and face. George and Adrien cry out in anguish, and in an attempt to flee from them, Adrien runs into the glass panes of the massive windows and cries out in pain.

"Get them off! Get them off!" George shouts, stripping off his suit jacket.

Victor stands at his throne as the entire room erupts in howls and cursing. Ubel has thrown off his cassock and is writhing on the floor as the locust-like bugs sting him over and over. Victor's back arches as if he's been seized from behind when several alight on his body. His voice rises above all the others as he swears and screams.

"Get them off!" Maria's voice is shrill as she flails at her head.

"A plague of demon locusts will torment you for five months!"

Victor stops cursing at the sound of the voice. It's one he's heard many times, and he turns to see Zerah on the screens, standing on the temple steps in Jerusalem. The crowd that has been standing in line

153

to worship Victor's image is now running away or flailing in agony as a menacing swarm of locusts swoops down on them. "You have chosen Victor Quade over Jesus Christ, and this is just the beginning of your torment," Zerah yells to the crowd. "You have given your souls to Satan."

"It is far worse than a scorpion's sting!" another voice on a screen says.

Victor glances at the screen and sees Elliott standing inside what is left of Chicago's Union Station, which is mostly inoperable now. Lines are always long as people wait for the few trains able to run each day, and Elliott is speaking over the pandemonium that has broken out amidst the pulsating black cloud in the station. "A scorpion's sting will feel like relief compared to your torment for the next five months. You will want to kill yourself, but as it is written in God's Word, death will flee from you. For those who can hear me and have not taken Victor's mark, this is your time to claim Jesus as Lord!"

Victor listens in misery as, on screen after screen, many of the 144,000 sealed servants of Jesus proclaim in Bolivia, Niger, Libya, Mongolia, Denmark, Laos, and around the world that Jesus is Lord, and that those with Victor's mark will be tormented for five months. Victor screams and rushes for a chair near the screens, bashing it against each one until Zerah and Elliott and the others can no longer be seen or heard. "I am god! I am savior! I am king!" Victor rages as the hordes from hell torment their own lord.

The Negev

Zerah rushes to the truck that has pulled in front of an incinerator. A Global Union Forces soldier opens the driver's-side door and falls from the seat onto the ground, where he thrashes about in distress as the locusts sting him and a tempest of a dust storm blows against him. Zerah strips him of his gun and runs to the back of the truck, opening the doors. "Go!" he says, shouting at the Jews through the raging sand. "Someone get behind the wheel and drive to Petra! Go now!" Three men scurry from the back of the truck, and Zerah hands the gun to one of them. They stop for a moment to watch the soldier scream and squirm on the ground. "Go!" Zerah yells at the men through the dust.

"But we will be stopped," says the one getting behind the wheel.

"All those with Victor's mark are being tortured by Satan's own demons. Their pain and agony is so great that they will be distracted. Just drive! You have a gun to help. Get out of here!" Zerah then bolts to the back of the truck and closes the doors before racing to the next one.

Elliott and several others of the 144,000 sealed servants have been translated back to Israel, where they drive through the streets, countryside, and deserts hollering for the Jews to flee. "Yeshua Messiah is Lord!" Elliott cries as he runs through the sandstorm and deep into a cave, where a large group of Jews have been hiding. "Get to Petra," he says, breathless. "There are trucks outside."

"It is light out," a man says, whispering and frightened. "We must wait until the night."

Elliott grabs the man by his shoulders. "Tormenting spirits have taken hold of your enemy for the next five months. All those who have taken Victor's mark are consumed with excruciating pain. There is a powerful sandstorm that will provide cover for you. Run now! Yeshua Messiah is Lord!"

"Yeshua Messiah is Lord," says the man as others run past them into the murky light.

CHAPTER 31

Singapore

The transmitter is crackling as John sits inside the darkened room. Believers throughout Singapore have been helping him find places to broadcast the news, but life on the run is taking its toll. He's weary, hungry, and ill, with yet another plaguing sickness galloping across the globe at this time.

"The Revelator says Mark will be pure agony for nearly half a year," he says, whispering into the microphone. "Locusts of hell attacking Mark and death will not come to those who know Mark, no matter how hard they try. Earthquakes in Japan, Singapore, Brazil, and Australia kill thousands, and volcanoes in Russia, the United States, Chile, Papua New Guinea, the Philippines, Mexico, and around the Ring of Fire kill thousands more as famine marches on. Millions upon millions of doves have flown, but doves and ash collection might be at temporary halt due to locust invasion. Ash collection stands at least eight million worldwide. Another pestilence winging its way through the air at fevered pitch. When will the bound angels described by the Revelator be released from the Euphrates? Keep standing. Things are looking up."

John sits for a moment with his head against the wall and knows it's only a matter of time before one of Victor's goons finds him. He prays for strength, then quickly puts his equipment inside the backpack before running out beneath the blood-red moon.

To discover more about the biblical facts behind the story, read Where in the Word? *on page 253, or continue reading the novel.*

CHAPTER 32

New York City
Two Weeks Later

When they realized that those with Victor's mark were being tortured for five months, Emma, Lerenzo, Brandon, and the children made their way back to live in New York City. They know that this five-month span, which is straight out of the book of Revelation, is a gift of mercy from God to all those who have yet to take Victor's mark, and they want to tell everyone they can about salvation in Jesus alone.

The city has suffered even more since the last time they were here, which was the day that Emma watched as Matt was killed. An earthquake that rocked the eastern half of the United States has left more of the city in shambles, and more rats, dogs, coyotes, and foxes roam the streets in search of food. The black swarms of menacing spirits fly through the streets in search of those with Victor's mark, and the anguished cries of those under infernal torment rise and pierce the air. The tortured roam about like ferocious dogs, wailing and seeking relief from their unimaginable woes. Their heinous voices saturate the city and their faces and bodies are ghastly, ghoulish, and distorted as the maniacal infliction twists and perverts their humanity.

The unceasing attacks of the demon locusts on those with the mark has kept the afflicted in a state of near debilitation, making it easier for those without the mark to find food. No one with the mark is interested in chasing someone down for swiping a loaf of bread when his body is racked in indescribable pain. For the first time in more than a year, Emma and the others have gone less than three days without eating and have been able to find one abandoned home or apartment after another to lodge in, keeping them out of caves and the woods for now.

A beautiful light show of red and green whirls about in the sky as Emma and the others walk through the streets of Queens, where they formerly lived. Emma's heart breaks at the sight of the gutted-out buildings she once loved, places where she had spent time shopping or sipping a coffee. "The bakery was there, remember, Brandon?" she says, pointing. "You and Rick and Matt and I would go there on Sunday mornings." It brings Emma comfort to know that her former fiancé claimed Jesus as Lord in his last moments on earth, but neither she nor Brandon know what had happened to Rick. She has prayed for him often, but he was so hardened to God's truth that she worries he has taken the mark. The possibility he may have done that brings tremendous sadness to both her and Brandon.

"For those who have ears to hear, call on Jesus and live!" Emma shouts, looking up into an apartment building where the top floors have slid onto the pavement as the result of a recent earthquake. "If you take Victor's mark, you will die. If you take the mark, you will be tormented right now just as the others are. There is only death in that mark. You will be separated from God forever! This is a time of mercy. Come out of hiding and come down here to listen to us. We know how you can live!"

The cries and groans in the street from those with the mark are so loud that it's unnerving. As they go by, they are constantly flailing their arms, batting about their heads, clawing their skin until it bleeds, grimacing and twisting their faces in agony, and twitching. Kennisha was brutally murdered by one of hell's angels in a singular attack; what is happening now is a continuous satanic onslaught against everyone who has the mark and is brutal to hear and watch.

In spite of the beautiful light show in the skies, the air is saturated with evil. The group feels as though they're walking among ghouls and goblins whose moans of affliction rise and fill all the streets. The commotion and clamor from those with the mark rattles their nerves, but despite the noise and distractions around them, they are filled with resolve to reach people for Jesus. Lerenzo stands next to Emma and looks in the direction of the apartment building on the other side of the street. "All who call upon the name of the Lord Jesus Christ will be saved!" he hollers. "He is coming again for all who believe in him!"

"Come down to us," Brandon says, cupping his hands around his mouth as he shouts. "We are telling you about how to live!"

Micah, Esther, Antonio, and Habib scan the apartment windows, and Micah points to one. "Up there!" he says, pointing to a window near the top of the razored-off building. The sunken face of an elderly man appears, and he puts his palm on the window, looking down at them.

"Over there," Esther says, pointing to another building. "Third floor. Two women."

"Come down!" Brandon yells again, louder this time. Moments later, a woman and her child open the apartment building door that leads to the street, and Brandon waves his arms to invite them over. Moments later, the elderly man and the two women approach from their buildings. "Come and live," Brandon says. The five apartment dwellers approach the group with caution, and Brandon smiles at them. "Only Jesus can give you eternal life," he says as a man contorted in pain runs past them. "If you take Victor Quade's mark you will die and be forever separated from God. If you proclaim that Jesus is Lord, you can live for eternity. Repent of your sin and call on him as Savior right now. And even though you die here on earth, you will live forever."

Emma pulls Esther closer to her side as the small group confesses Jesus as Lord. Even though the sunlight is dim and voices of torment surround them, right now it feels like heaven is shining down on these few square feet of pavement. As the group walks to the next set of apartment buildings, Emma says to Brandon, "Your mom would be so proud to know what kind of man she raised." Brandon responds with a sad smile. He had spoken to his mom once after the mass disappearances, but since the nuclear attack and loss of the power grid, he has not spoken to her again. He continues to pray that she knows Jesus and that he will see her again when Jesus returns. "Elliott would be proud too," Emma says. "Wherever he is in the world, we all know he's saying those same words you just did."

They keep up a quick pace as they walk, always watching for anyone who might attack them as they stop outside another apartment building to proclaim the gospel. It is exhausting to preach all day in a city flooded with evil, and as dusk begins to fall, they head back to the abandoned retail store where they had slept the previous night. With fewer stars and the sun and moon both darkened, they know they need to walk briskly so they aren't left on the streets in the pitch black of night. Although she is holding Habib's hand, someone grabs him from behind, scoops him off his feet, and runs away as Emma and Esther scream.

"Stay here!" Lerenzo shouts to Emma. He and Brandon give chase through the littered street as Habib shouts and tries to wrestle free from his abductor, pounding him in the head with his fist and screeching in his ear. The infernal attack on the man's body is too much to endure along with Habib's relentless screaming and pounding, and the captor falters enough for Lerenzo and Brandon to catch up. Brandon struggles to remove Habib from the man's grip as Lerenzo bashes him in the head with his fist, causing the man to bellow. Moaning in pain, he releases his grip on Habib, and Brandon clenches the boy protectively. "He's not one of yours," Brandon says. "He belongs to Jesus."

Lerenzo and Brandon then rush back to Emma and the other children. Emma wraps her arms around Habib, thanking God that he is safe. They then race as quickly as they can through the ever-darkening streets. As they pass a row of shuttered retail businesses, Micah comes to a halt. "Listen," he says, holding his hand up so the others will stop. They each look into the mostly hollow remains of a store and can hear voices coming from the back. "Is someone calling for help?" Micah asks.

"Wait here," Lerenzo says, signaling for Brandon to follow him. They step into the building, and glass crunches beneath their feet. They can hear rats scurrying past them, and the sun is too weak to shine into the back of the store, making it hard for them to see. As they move cautiously down a dark hallway, the voices become louder. Lerenzo tries to open a door, but it is locked. He and Brandon can hear the cries of what sounds like young girls. He tries a couple times to break down the door with his shoulder but fails.

"Here," Brandon says, handing him a brick that was on the floor.

Lerenzo whacks at the doorknob until it breaks and falls to the floor. Pushing the door open, he says, "It's okay. We're here to help you."

Soft shuffling can be heard as two young girls step into the dim light of the hallway, followed by a teenage girl. "Are there more of you?" Brandon asks.

"No," the teenager says.

"Let's get out of here before whoever locked you in here comes back," Brandon says. Brandon exchanges glances with Lerenzo as they rush the girls out of the building. They both know they have saved three more lives from eternal darkness and rush through the streets to get the girls to safety.

CHAPTER 33

Petra, Jordan

A group of 60 emaciated and sickly Jews jump out of the back of the truck and run into the mile-long Siq. At the end, they are greeted by what looks like thousands and thousands of other Jews. The newcomers, young and old, fall to their knees weeping as water is rushed to them—water that has been collecting inside the cisterns that were carved out of this rock two millennia ago. Baskets filled with some sort of wafer are passed around, and their hands shake as they bring the food to their hungry mouths. One elderly man studies the wafers in his hands, then looks up at the young woman holding the basket in front of him. "Is this...manna?"

The young woman's face comes alive with joy. "It falls every morning!" The old man clutches the wafers to his chest and sobs. "Adonai is providing all our needs," she says, touching his shoulder. "Just as he did for our ancestors in the wilderness. There is plenty of water, we have sheep and goats in abundance, and there are thousands of caves, which protect us."

"Praise be to Adonai!" the man says, whispering. He bends over on his knees with his face to the ground, takes a bite of manna, and closes his eyes. It has been days since he last tasted any food. "Praise be to Adonai!" he says louder this time as he rocks back and forth on his knees. He puts the rest of the wafer into his mouth and sits up straighter, saying even louder, "Praise be to Adonai!" He then stands to his feet and shouts, "Praise be to Adonai! Praise be to Yeshua Messiah!" Finally, he looks up to the sky and cries out, "Maranatha!" Others recognize this to mean "Our Lord Comes!" They stand and join him, raising their voices in praise and pleading, "Praise be to Adonai! Maranatha! Maranatha!"

CHAPTER 34

Rome, Italy
Three Months Later

Victor paces like a caged animal inside his palace while dark clouds are racing across the sky, as if someone is rolling them from one end to another. Another physician has been summoned in the hopes that he can ease the pain that innumerous other doctors have been unable to alleviate. Victor attempted to kill those doctors due to their failure to help him, and although they would have welcomed death, it cannot come to anyone with the mark right now. For three-and-a-half months, Victor and his followers have been inhumanely afflicted while those without the mark continue to live and tell people about Jesus all over the earth. Refusing to be seen this way, Victor has not made any appearances on the news, but he continues to send out voice recordings letting his subjects know that all is well and that peace and security are at hand.

Three generals file into Victor's palace and attempt to stand at attention in front of him, but it is impossible to do so while they are under constant attack and they twitch and cry out in agony. "Tell me those Jewish parasites who are preaching against me are dead!" Victor says, his eyes flashing with rage.

"We have not been able to kill them, my lord," says General Abar, falling to his knees in pain.

Victor strikes him with the back of his hand, then puts both hands

167

on his neck to strangle him, but he can't. He cries out, then holds his hands against his own head in an attempt to stifle his suffering. "Their false prophet has sent his wicked angels to terrorize us, and you are worthless in bringing an end to our misery!" Victor tears at his own arm, which is already bloody from his endless clawing, and the blood drips onto the luxurious Persian rug below.

"We have tried countless ways to kill them," General Abar says. "They have survived them all."

Victor grips the general's chin, and the blood from his arm drips onto the general's uniform. "You won't survive, General. When this diabolical attack from their dead prophet ends, you and so many others will be executed. Get out!" He pushes the general's chin so that he falls backward, and Victor screams louder for all of them to leave. "You are useless to me!"

The generals flee from the room as the new physician enters, twitching and wailing in his own despair. Victor curses at the sight of him. "I will kill you if you cannot relieve my pain!" he shouts. "Just as I told my generals, I may not be able to kill you now, but I will execute you later." Victor writhes and strings together obscenities that shake the doctor more than his own demon locusts.

He approaches Victor with a needle filled with enough heroin to kill a man, and his hand quivers as he attempts to inject it into one of Victor's veins. Victor bellows as the needle stabs him over and over before it finally plunges into the intended vein and the drug courses through his body, increasing his heart rate and throwing him to the floor in convulsions. Terrified, the doctor races from the room, down the stairs, and out the palace door. Aides rush to Victor's side and try to help, but the twitching and pangs of their own bodies prevent them from being able to restrain Victor from thrashing. Screaming, Victor jumps to his feet and attacks one of the aides, choking the young man until all strength leaves his hands. The aide is unable to die, and Victor lets him go. The young man and the three other aides bolt from the room as Victor trashes the room in his rage. "I am god!" he screams, throwing and breaking expensive artwork and artifacts that were sent as gifts to him from around the world. "I am god!"

CHAPTER 35

New York City
One Month Later

Emma and her group have been able to find many other believers who are canvassing the boroughs of New York in an effort to tell people about salvation in Jesus and to rescue abandoned children or teens who may be on the streets. The city has grown even more savage since their arrival four-and-a-half months ago. The demonic locusts dip and swarm, droning and buzzing by the millions, shielding the sun and making the air appear thick and gray. The whirring pests fly into Emma and the others, but the salvation of Jesus covers their bodies and the locusts bounce off them and onto those with the mark. Between the locusts, the wild animals that prowl the streets, and the demonically possessed, the city is more deadly and dangerous than ever.

Yet Emma and her group have discovered ways to survive. Scouts among the believers have been able to obtain enough food every day or so to feed these street evangelists. When food trucks are able to make it into the city, the scouts wait and watch for a vicious locust strike on those unloading the trucks. These strikes throw the workers into convulsions and cause them to howl in horror, and each time they drop or scatter food, the scouts grab as much as possible before darting away.

Many believers sharing the word of Christ have been killed by those who seem more like wild beasts than humans. They have been run over, shot at, beheaded, and stabbed, but the deaths of these martyrs haven't stopped Emma and the others. They know that this five-month time of judgment poured out on those with the mark will soon come to an end, and they sense the urgency of spreading the gospel to those who haven't taken the mark. They have listened to John on the shortwave radio, and he has relayed how doves are chirping and singing across the planet and saving lives from Victor's mark. Just knowing that believers all around the world are putting their lives on the line as they tell the lost and dying about Jesus gives Emma and her group the determination and courage to press on each day.

When it is possible to do so, the groups of believers in New York City come together inside an abandoned building or home to encourage one another, pray, and discuss how best to help the children who are found on the streets. There are about 100 of these Christ followers, from elderly people to young children, who travel through the city in teams and shout that Jesus is Lord to anyone who might hear them.

Before heading out this morning, many of them gather inside a ghost of a building in Manhattan to listen to a shortwave radio. They do this each day so that they know what's happening in the world and how to pray. "Mark has terrorized and tormented, and the time of mercy is ending soon," John says. "Now is the time to call on Jesus and be saved! Ashes are not collecting in the desert right now. Wings from around the world continue to fly Jacob's lot to the rocks, where it is reported that Jacob is cared for by I AM."

"More Jews have made it to the mountains," Emma says, looking at the others standing around the radio.

"Loser trying, but can't find the rocks," John says on the shortwave radio.

"Victor's troops can't find the Jews in Jordan," Brandon says, deciphering what John said.

"Deadliest virus has struck the earth," John continues, keeping his voice low as if he knows he could be heard and stopped at any moment. "Countless dead. Earthquakes, famine, and plagues are increasing and happening more frequently across the planet. Something is about to be birthed."

The signal goes dead, and Emma knows that John has stopped transmission. "Something is about to be birthed," she says. "We're closer and closer to Jesus's return."

A booming voice from outside the building startles them, and the group stands frozen in silence, wondering where it came from. They hear it again, and they rush to the door, spilling out into the rubble-strewn street buzzing with demon locusts. "Jesus is the way, the truth, and the life!"

"There!" Esther shouts, pointing upward.

The sky is flashing from one brilliant color to another, and Emma gasps at the beauty of a majestic angel high up in the air. She can barely look at his brilliance as he moves overhead. "Repent while there is still time and call on the name of Jesus as Lord," the angel shouts. He then proclaims the gospel, and Emma's knees feel weak as she takes it all in.

"How could anyone see and hear that and still deny Jesus?" she asks as she watches the angel. She remembers what Revelation says about angels proclaiming the everlasting gospel throughout all the earth so that no one will be without excuse; all ears will have heard the gospel of Christ.

She leads everyone back inside the building and reaches quickly for the Bible in Brandon's hand, and turns to Revelation 21, where she scans the page and holds up her hand to get everyone's attention. "Listen to this," she says. "We are closer than ever before to the return of Jesus." She looks down and begins to read in verse 3: "I heard a loud voice from the throne saying, 'Behold, the dwelling place of God is with man. He will dwell with them, and they will be his people, and God himself will be with them as their God. He will wipe away every tear from their eyes, and death shall be no more, neither shall there be mourning, nor crying, nor pain anymore, for the former things have passed away.'"

A lump forms in Emma's throat and she pauses, unable to read as the words bring her to tears. She hands the Bible back to Brandon so he can finish the passage.

He looks down at the page, and picks up at verse 5: "He who was seated on the throne said, 'Behold, I am making all things new.' Also he said, 'Write this down, for these words are trustworthy and true.' And he said to me, 'It is done! I am the Alpha and the Omega, the beginning and the end. To the thirsty I will give from the spring of the water of life without payment. The one who conquers will have this heritage, and I will be his God and he will be my son.'"

Brandon looks up, and many have tears in their eyes. "This is our hope," he says.

CHAPTER 36

Tel Aviv, Israel

Victor bursts through the doors of what was once Israel's Ministry of Defense and storms down the hallway to the situation room, where General Durand is assessing intelligence out of Jordan. The locusts fly about the room, landing on and stinging General Durand, causing him to bellow. The general's face looks hideous; his skin is inflamed and broken and bleeding from his attempts to remove the pain from his flesh. He is rocking back and forth and moaning when Victor enters, cursing at him.

"Show me what's happening," Victor snarls, swatting at the locusts that zoom for him. He is enraged by the sight of General Durand. "You are a disgrace." The general pulls out a handkerchief and tries to wipe the blood from his face, but the infliction increases, and he begins to tear at his face again. Victor twitches as the locusts sting him and he scoffs, looking at the general. "You disgust me. Show me," he snaps, indicating the intelligence.

"We believe the Jews are hiding in Jordan," the general says.

Victor scans the screens throughout the room. "All I'm seeing is mountains. Where are the Jews?"

General Durand's back stiffens as if he's been stabbed from behind. Several locusts bite into his flesh, and he cries out like a wounded animal.

He points to a mountain range on one screen and says, "We have never seen them, but we believe they are hiding there among the rocks."

Victor's rage is palpable. "How many?" The general is too slow to respond, and Victor swears, shouting at him. "How many!"

"We believe there could be several thousand, my lord." The truth is that General Durand believes there are well over four million Jews who have escaped to the mountains of Jordan.

"Then fire a nuclear missile and kill them!" Victor says, feeling as if he's losing his mind. He cannot let these Jews get away. Every single one must be annihilated once and for all.

"We have sent missiles, but they disappear in the atmosphere." The torture caused by the locusts is too much for the general and he begins to paw at his arms.

"No, no, no, no!" Victor screams as his own demonic locusts terrorize him. "Send a nuke now!"

General Durand makes a quick call, and together they watch a screen on which a nuclear weapon is launched from Israel into Jordan. The missile disappears from view, as if it disintegrated midflight.

Victor's eyes are black with rage. "Send another one!"

General Durand makes the call, and another missile flies into the sky before vanishing. "We've tried flying into Jordan to attack from the air, but our planes can't get through the airspace."

Victor howls in pain and he shakes his head fiercely in response to the wretched stings. "Get tanks into those mountains now!"

General Durand taps a button to change the footage on the screens. "The tanks can't move across the border, my lord." Victor can't fathom what he is seeing. More than 100 tanks are sitting at the border. "The tanks are running, but they can't move forward or backward."

Fury seethes through Victor. He is not going to be outdone by a few runaway Jews. "Get me there."

A Black Hawk helicopter is summoned and takes Victor and General Durand to the Jordan border. Victor jumps out amidst a black cloud of locusts and bolts to the line of armored tanks that are lined up as if for a child's playtime race. "Move these tanks into Jordan!" he shouts at the Global Union Forces commanders around him.

"We keep trying, Emperor," one commander groans. Once again he issues the command for the tanks to move, but they are unable to.

Infuriated, Victor climbs atop a tank and descends through the hatch, yelling at the driver, whose face is swollen and bloody from the locusts inside the small space. "Move this tank!" Victor watches in desperation as the crewman engages switches and levers, but the tank doesn't budge. "Move it backward!" The pain-inflicted driver does as commanded, but it is useless.

Victor shoves him out of the way and engages the controls himself, but to no avail. Hurling a slew of obscenities, he climbs back up through the hatch and down onto the ground again, looking at General Durand and the commanders through the haze of flying insects. "Get my forces over this border and into those mountains and use whatever means necessary to destroy those Jews! Your lives depend on it!"

CHAPTER 37

Jerusalem
One Month Later

Victor and Ubel stand outside the temple and smile at the hundreds of reporters gathered from his global broadcasting affiliates, as well as the line of pilgrims who have resumed traveling to Israel to worship Victor. "Our glorious one ended our horrendous suffering two weeks ago," Ubel declares. "As you know, the false prophet Christ left behind his depraved spirits when he was killed on that beautiful cross, and they thought they could inflict so much of their evil upon our lord's world that he would give up. They thought they could drive him from where he is worshipped," he says, pointing to the temple. "These plaguing spirits didn't think that our savior would fight back or be victorious, but he has overcome them." The reporters and pilgrims burst into cheers, and Victor levitates into the air so those in the very back can see him. They all bow down and worship him, their voices rising in adoration and awe.

"We have all survived their torment. Not one of my sheep has perished," Victor says, floating above the deafening roar of praise. "We are all accounted for and stronger than ever. We are flourishing under my leadership, and my temple is open once again for your worship." More cheers come from the reporters as they broadcast Victor's words everywhere.

"But we have much work that remains to be done," he says, smiling. "The false prophet's torturing spirits are gone, but his followers are still trying to sabotage my good and precious work. And the Jew termites are still attempting to destroy the foundation of my world. We must work together as never before and slay them all. These beasts of prey are our biggest threat to peace, and all of space and earth is trying to expel them but need our help. Earthquakes will end when all Christ followers and Jews are dead. Hurricanes, volcanoes, tsunamis, famine, and all sickness will end when these foul animals bleed out. Peace and security will come to the entire universe when these cockroaches are crushed beneath our feet." His body descends back to the ground, and the reporters and crowd of worshippers burst into applause with the taste of the blood of Jews and Christians filling their mouths.

"They are not worshipping our holy one," Ubel says, his chest puffing out as he addresses the masses. "They are not worshipping the only one who is worthy to be praised." He walks down a few stairs to get closer to the reporters. "As we repeatedly say to you, you are our savior's messengers of hope. You are the truth-tellers. No one will know what to think or believe without you telling them what our beautiful one says. You must repeat it often. Repetition is how it becomes truth for the sheep. Our lord's sheep must know how urgent this hour is. We are at a time like no other in history. We are on the cusp of eternal greatness, but it can only come through the demise of those who are rising up against our lord and savior and the peace that he alone brings. There must be round-the-clock news of our enemy's end. Their death brings resurrection to our world. Their death brings life eternal to our planet. Find them wherever they are hiding. Root them out. Cut off their heads. Shoot them in the back. Drown them. Stab them in the heart. Because when you kill them, you are storing up eternal rewards for yourself in our savior's kingdom. When they die, we will live like never before! All praise to our great god and king!" The applause and noise is thunderous as the reporters, the pilgrims, and Ubel scream and shout Victor's praise.

As the applause continues, a great shadow darkens the temple area and the large crowd looks up to the sky to see a tremendous gleaming figure flying above them. "Repent today and call on the name of the Lord, Jesus Christ of Nazareth, who died for the sins of the world and rose from the grave and is coming again on the clouds. Salvation is found only in the Lord Jesus Christ and no other." The angel glides over the crowd, booming the message of everlasting salvation as he flies. Then the shadow moves onward as he continues proclaiming the gospel message through the skies.

Victor raises his fists to the angel and curses at him, blaspheming the holy name of God. "Salvation is found in no one but me! No one but me! I am the savior of the world!"

To discover more about the biblical facts behind the story, read Where in the Word? *on page 261, or continue reading the novel.*

CHAPTER 38

Petra, Jordan

Zerah runs through the Siq's mile-long entrance and, at the end, he stumbles to the ground at the sight of Petra. While out-of-place auroras create a dazzling show in the skies above, his fellow Jews are collecting something from off the ground and eating it. Some are roasting lamb over open fires or collecting water from cisterns. Tears spring to Zerah's eyes. The last time he saw many of these faces, they were filled with horror and fear. His hand brushes against something beside his knee, and he looks down and begins to laugh. Picking up a piece of manna, he breaks it in two and bites into one of the pieces. It tastes sweet like honey, just like it did for his ancestors.

"You're Zerah, right?"

Zerah looks up to see the silhouette of a young man standing in front of him. He rises to his feet to get a look at the man's face and he smiles. It is Amsel, a computer tech from Hadassah Medical Center who had worked on the same floor as Zerah. They ran into each other on the day of the mass vanishings but have not seen each other since. "Amsel!" Zerah cries, embracing him. "You have followed Yeshua Messiah! How did it happen?"

Amsel strokes his shaggy beard, then says, "The day that Yeshua seized his followers, you were looking for Dr. Haas, wondering if she had disappeared." Zerah nods, remembering. "I couldn't forget that, and I started digging for answers about what happened to her."

"And that led you to Yeshua," Zerah says, pleased. He takes another bite of manna. "Unbelievable."

"Every day," Amsel says. "Adonai's goodness to us is overwhelming. We have water and sheep and goats. We have been able to grow some vegetables. Adonai has not forsaken us."

Zerah eats the remainder of the manna and watches as the Jews work together at various tasks. "How many are here?"

"Between four and five million," Amsel says. Zerah's mouth drops open and he covers it with his hand, beginning to cry. "Some were flown here from all over the world during the five months of torment on those with the mark." Zerah shakes his head; he can't believe what he's witnessing. For years he's been warning Jews to flee to the mountains, and here they are, being protected and cared for by Adonai. "You're the reason so many of us are here, Zerah. You and others of the sealed servants of Yeshua."

"Have you seen some of the other servants here?" Zerah asks, anxious to know.

"Every now and then. They each said Adonai translated them to help us here."

Zerah smiles, thinking of the many ways his brothers helped him save the Jews from death. He is overwhelmed at the number who are living among the rocks here. "Your family, Amsel?"

Amsel shakes his head. "Only my wife. My parents and brothers would never believe."

Zerah looks beyond them to the multitude of Jews spread throughout the mountain crevices. "You're sure none of them are here?"

"No. Whenever new people arrive, everyone stands here and greets each survivor. Each time, it has been more celebratory than any feast day we've ever experienced. But I fear that my family is gone. Lost to Satan's lies. What about your family?"

Zerah continues scanning the crowds in the hopes of seeing the faces of his mother, father, dear sister Rada, and her beautiful children. "They were supposed to come here. I don't know if they made it."

Amsel points in the direction of many of the caves in the walls. "Come. I'll help you look."

They barely begin to move when people recognize Zerah and rush to him, crying and hugging him. So many of them know Yeshua because of Zerah, and so many others are safe within these rocks because of him. He is caught up in the laughter when he hears a familiar voice cry out, "Zerah! My son!"

Zerah's father, Chaim, is pushing his way through the crowd. "Papa!" Zerah shouts, running to him. His father's face is wet with tears as he grabs Zerah, kissing his cheeks. Zerah's mother, Ada, his sister, Rada, and her two children wail at the sight of him and cling to him.

"Adonai is mighty to save," Chaim shouts, lifting his hands into the air. He opens his mouth to say it again, and the multitude of Jews around him join in. "Adonai is mighty to save!"

Zerah laughs as he hears their voices rising together in praise. "Come, Yeshua Messiah!" He joins them as they shout all the louder. "Come, Yeshua Messiah! Come, Yeshua Messiah!"

CHAPTER 39

Petra, Jordan

Zerah stands on the side of a mountain and still can't believe the number of Jews in Petra who have been saved, supported, and sustained by Adonai himself against every attack of Satan. Their bodies are thin and their faces are wearied by all they have been through, but they are all standing and many are praising Yeshua Messiah with one voice. "No weapons formed against you have prospered!" Zerah says to thunderous cheers. "Yeshua Messiah is returning!"

"Come, Yeshua Messiah!" many shout together. "Come, Yeshua Messiah!"

Zerah knows that many of those who fled to this place did so to spare their lives, not because they believe in Yeshua. He opens the Bible he found in Dr. Haas's house all those long years ago. "This is what a Jew named Paul said in the first century: 'What shall we say, then? That Gentiles who did not pursue righteousness have attained it, that is, a righteousness that is by faith; but that Israel who pursued a law that would lead to righteousness did not succeed in reaching that law. Why? Because they did not pursue it by faith, but as if it were based on works. They have stumbled over the stumbling stone, as it is written, "'Behold, I am laying in Zion a stone of stumbling, and a rock of offense; and whoever believes in him will not be put to shame.'"'"

He looks up from the Bible and continues: "For generations, Israel sought a relationship with Adonai by way of righteousness through the keeping of the law, not a faith relationship with Adonai through Yeshua. We worked hard at our relationship with Adonai by doing what the law prescribed, but that required us to keep the law perfectly, and that is impossible. Yet we refused to admit our failure in keeping the law perfectly and recognize our need to turn to Adonai for forgiveness. We rejected Yeshua as Messiah because he did not fit our preconceived thoughts and notions about Messiah—and just as Paul said, we stumbled over him." He flips through his Bible and taps a page.

"A Jew named Peter also said this in the first century: 'Repent, therefore, and turn back, so that your sins may be blotted out…and that he may send the Christ appointed for you, Yeshua.'" Zerah looks up from the Bible at his beloved countrymen. "Repent, my dear brothers and sisters. Repent so that your sins may be wiped out and so Hashem will send Yeshua Messiah. He is coming. Salvation is found in no one else. Yeshua said, 'I am the way and the truth and the life. No one comes to the Father except through me.' Yeshua is our salvation." Zerah's voice echoes off the mountain walls, and the Jews scattered throughout listen with tears in their eyes.

"The prophet Isaiah gave us an amazing revelation of Adonai," he says, reading. "'I bring near my righteousness; it is not far off, and my salvation will not delay; I will put salvation in Zion, for Israel my glory.'" The applause and cheers are deafening. "Yeshua Messiah says, 'Truly, truly, I say to you, whoever believes has eternal life. I am the bread of life. Your fathers ate the manna in the wilderness, and they died. This is the bread that comes down from heaven, so that one may eat of it and not die. I am the living bread that came down from heaven. If anyone eats of this bread, he will live forever. And the bread that I will give for the life of the world is my flesh.'

"Believe on Yeshua Messiah, and you will have eternal life!" The crowds all through the mountains begin to roar with the sound of repentance and wailing, and emotion lodges in Zerah's throat. Never in his life did he ever imagine he would hear such a beautiful sound. He allows for Adonai to care for each of his children in this moment and stands aside, praying.

When the sounds of crying and praise fade, Zerah bends down and picks up a piece of manna from the ground. "On the night when our Yeshua Messiah was betrayed, he took bread, and when he had given thanks, he broke it, and said, 'This is my body, which is for you. Do this in remembrance of me.'" Zerah takes a bite of the manna and the crowd follows, millions of them, standing together in faith throughout the mountain crevices; many of them repeat what Zerah has said. He waits until he no longer hears the voices, then says, "In the same way also he took the cup, after supper, saying, 'This cup is the new covenant in my blood. Do this, as often as you drink it, in remembrance of me.' For as often as you eat this bread and drink the cup, you proclaim the Lord's death until he comes." Zerah then takes a drink of water from a ladle that has been handed to him, and passes it on to a man standing just below him on the rocks.

Cups and ladles are passed from one Jew to another, and then they drop to their knees, crying out together. "Come, Yeshua Messiah! Come, Yeshua Messiah!"

CHAPTER 40

Pennsylvania
Three Months Later

Y ou are doing a powerful and cleansing work." Emma recognizes the
voice of Ubel coming through the shortwave radio. They are grateful for the many batteries they found in New York, which has enabled
them to keep listening for John, who gives the real news and not Ubel's
or Victor's propaganda. But they can't find him today.

"Reports around our lord's planet reveal that Jews are still being
rooted out of their pathetic rabbit holes and killed for insurrection
against our glorious one," Ubel says. "Not one of them will remain!
From New Delhi to New Zealand, despicable and deadly Christ followers have been slain in the most beautiful fashion, and our world
breathes easier without them. Can you feel the peace? The tranquility
that's coming over our planet?"

"Turn it off," Emma whispers, looking down at Esther, who is lying
on the floor of a barn that looks flimsy at best after the most recent
earthquake to shake the earth. Antonio and Habib are now with other
couples or groups they met while in New York who didn't have children. Although it was painful to say goodbye to them, Emma knew it
was best for the boys to go with a smaller group, as food would once
again be difficult to find.

When she, Lerenzo, Micah, and Esther left New York, there wasn't an inch of the city that hadn't been covered by the teams that went out every day preaching the gospel. On their last day, Emma and her group found themselves in Brooklyn and standing in front of what remained of Salus, the building they had used for months to house rescued children and teens. An earthquake had left the building in shambles and Emma stood there in sadness, but then she smiled and straightened her shoulders. "This building couldn't survive," she had said, peering over the wreckage. "But what we did in there survives. The word of God endures forever."

"I can keep going," Esther says, laboring to breathe on the barn floor.

Feeling Esther's forehead, Emma smiles down at the young girl who has been so brave since the moment she was found, but this fever isn't going down. Emma pats her hand. "We're not going anywhere without you. Wherever you are, we are."

"But if I go to heaven, you'll still be here," Esther says, gasping for breath. "I'd feel so bad leaving you here."

Emma strokes her hair. "Don't feel bad for us. You know what we believe: We'll see you soon."

Esther looks up at her. "What do you think heaven will be like?"

"Beyond anything we could ever imagine," Emma says.

"Amazing food!" Brandon says. "We'll never be hungry again."

"Perfect health," Lerenzo adds, squeezing Esther's hand. "No more fevers, sicknesses, diseases, or plagues."

"No more crying," Micah says. "No more fear. No more earthquakes or sleeping in barns or caves. No more wild animals to fight off. No more running. And no more evil. Jesus wins."

"Thank you for loving me," Esther says, looking at each one of them. "I was so afraid, and you became my family."

Tears form in Emma's eyes as she squeezes Esther's hand. "We *are* family, sweet one. And you are always so brave."

"Like you and Kennisha," Esther says.

Emma smiles through the tears and shakes her head. "I'm not nearly as brave as you or Kennisha. But someday I hope to be."

"I'm so tired. I need to sleep."

Emma nods and continues stroking her hair. "All right, sweetheart. You get some rest, and we'll see you soon."

CHAPTER 41

Tel Aviv, Israel
Four Months Later

Several generals with the Global Union Forces stand inside the war room awaiting Victor's arrival. Generals Bernard, Durand, and Abar had all committed suicide when the demonic attacks on those with the mark ended, and many of Victor's aides and doctors also ended their lives so they wouldn't have to face Victor, who had promised repeatedly that he would kill them. Victor arrives, and the generals bow to their emperor and lord.

"Show me," Victor barks. General Schmidt taps a computer in front of him, and the screens across the front of the room fill with images of the 144,000 Jewish evangelists who are preaching in Norway, Togo, Wales, the United States, Myanmar, Panama, Peru, Afghanistan, and many other places all over the world. "What now? Turn one of them up!"

General Schmidt taps a button, and Elliott is seen preaching atop the rubble of what is left of a high-rise beach condo in Miami, Florida. The coastline had been ravaged years earlier in a devastating earthquake and tsunami, which radically changed the shape of the state and left many inhabitants scrambling for housing. Small tents and lean-tos are now found in many streets and on the beach, and Elliott stands in the midst of them as the ocean waves roll behind him. Those living in the tents try to forcibly remove him or kill him, but there is no use. Nothing can stop him, and he continues to preach.

"Jesus said, 'Behold, I am coming like a thief! Blessed is the one who stays awake, keeping his garments on, that he may not go about naked and be seen exposed.' And they assembled them at the place that in Hebrew is called Armageddon."

Victor's eyes darken as he listens to Elliott and he curses beneath his breath. "Is he talking of war?" he says mostly to himself.

"Jesus is returning!" Elliott proclaims to angry passersby who are dead in their deception. "He will step onto the Mount of Olives in Israel, and it will split in two."

"Do you still want to hear these myths and fabrications, my lord?" General Schmidt says, reaching for a knob to turn the volume down.

"Leave it!" Victor snaps, stepping closer to the screens.

Elliott opens his Bible to Revelation 19 and shouts as he reads so everyone inside their tents or on the beach can hear him. "I saw heaven standing open and there before me was a white horse, whose rider is called Faithful and True. With justice he judges and wages war. His eyes are like blazing fire, and on his head are many crowns. He has a name written on him that no one knows but he himself. He is dressed in a robe dipped in blood, and his name is the Word of God. The armies of heaven were following him, riding on white horses and dressed in fine linen, white and clean. Coming out of his mouth is a sharp sword with which to strike down the nations. 'He will rule them with an iron scepter.' He treads the winepress of the fury of the wrath of God Almighty. On his robe and on his thigh he has this name written: King of kings and Lord of lords."

Victor paces as he listens to Elliott; his head rotates 360 degrees, and his eyes turn black in rage. He's ready to strike Elliott and all of the 144,000 dead.

"Then I saw the beast and the kings of the earth and their armies gathered together to wage war against the rider on the horse and his army. But the beast was captured, and with it the false prophet who had performed the signs on its behalf. With these signs he had deluded those who had received the mark of the beast and worshiped its image.

The two of them were thrown alive into the fiery lake of burning sulfur. The rest were killed with the sword coming out of the mouth of the rider on the horse, and all the birds gorged themselves on their flesh."

Incensed, Victor erupts in obscenities and furor over what he's heard. "He's calling for war!"

"He and the others are not able to overcome your military, my lord," General Schmidt says.

Walking back and forth, Victor shakes his head and points to the screen where Elliott is still preaching. "It's not them. It's Jesus."

General Schmidt exchanges glances with the other generals. "Their false prophet?" he says. "He's a myth. He's a lie. They're all liars, my lord."

Victor isn't listening but is stark raving mad, talking to himself and devising a plan out loud. "He's coming back here. There are still too many Jews alive! He's coming to rescue them. He has to be stopped!" Victor's pacing takes him to General Ricci. "How many Jews are still alive throughout the world?" he asks.

The general shakes his head. "There is no way to know that, my lord. They hide as do the followers of this Jesus myth."

Anger inside of Victor boils over and scalds General Ricci and the others with curses as he screams at their incompetence. "Get me to the Mount of Olives!"

After the short flight, Victor steps out of the helicopter near the Mount of Olives and walks to it, finding it unextraordinary and hardly the place to make a grand entrance. "Apollyon!" he shouts into the air. "My great warrior Apollyon! Come to me!"

General Ricci and the helicopter pilot wait by the chopper as Victor raises his voice to summon his army of darkness, and they are both taken aback when an abhorrent being with an abominable twisted face, elongated head, and great black wings appears hovering just above Victor. A putrid odor of sulfur fills the air, and the general and pilot cover their noses, trying to block the smell.

"War has been declared," Victor says to the satanic overlord Apollyon. "Jesus says he will return here. On this mountain. He must be stopped."

Apollyon screeches and monstrous curses penetrate the air, making General Ricci and the pilot protect their ears from the ghastly sound. "Only a fool would dare fight our lord. There will be *no* war against our lord's army! Victory belongs to you, my lord!"

Victor sneers at the words that are normally precious to his ears. "Go throughout the face of the earth and annihilate the Jews—wherever they are! Many are hiding somewhere in Jordan. Exterminate them all, Apollyon. Jesus would return for even one, so not one must be left alive."

A gruesome noise comes from the mouth of the hideous creature and the air is thick with the foul, sulfuric stench of the abyss as the sky blackens with hundreds of thousands of grotesque winged beasts wearing fiery breastplates and riding horse-like creatures. The nether animals have the head of a lion and the tail of a great serpent, and their mouths have fangs capable of killing their prey. A maniacal and appalling roar comes from the beasts and fire, smoke, and sulfur permeate the atmosphere, bloating it again with depraved, hellish sounds as the dark army looks to their general for orders.

"Go forth, my beautiful army!" Victor cries, raising his arms to the infernal infantry. "Seek! Kill! Slaughter all the Jews!"

Petra, Jordan

Apollyon leads a legion of dark warriors over Jordan in search of Jews, and they cast a deadly shadow across the land. Apollyon howls when he discovers the Jews hiding in the mountain caves and crevices at Petra. "Death is coming to your enemy, my lord!" he shrieks as the entire army joins him in surrounding the mountains. Apollyon roars in hunger and the other beasts follow, their malicious sounds perverting the atmosphere.

They all fly round and round overhead like carrion vultures circling their prey, and a chill falls over Petra as darkness descends and the smell of death spreads throughout the mountains. The Jews scream in terror as fire, smoke, and sulfur pour forth from the mouths of the demoniac horse creatures and they run for the clefts in the rocks, crying out to Adonai. "Have mercy!" they plead. "Save us, Yeshua!"

Apollyon shrieks as he hears the Jews cry out the name of Yeshua. "Kill them!" he orders, leading the charge of the satanic soldiers. They guide their beasts to head for the center of the mountains, but a barrier from God blocks them, incensing Apollyon, and he curses at his troops to carry out their mission. Their shrill voices echo off the rocks and the Jews tremble in terror as the hordes of hell aim for them again.

"Adonai saves!" an elderly Jewish woman shouts when she realizes what is happening. She steps out from the safety of a crevice and raises her arms in praise. "They can't reach us! Adonai is protecting us! All glory, honor, and praise to Adonai!"

One by one, the Jews look overhead at the menacing throng of beasts that whir about in one failed attempt after another to exterminate them, and they begin to shout praises on top of one another.

"Though an army should encamp against me, my heart shall not fear!"

"Though war should rise against me, even then I will be confident!"

"Adonai is all-powerful to save!"

"Blessed be the name of Adonai. Blessed be the name of Yeshua Messiah!"

"Come quickly, Yeshua! Come quickly, Yeshua!"

Apollyon and his beastly battalion wail in outrage as they flail above the mountains, so close to their prey but doomed to failure.

CHAPTER 42

Pennsylvania
Three Months Later

Lerenzo and Brandon leave Emma, Micah, and a dog named Hero that adopted them as family two months ago. They depart from a cave to go for a short walk to a row of pear trees; they found this cave shortly after Esther died and are grateful that it is near a stream. The pear trees had provided them with some nourishment, along with berries and wild foliage like dandelions, paw paws, mulberry, and wild mint. They had also been able to live on birds and other small wildlife they had shot with the bow and arrow.

They are approaching the trees when the skies unexpectedly darken, and Lerenzo sniffs the rank scent that pervades the air when an army from hell is nearby. He motions to Brandon, points to a barn, and together, they sprint toward it.

Gasping for breath, they barely make it to the side of the barn when they spot several of Satan's fiends flying nearby on their terrifying beasts that breathe out sulfur and brimstone. For the last three months, the air has been charged with the cries and screams of earth dwellers as Victor's demonic cavalry wages war, killing not only Jews, but anyone in their path of destruction. Nations have risen against the beasts, firing missiles and nuclear weapons, but at last count, at least one-quarter of the world's population has died from this most recent warfare. Emma and the others have seen the nether creatures every now and then and have been able to retreat to the safety of the cave each time.

The infernal infantry flies toward the barn, and Lerenzo and Brandon crouch down on the ground and remain still, knowing that any movement will alert hell's angels of their whereabouts. They each can hear their hearts beating and their breath comes out in short, ragged gasps. If they can get inside the barn, they won't be seen, and the hellish creatures will move on. A foul, sulfurous smell invades the air around them and Brandon looks up as a ghastly lion's head appears above. "Go!" he yells, pushing Lerenzo to run for the barn's entrance. A blast of brimstone laps at Brandon's backside as they run around a corner and enter through the barn's open door and into an empty stall. Brandon falls face down in excruciating pain, and the barn is saturated with the repugnant stench of death from the mouth of the lion.

Lerenzo kneels beside Brandon, keeping him quiet as he watches through the slats of the barn walls and listens for the wretched screech of Satan's brigade. As light filters into the barn and the screeching sounds fade into the distance, Lerenzo knows the dark corps has moved on. He turns his attention to Brandon. The back of his shirt and jeans have been burned off; the skin on his back, legs, and arms is burned so severely that it looks as if bone is exposed. "It's all right," Lerenzo says, taking off his own shirt to drape it over Brandon's back. "Let's get back to the cave with Emma and Micah."

Brandon's face is pressed against the barn floor and he attempts to shake his head. "I can't."

Lerenzo feels his throat tighten. "Yes, you can. Come on, Brandon. Let me help you." He struggles to help Brandon rise, but he's dead weight.

"I can't," Brandon says feebly.

Tears burn in Lerenzo's eyes and he sits on the floor of the stall, bending over so his face is close to Brandon's. "Come on, man. We're so close to the end. Jesus is coming, Brandon! Let's enter the millennial kingdom together."

Brandon gently turns his face so he can look at Lerenzo. "I'm ready. I'm ready for Jesus, Lerenzo. Before the vanishings, I never said his name unless I was cursing, but now I say his name like a prayer. Jesus. Come quickly, Lord Jesus." He smiles as Lerenzo wipes a tear from his cheek. "Satan's army marches on across the world. He thinks he's got us, Lerenzo. Satan thinks he's won with his army, but the gates of hell cannot prevail, can they?" Lerenzo shakes his head. "Death has no power over me. Over any of us who believe. Hell has already been defeated."

"Amen, Brandon."

Brandon stiffens in pain and Lerenzo puts his head down, scarcely able to watch him. "Emma would be mad if I died here, wouldn't she?"

Lerenzo smiles and nods. "She'd have a hard time with it, yeah."

"I'm so glad she found you, Lerenzo. You're my brother." He reaches out his hand and Lerenzo grabs hold of it. "You know, I feel that I'm going to see my mom in heaven."

"Yeah?"

"I've been praying for her ever since the disappearances—that she would hear about the salvation of Jesus, and somehow, I believe that she did. I'm going to see her again, Lerenzo. I can feel it."

Lerenzo brushes another tear off his cheek and rubs his nose along his sleeve. "You're the greatest man I've ever met, Brandon. We couldn't have rescued kids off the street or lived from one day to the next without you." He squeezes Brandon's hand. "Will you hold on so I can run and get Emma and Micah?"

"Because she'd be mad if I left without saying goodbye, right?"

Lerenzo laughs. "She'd be awfully mad."

Emma races into the stall and covers her mouth with a hand, gasping. "Brandon," she says, falling next to him as Lerenzo and Micah gather around him. She gently touches his face and tears pour over her cheeks. "Brandon, no. Please."

"You led me to Jesus, Em," Brandon says, making her cry harder. "Don't cry, Emma. You know what we believe. I'll see you soon. I'm just a little while from seeing Kennisha and Jamie and Esther and all the others. One day, we'll all see Elliott again, and I can't wait to hear his stories. Just a little more pain here, and then victory."

Emma sobs. "You're making me jealous," she says, grabbing his hand. "I love you so much, Brandon. You have always been such an amazing friend."

"My friend and my sister," Brandon says. "I don't know what I would have done without you. Without any of you." He tries to turn so he can see Micah, and Emma directs Micah to move so Brandon can see him. "Does Satan have the same power as Jesus?" he asks, looking at Micah, standing with the dog.

"Not even close," Micah says, petting Hero's head and recalling what Brandon has taught him and the other children over the last few years. "He cowers at the name of Jesus."

"Brave warrior right here," Brandon says, attempting to smile. He winces in pain, and Emma whispers a prayer of mercy over him. Hero nudges him with his nose, and Brandon weakly rubs the back of the dog's head.

For years now they've read the Bible together, and Lerenzo opens his Bible to read out loud to the others—this time from Revelation 22. "Look, I am coming soon! My reward is with me, and I will give to each person according to what they have done. I am the Alpha and the Omega, the First and the Last, the Beginning and the End. Blessed are those who wash their robes, that they may have the right to the tree of life and may go through the gates into the city. Outside are the dogs, those who practice magic arts, the sexually immoral, the murderers, the idolaters and everyone who loves and practices falsehood. I, Jesus, have sent my angel to give you this testimony for the churches. I am the Root and the Offspring of David, and the bright Morning Star."

Lerenzo looks down, and Brandon's eyes are closed.

"Go on," Brandon says weakly.

Lerenzo clears his throat and keeps reading. "The Spirit and the bride say, 'Come!' And let the one who hears say, 'Come!' Let the one who is thirsty come; and let the one who wishes take the free gift of the water of life. I warn everyone who hears the words of the prophecy of this scroll: If anyone adds anything to them, God will add to that person the plagues described in this scroll. And if anyone takes words away from this scroll of prophecy, God will take away from that person any share in the tree of life and in the Holy City, which are described in this scroll. He who testifies to these things says, 'Yes, I am coming soon.' Amen. Come, Lord Jesus."

"Come, Lord Jesus," Brandon whispers.

"Come, Lord Jesus," Emma says, wiping a tear from her cheek.

"Come, Lord Jesus," they all say together.

Emma leans against the barn wall, and Lerenzo and Micah help position Brandon so his head is on her lap. Then they sit closely, each putting a hand on Brandon as they pray together. They stay this way for hours, praying and taking turns reading the Bible before sleep overtakes Micah and he lays down next to Hero.

"We're still here," Emma whispers to Brandon in the darkness. "We're not leaving you." She can feel him breathe, but talking is no longer a possibility for her dear friend. Lerenzo sits next to Emma in the pitch-black darkness of the barn and puts his hand on Brandon's head, praying.

When light sneaks its way between the barn wall slats, Emma's eyes flash open. She wonders how long she has been sleeping and looks down at Brandon, who is still and lifeless. She shakes her head and wipes her eyes. "You waited until I fell asleep, didn't you?" She nudges Lerenzo awake, then leans forward to kiss Brandon's forehead. "My friend. My sweet, sweet friend. You're home."

CHAPTER 43

Singapore
Four Months Later

The transmitter crackles as John plugs in the microphone and sits on the floor of the deserted building. The skin on his face and hands is burned and white with infection from the sulfur and brimstone that had filtered its way into his hiding spot by hell's beasts. He speaks in whispers. "Hundreds of millions dead across the planet as hell's minions killed one-third of population," he says, looking down at the putrid flesh on his own hands. "Jacob is safe in the mountains. No weapon of hell formed against him could prosper! The Revelator told us that those who survived hell's onslaught would not repent, but still worship darkness. The Euphrates is drying up. The Revelator tells us that the final battle is near. Our King is coming." He hears a noise but doesn't stop broadcasting this time, and his voice gets stronger. "Victory belongs to the Lord. Blessed are the dead who die in the Lord, for you will rest soon from your labors. Be of good courage! He has overcome the world and will return to make all things new. Blessed be the name of the Lord! His mercy endures forever."

Two men wielding swords burst through the ramshackle door and John smiles. His journey is complete. "Call on the name of Jesus Christ and be saved!" He shouts his final words into the microphone with all his strength, and the transmission ends.

CHAPTER 44

Victor City, Italy

Generals with the Global Union Forces stand inside the throne room and watch the screens with Victor and his court. Tanks, foot soldiers, warplanes, drones, and nuclear warheads yet again attempt to attack Jordan without success. "It is impossible," George says, looking on in dismay. "It is as if the missiles disintegrate. How many have you launched?"

General Nygard gives a half-shrug and replies, "I don't have the exact count with me, but thousands."

"Then make it millions," Victor says, standing and walking closer to the screens. "Millions upon millions upon millions."

"We don't have that many in our arsenal, my lord," General Nygard says.

"Then produce them," Victor says, turning to him. "Manufacture however many it takes to exterminate the rats burrowing among those mountains! Bring in warheads from across the planet. Do whatever is necessary to blow up those terrorists."

Adrien cries out in pain and Victor turns to him, incensed by his interruption. Maria screams in misery as the entire court and generals begin to wail in torment. Victor watches as great, horrendous sores break out over all of their bodies. He howls when the affliction spreads over his own flesh, and his voice is shrill and full of hell itself as he screams.

Seattle, Washington

"God's final judgments are falling," Elliott shouts from what's left of Bell Street Pier, where people have been desperate for healthy fish following the corruption of so many more than three years ago when the waters were afflicted. The people's cries of agony fill the atmosphere not only because of the excruciating sores breaking out on their bodies, but because the water looks as if it has turned to blood and dead fish float over the surface.

"Harmful and painful sores have come upon all those who bear the mark of the beast and worship its image," Elliott yells. "And the sea has become like the blood of a corpse, and every living thing that is in the sea is dead." The people howl and sob at what is happening, and fear turns to violence as each man and woman turns against the other. "The Lord God Almighty is true and just in his judgments!" Elliott shouts. "Jesus said, 'To the thirsty I will give from the spring of the water of life without payment. The one who conquers will have this heritage, and I will be his God and he will be my son.'" Amid the fighting and brutality, Elliott looks up to the heavens and shouts, "Come, Lord Jesus! Come, Lord Jesus!"

To discover more about the biblical facts behind the story, read Where in the Word? *on page 265, or continue reading the novel.*

CHAPTER 45

Pennsylvania
One Day Later

Emma, Lerenzo, and Micah are gaunt and weak; it has been nearly three weeks since they've eaten anything beyond burdock root, wild mint, and honeysuckle. They lost their remaining arrow when it didn't kill a deer that was struck, and the deer ran away. Each attempt to make their own arrows over the last few days has failed, leaving them without a means to use the bow. The nearby vines and trees are no longer producing fruit, and even when they were, it wasn't enough to sustain them for days on end. Sitting outside the cave and resting against the hillside, Emma looks at these two incredible men who have been reduced to skin and bones. In a world that praises evil, they remain faithful to Christ. Micah, whose childhood had already been stolen from him before his ninth birthday, has grown up in a world that destroys everything that is precious and good and innocent. He has put his own young life on the line to rescue other children and teens from the jaws of hell and has evangelized like Peter himself on the streets of New York City. "I love you, Micah," Emma says, her eyes welling with tears.

He looks at her with sunken eyes, and rubs Hero, who has returned after being gone for days looking for food. "I love you, Mom."

Emma never had the chance to become a mother in the way she

had always imagined, but every time Micah or any of the other hundreds of children they rescued called her Mom, her heart would swell. Someday soon, she hopes to know the exact number of children she mothered during these past seven years.

"It won't be long now," Lerenzo says, squeezing her hand. "Our Savior is coming."

"And I'll see my mom again," Emma says, her voice quivering as she speaks. "And Sarah." She wipes the tears from her face. "I just know that my sister has followed Jesus. I know that I'm going to see her again."

Lerenzo moves closer to her and kisses her forehead. He looks at her face and body, which are angular and thin; seven years of near starvation has eroded the gentle curves, but her eyes are still full of compassion and love for him and Micah and for the world that hates the Jesus whom she loves. "We need to try to find something, anything to eat." He helps her to her feet, and the three of them and Hero trek away from the cave opening to the nearby stream.

They each get down on their knees and use their hands to lap up the water and take several drinks before the clear liquid starts to turn crimson. "What is…" Emma says, dipping her hand into the stream again and raising another palmful of water. "It's blood!" Her eyes are full of fright as she looks at Lerenzo, who dips both hands into the water, lifts them up high, and lets the bloodied water trickle through his fingers in front of them.

Micah quickly moves to another part of the stream and dips his hands. "It's bloody throughout," he says, immersing his hands again and again. Hero tries to take another drink and stops at the taste, looking up at Micah.

"The final judgments are falling," Lerenzo says. "Blood has obviously already struck the seas because now it has struck the rivers. The return of Jesus is…"

"We're almost home," Emma says, getting up and reaching for him and Micah. They extend their arms and hold on to one another. "Come, Lord Jesus!" Emma says, her voice quivering with strength.

"Come, Lord Jesus!" they say together.

CHAPTER 46

Tel Aviv
One Day Later

Victor strings together blistering profanities as he watches the screens. His body and the bodies of those with him are covered with hideous, painful boils, and maggots like Zerah continue to preach in many locations all around the world, which is a torture far worse to Victor. "Turn that one up!" Victor barks, pointing at the screen with Elliott. Ubel is closest to the screen and turns up the volume.

"Jesus Christ is coming soon," Elliott says into a bullhorn while inside the international airport in Toronto. The crowd is bent on killing him, but his body is impervious to all their attacks. The mob brawls and fights to remove him and stop his cursing of the name of their lord, Victor, but despite their most vicious efforts, they are unable.

"His armies and saints will be with him," Elliott says. Victor's face morphs into many as it changes in front of the generals and his neck elongates, extending his head closer to the screen as he watches Elliott. "The Word of God tells us that Jesus will strike down the nations with the sharp sword coming from his mouth. He alone will destroy evil!" The snarling mob inside the airport screeches at the name of Jesus, and Elliott uses the bullhorn to shout over them. "All those who have not called on Jesus as Savior will be food for the birds of the air. Victor and Ubel will be cast alive into the lake of fire." At this, Victor and Ubel begin to rage, screaming inside the war room. "The time is at hand," Elliott says to the deranged crowd. "If you can hear my voice anywhere in the world today and have not taken Victor's mark, call on the name of the Lord Jesus Christ of Nazareth and be saved."

"He cannot return without an Israel to return to," Victor snaps, his breath coming out ragged and poisonous.

General Schmidt glances at the other generals. "Who cannot return, my lord?"

"Their false prophet!" Victor screams. "You will not win! The earth is mine," Victor says, swearing and mumbling beneath his breath as he flings himself from the walls to the ceiling. "The earth was given to me and all that is in it." The generals stand uncomfortably, wondering who Victor is addressing. "Victory is mine!" he shouts, making the generals flinch.

"Jesus is returning soon in power and might!" Elliott says on the screen.

"Destroy Israel!" Victor yells.

General Schmidt pauses, unsure if Victor is talking to the generals or himself. "Did you hear me?" Victor seethes. "Destroy Israel! He can't return to a country that doesn't exist!"

"But my lord," General Schmidt says. "The Global Forces are based there. Your temple of worship is there and many thousands of pilgrims are there. The technology that we rely on for our weapons, artillery, and even your mark all are there, my lord. Some of your greatest riches in oil and gas are there, which keep Rome and Victor City and much of Europe supplied. If we destroy Israel, we are destroying your most valuable resources. The country is cleansed of the vermin. We have swept the land many times and the stink is gone, my lord. Only the riches remain. You have said that the false prophet Jesus is a myth…"

"I want you to destroy Israel." Victor says, cutting him off. "It is only when that land is going up in smoke that we can be sure that every Jew is dead and he won't be able to return. Get all global forces here!" Victor commands him. "Get them to the Jezreel Valley for war against the false prophet Jesus, who will attempt to overthrow my kingdom." He looks at Ubel. "I need to address the world." Ubel nods, and leads

Victor outside the building. Ghoulish-looking reporters whose faces are covered in boils are waiting as usual to help transmit his words and, in a moment's time, the cameras are running.

"My great citizens, followers, worshippers, and friends," Victor says, looking weak and sickly. "You know all that I have done to keep us from war, but at this time it is of utmost urgency that I call upon all soldiers throughout my entire kingdom. The false prophet Jesus will be attempting to overthrow my kingdom of peace. His rhetoric and his followers have always been our greatest danger and the most immense threat to mankind. His minions around the world are saying he will wage this war against me in Israel. I will not allow him to take your peace. I will not allow him to take your pride. I will not allow him to take your freedom. I will not allow him to soil this earth that we have purged and cleansed of evil. Rise up, all soldiers! Fight for my world! Fight for your lives! Fight for your freedom! The powerful army of Satan will fight with you, and together we will kill Jesus once and for all. We will execute his followers. We will murder their hopes and faith. We will eradicate all that is wicked, and the earth will rejoice! My armies of the world, come at once to the Jezreel Valley in Israel and fight, fight, fight! We will have a glorious war unlike the world has ever seen and we will slay the false prophet Jesus and all of his pathetic followers in one magnificent battle!" The reporters burst into cheers, and Victor's words are broadcast around the planet.

"The Lord will gather all the nations against Jerusalem to battle!" Zerah shouts as he walks from behind the reporters to the front, where Victor is standing.

General Sarpara calls for all the soldiers stationed in Tel Aviv to come at once, and within moments, many can be heard running toward them. "Finish him!" Victor commands his generals and soldiers as he trembles with fury, pointing at Zerah.

The reporters flee as dozens of soldiers open fire on Zerah, but his voice rises like a trumpet above the noise. "The day is near!" he says through the smoke from the gun blasts. "The Lord will go out and fight against the nations. His feet will stand on the Mount of Olives and it will split in two."

Victor and Ubel are both enraged at Zerah's words. "Kill him!" Victor orders again. The soldiers open fire once more, aiming hundreds of rounds of ammunition at Zerah.

Zerah is unhurt and unfazed and continues to preach into the cameras. "My Lord Jesus will come, and all his holy ones with him." Victor blasphemes God and attempts to attack Zerah himself using all the power of Satan but is unable to get near him. Zerah turns to look Victor in the eyes. "Jesus said, 'Behold, I am coming soon. I am the Alpha and the Omega, the first and the last, the beginning and the end.'"

"He is not coming!" Victor shouts in agony.

"Shoot him again!" Ubel commands.

The soldiers open fire on Zerah as he proclaims, "And the Lord will be king over all the earth."

"No!" Victor yells over the shots. "He is not lord! I am god! I am lord over the earth!"

At that moment, the sun suddenly begins to scorch fiercely upon the entire assembly, searing everyone with unimaginable heat and causing even the pavement beneath their feet to buckle and sizzle. Victor, Ubel, the generals and soldiers, and all the reporters wail and curse as they bolt for shelter, away from the unbearable rays. Zerah stands and watches as they scurry away; the sun does not affect him.

He raises his arms to the sky and smiles. "Come, Lord Jesus!"

CHAPTER 47

Tel Aviv

Victor and his court, Ubel, and the generals watch the screens as his armies from around the world make their way to Israel, but the troops are withering beneath the sun's blistering beams. The entire planet is broiling and obscenities explode throughout the war room. The sores on their bodies are even more painful in the searing heat and they curse God for the fiery rays. Victor raises his fists to the ceiling and shouts, "You will not win! I have already won! The earth is mine!"

Suddenly, the entire room is blanketed with a darkness that can be felt, and all cursing is silenced at the abruptness of night. "Check the fuses," Ubel says, ordering anyone who will listen.

The sounds of several people feeling their way to the door can be heard as Victor moves toward what he thinks is a window. He steps along the wall until he gets to the window and looks outside. There is no sun or moon or stars or even streetlight. The pitch is so deep and so black that he can't see his hand on the glass pane or what is just beyond it. Cries and wails are heard from the screens inside the war room as Victor's entire world has been plunged into utter darkness and the tortuous sounds grate against his ears. As the room erupts into screams of terror, Victor raises his fists again toward the ceiling as he swears. "You will not take my kingdom! It is not yours to take!"

As hours pass by, the pain of darkness is too great a burden to handle, and Victor's court and generals, along with those who bear his mark around the world, feel as if they're losing their minds and they gnaw their tongues in anguish, cursing God for their afflictions.

Tel Aviv, The Next Morning

Light bursts through the windows of the war room, and Victor, Ubel, and the court and generals cover their eyes as they stand to their feet. The night was longer than any they've ever known and filled with inexpressible anguish and suffering. Images on the screens reveal that the Euphrates River is drying up, and Victor smiles in victory, pointing out what's happening. "Look at this," he tells his generals. "My lord Satan has provided a miracle—a perfect path for my armies to get into Israel. Inform the commanders right away." Generals Ricci and Schmidt begin to make the calls as Victor laughs. "Such a marvelous miracle," he says, mesmerized by what he's watching as the waters recede from the Euphrates, as if they're being sucked up into the atmosphere. "What other miracles will my lord Satan provide me?"

Maria starts for the door but stops when a pain deep in Victor's throat brings him to his knees. On the other side of the room, Ubel falls to the floor, holding his abdomen. They both make retching sounds and everyone moves back, stepping away from Victor and Ubel. They both open their mouths as if to vomit and evil spirits fly out. Maria and the others scream as the evil spirits throw each person to the ceiling, where they remain pinned tight.

"Gifts from my lord!" Victor says, spellbound and delirious with joy at what is happening. "Go!" Victor commands the spirits. "Go assemble the troops of my world to the Jezreel Valley! Israel must be destroyed now!"

The demonic spirits flee the room, and everyone falls back to the floor. Flying all over the globe, the spirits energize the leaders and warriors of the planet to come against Israel. Apollyon, the chief fallen angel, summons his troops to fight alongside the earth's troops. All are armed to the teeth and heading for Israel.

CHAPTER 48

Petra, Jordan
One Day Later

The skies above the mountains are black with warplanes and hell's forces. As the sinister shadows pass over, the Jews are on their knees, praying. The earth trembles beneath them as millions of enemy tanks and abyss dwellers converge on Israel to assemble at the Jezreel Valley. Satan's armies are bent on wiping Israel from the face of the earth before the false prophet Jesus can return, and the air is filled with nerve-stripping howls and shrieks. Zerah, Elliott, and others of the 144,000 sealed servants of God run throughout the mountains and lead the Jews in crying out, "Come, Yeshua Messiah! Blessed is he who comes in the name of the Lord!"

Rome, Italy

Flames of fire fall like rain from the sky and lick their way up Victor's palace, swallowing it in a massive gulp. The port where cargo ships came and went each day carrying loads of precious gems and goods from all over the world and where men, women, and children were sold into slavery is engulfed in a fiery, orange blast as dozens of ships at the port and on the sea go up in blazes and people scream, running for their lives. Inside Victor City, the thrones in the throne room ignite, and posh hotels, casinos, sex bars, and Victor's statue in Victor's Square all go up in smoke, the infernos rising as high as the naked eye can see. The entirety of Rome lights the sky as a torch and within an hour is no more.

CHAPTER 49

The Jezreel Valley, Israel
One Day Later

The number of Satan's armies descending upon the valley must be at least 200 million. They are inside tanks, warplanes, carrying the most advanced weaponry in the world, or riding atop hell's beasts breathing out sulfur and brimstone as they get into position, waiting for the false prophet Jesus and his army. Victor smiles from high atop the valley, his heart racing at the sight. He walks back and forth, cursing in gratitude as he watches them. "Look at them, my lord Satan!" he shouts into the air. "Look at what we've done."

Ubel is weak in the knees and his skin tingles as he looks over at the magnificent sight of Satan's and Victor's troops from around the world. The mighty Apollyon and his army from the abyss paint the skies black as they fly overhead. Never before have so many warriors gathered for so glorious a cause. He bows before Victor, shaking as he does. "You will be praised for eternity, my king and savior."

Jerusalem

The line to get inside the temple stretches down the temple stairs and into the streets. Pilgrims have come in increasing numbers to worship and give gifts to the king as he prepares for battle. Curses, cheers, horns, and sounds of celebration can be heard throughout the city as Victor's followers call on the name of Satan to fully equip their lord and savior for this great battle. Their voices rise louder and louder in an effort for their praises to carry to their king, who is at the Jezreel Valley preparing his troops. As the sounds of profanities and revelry ring throughout Jerusalem, the ground begins to shake. The trembling is so violent that the voices of praise and worship turn to screams of terror as enormous chasms open up in the ground. Voices are silenced as the earth swallows the crowds and buildings collapse on them.

All over the world, the earth convulses and heaves as if vomiting the evil and wickedness from its bowels and reduces every city from Paris to Dallas to rubble. So tremendous is the shaking that not one city on earth is left standing. Every island flees from its spot, as if trying to hide, and every mountain on the globe disappears, and people curse and scream at all that is happening. As they run for shelter, the heavens open and pound the earth with giant 100-pound hailstones that fall from the sky and batter what is left of the earth's topography that hasn't already been decimated. There is no place left for anyone to hide, and all those with Victor's mark blaspheme God, refusing to repent.

CHAPTER 50

The Jezreel Valley, Israel
One Day Later

As word continues to reach Victor of the demise of his world, he is out of his mind with rage. He paces at his post atop Mount Carmel with Ubel and several of his generals and is energized by the monstrous sound of the troops below—he is ready for war. Enflamed with fury, he screams curses at God. "Come on!" he shouts, raising his fists to heaven and uttering blasphemies. "Come down, you coward! You're not taking my world. It is mine! I am god! I am savior and lord and king over all the earth! Not you! You are nothing!"

Petra, Jordan

Protected from the calamities that are destroying the world, the Jews have been on their feet or on their knees as they wail day and night. They stretch their arms heavenward as they shout with all their strength, "Come, Yeshua Messiah! Blessed is he who comes in the name of the Lord! Blessed is he who comes in the name of the Lord!" Although they are more than 130 miles away from the Jezreel Valley, they can hear the sounds of the massive gathering of troops all the way to the mountains of Petra. This inspires the Jewish remnant to call out all the louder. "Come, Yeshua Messiah! Blessed is he who comes in the name of the Lord!"

As they cry out, the heavens disappear above them. The roar of rejoicing is deafening as the Jews look upward and their hearts nearly burst as they revel in the glory that is more beautiful and magnificent than they ever imagined.

The Jezreel Valley, Israel

The horrific and terrifying sight sends Satan's troops reeling and they wail and run for their lives. Around the world, those with Victor's mark cry out in anguish as they look upward into the sky. Victor and Ubel curse the troops for attempting to flee, and Victor shouts for his demonic legion to use every weapon in their arsenal. He lifts his fists in rage but is struck with terror at the horrifying scene unfolding above him.

Pennsylvania

Emma, Lerenzo, and Micah stand to their feet and wave their arms in the air, weeping and shouting as they hold on to one another and praising God for who they are seeing.

It is Jesus!

To discover more about the biblical facts behind the story, read Where in the Word? *on page 271.*

WHERE
IN THE
WORD?

DEEP WATERS

A few years ago, my husband Troy and I went to Maui for our twenty-fifth wedding anniversary. One day, we took a walk along the ocean and came upon a bay where a few people were sunbathing on the beach and fewer still were snorkeling in the water. A man and his wife walked out of the water and told us it was the best snorkeling in the entire state. At only five dollars an hour, how could we resist? We paid for our two-hour slot, put on our flippers and masks, and as soon as we submerged our faces in the water, we knew the man was right! We saw countless colorful fish, a couple of eels, a reef shark, and it was impossible to swim after all the sea turtles that were keeping us company.

When our two hours were nearly up, we started swimming back toward the beach. I was about to stand up out of the water when I saw the most enormous turtle I had ever seen. It was magnificent! It was so big we could have set plates on top of its shell and had lunch. Not five feet behind me were three little girls who were playing in the water with their dad, and right next to me were a man and woman who were standing there in thigh-deep water, looking out over the bay. Nearby, another couple was putting on their snorkeling gear and I popped up out of the water and talked with them, telling them about the massive turtle that was literally right here below the surface. I stuck my head back in the water, and Troy and I watched as the turtle's ginormous flippers gently moved through the water as it hovered over a rock, munching on algae. By this time, our two hours were complete, and we got out of the water. The little girls were still playing, the husband and wife were still standing there looking out over the bay, and the other couple was putting on their masks.

We turned in our snorkeling gear and as we walked away, I saw the couple with the snorkeling gear walking to another part of the bay. "Where are they going?" I asked. "They're missing the turtle."

"Maybe they don't want to see the turtle," Troy said.

"But I *told them* how beautiful it was. I told them exactly where it was and how enormous and amazing it was." I stopped and watched as the couple finally got into the water and headed off in an entirely different direction. "What in the world are they doing? Where are they going? They're missing the turtle!"

"Again," Troy said, "maybe they *don't want* to see the turtle."

"*Who* wouldn't want to see that turtle?" I asked, exasperated.

As we walked away, I realized that all those people were so close—just within a couple of feet—to beauty, wonder, and magnificence… and they all missed it. If any one of them would have just looked in the water, they would have been face to face with this awesome creature.

That's the story for a lot of people today. So many are within feet of the wonder, the beauty, and the greatness of God, but like the little girls who were playing within feet of the turtle, they are too caught up in the pleasures of their own world to notice. Others, like the couple standing in thigh-deep water and looking out over the bay, are so close to the very presence of God, but they stand by complacently, not interested enough to go deeper into the water. (A.W. Tozer said, "Complacency is a deadly foe of all spiritual growth.") And then there are those, like the couple about to go snorkeling, who are within reach of God, but even after being told of His amazing beauty, enormity, majesty, power, awesomeness, and exactly where to find Him, choose to go away from Him in a different direction altogether.

But there is one other set representing many people today, and that is those who are paying attention. They are in the water, face to face with the Almighty. As deep calls to deep, God is calling each one of us into a deeper relationship with Him to experience His wonder and love in these final days before Christ's return. It is there, in those deep waters with Him, where everything changes. We see Him for who He is. We sense His power and know that He and His Word are real.

A LOST MESSAGE

In His greatness, God told us "the end from the beginning" (Isaiah 46:10). He told us what this world would look like as we got closer to Christ's return (Matthew 24; Mark 13; Luke 21). He told us that people within the church would fall away, and that others would scoff at the return of Jesus (Matthew 24:10; 2 Peter 3:3). In a world that is chaotic and turbulent and feels as if it's gone mad, Jesus said, "Behold, I am coming soon" (Revelation 22:12). Unfortunately, that isn't a message you'll hear at most churches or on most Christian radio programs. I recorded an interview for my first novel in this series, *The Time of Jacob's Trouble*, that never aired because I was told that there are different views of Christ's return and not all listeners would have agreed with what was presented. I can't think of any topic that all listeners would agree on! Sadly, the message of Christ's coming has been ignored or overlooked by many like this Christian program. But you are reading this book because you sense or are aware that something is happening; things are happening in the world that have prompted you to search for answers.

WHAT TO EXPECT

Within this "Where in the Word?" section, we will go into the Scriptures to learn more about some key characters and events of what the Bible calls "the end of the age" (Matthew 24:3; 28:20). The novel portion of *Daniel's Final Week* is a fictionalized account of the final three-and-a-half years of the world before Jesus returns and makes all things new. Did I fully describe all the events that will take place? No. Did the characters portray all the real-life situations that will occur during that time? No. Did I come close to capturing all the supernatural aspects of what will happen during the tribulation? No. God has given us prophecies that tell us about earth's final days, but He has not revealed all the details, so we can only imagine how they will ultimately play out, and that is the purpose of the novel.

The intent of the "Where in the Word?" section is to take us into the Bible and learn what God has told us. In Revelation 10, John is told by an angel to eat a mysterious little scroll (we aren't told what is written on it), and we read that it tastes sweet in his mouth but is bitter in his stomach. The Word of God tastes sweet to believers but is also bitter because we know what the truth of Scripture means to those who refuse to believe; it means eternal separation from God. I pray this section will help you realize that if you are in Christ, your victory is certain. That is the sweetness. If you don't know Jesus, the Word of God may taste bitter to you, but I pray this portion of the book will lead you to consider God and the salvation He offers in His Son, Jesus Christ.

KNOWING THE END FROM THE BEGINNING

In *The Time of Jacob's Trouble*, we discovered that the Bible is the only ancient or modern religious text to include fulfilled prophecies within it. There is no other religious text that has even one fulfilled prophecy, let alone 500, proving that God alone is the one true God.

In Isaiah 46:9-10, the Lord says, "I am God, and there is no other; I am God, and there is none like me, declaring the end from the beginning and from ancient times things not yet done, saying, 'My counsel shall stand, and I will accomplish all my purpose.'"

In His goodness, God told us about the end of all things, which will culminate in a new heaven and a new earth (2 Peter 3:13; Revelation 21:1). When God prepared to destroy the cities of Sodom and Gomorrah, he told Abraham of His plans. Why? Because Abraham was a friend of God (2 Chronicles 20:7; Isaiah 41:8; James 2:23), and God takes His friends into confidence and tells them what He will do. In Genesis 18:17, we read, "The LORD said, 'Shall I hide from Abraham what I am about to do…?'" In the same way, God has not hidden what He will one day do with this present world, but has revealed His plans and purposes to us in His Word. He has taken us into His confidence just as He did with Abraham.

WHAT IS THE GREAT TRIBULATION?

The Bible tells us that as long as we're on this earth, we are going to have what we can call "lowercase *t*" tribulations. John 16:33 says, "In the world you will have tribulation." By "lowercase *t*" tribulations I mean pressure, affliction, anguish, trouble, burdens, and persecution.[1] Everyone experiences those tribulations in life.

That stands in contrast with what we can call the "uppercase *T*" tribulation, or the tribulation period, a future time that is called many things in the Bible: the day of the Lord, the day of wrath, the day of vengeance, the time of Jacob's trouble, the day of darkness and gloom, the day of the Lord's anger, the hour of trial, the hour of His judgment, and so many other names. This will take place during the earth's final seven years (we will soon examine where those seven years are mentioned in the Bible), and the final three-and-a-half years of the tribulation are called the "great tribulation" by Jesus: "There will be *great tribulation*, such as has not been from the beginning of the world until now, no, and never will be" (Matthew 24:21).

Daniel 12:1 tells us that this time of trouble is unlike any in history for the Jews. This period will also be marked by the martyrdom of Christ followers: "These are the ones coming out of the *great tribulation*. They have washed their robes and made them white in the blood of the Lamb" (Revelation 7:14). We will look deeper into this martyrdom and persecution later.

These final years will be the darkest in all of human history. Luke 21:26 gives us a hint of what to expect during those days as men's hearts fail them "from fear and the expectation of those things which are coming on the earth" (NKJV). J. Dwight Pentecost said, "No passage can be found to alleviate to any degree whatsoever the severity of this time that shall come upon the earth."[2]

WHAT WILL HAPPEN?

Revelation chapters 6–19 give us an account of the events, people, and places of the tribulation period, and I encourage you to read these chapters. When a Scripture passage seems too fantastical to be true, please remember that we are told seven times (the number seven represents completion and perfection in the Bible) within the book of Revelation that it is prophecy. It isn't allegory, myth, or science fiction, as many people claim. The Bible says that Revelation is prophecy and everything within it will be fulfilled in God's time and according to His will.

Revelation 6–19 reveals that a total of 21 judgments will fall during the tribulation, and it is obvious people know that it is God's wrath that has come upon the world as they cry out to the mountains and rocks, "Fall on us and hide us from the face of him who is seated on the throne, and from the wrath of the Lamb, for the great day of their wrath has come, and who can stand?" (Revelation 6:16-17).

Although people will indeed know that God's wrath has come, we are told of how they will respond: "People gnawed their tongues in anguish and cursed the God of heaven for their pain and sores. They did not repent of their deeds" (Revelation 16:10-11). The hearts of people will be so wicked that even though they know His wrath is falling on them and that time is running out, they will not repent of their sins and turn to Him.

We also learn in these chapters that God's judgments on a rebellious world will not be poured out all at once but come in waves. It is impossible to depict how horrible those days will be for those who live on earth, but the Bible compares them to birth pains, becoming more frequent and intense as the return of Jesus gets closer (Matthew 24:8; 1 Thessalonians 5:3). Jesus said that if those days had not been cut short that no human being could be saved (Matthew 24:22).

WHO IS INTRODUCED IN REVELATION?

Every book, movie, or TV show has what is called a backstory, where we meet those who are part of all that takes place. All during the time God's judgment is falling in Revelation chapters 6–19, the apostle John takes time to introduce us to the 144,000 (who are explained in *The Time of Jacob's Trouble*—see pages 216-222), the two witnesses (who are covered in *The Day of Ezekiel's Hope*—see pages 235-242), the great dragon, Antichrist, and the false prophet, whom we will examine in the final book.

WHY SHOULD WE CARE?

If we are part of the bride of Christ, those who are truly "in Christ" and follow Him as Lord and Savior, we will be saved from "the wrath to come" (1 Thessalonians 1:10). *The Time of Jacob's Trouble* goes deeper into what it means to be "in Christ" (pages 269-275), the snatching away (pages 243-251), and God's wrath that is yet to come (pages 249-251), so I won't cover that again in this book. Even though Christ's bride won't be on earth during the tribulation, there are several reasons why we should take the time to study the Bible and know about what will take place.

God Shared It with Us in His Word

In Genesis 18, God didn't have to tell Abraham that He was going to destroy the cities of Sodom and Gomorrah. After all, Abraham didn't live in that region. But his nephew Lot did. Abraham would want to see his family in Sodom and Gomorrah saved from God's wrath in the same way we would want to see our own family members safe from God's coming wrath. God has revealed His plan for the end of the age so we can tell others about His redeeming plan of salvation.

We Realize that the World Really Is Heading to an End

When we study the Scriptures about what the Bible refers to as the "end of the age" (Matthew 24:3), we learn that God has a plan to redeem the world from the sin-sick state it's in and make all things new (Revelation 21:5). We understand that He will pour out His wrath on a rebellious and deceived world but that millions will turn to Him in the greatest revival in history (Revelation 7:9-14).

We Become Aware of Satan's Schemes and Intentions

As we study about the end times, we not only come to understand God's plans for the future, but we also become aware of Satan's schemes and intentions, and this inspires us to strap on the armor of God (Ephesians 6:10-18) and use the weapons of our warfare (2 Corinthians 10:4) to resist the devil (James 4:7) and his deceptive ways.

We Understand We Are Living in a Time of Signs

When we are aware of the season that we're living in, we come to realize that we are living in a time of unprecedented signs. We are seeing more signs of Christ's return than were seen by any generation before us (I covered some of these throughout the "Where in the Word?" section in *The Day of Ezekiel's Hope*). These signs aren't happening sporadically but are converging all at once. This recognition shouldn't strike fear in us, but as Jesus said in Luke 21:28, it should lead us to lift up our heads because we know that His return is closer than ever before. God has trusted us with His Word, and what a privilege it is to know His plans for the future! We know that things are looking up!

SATAN

Just as the Father, Son, and Holy Spirit are the holy Trinity, in the earth's final days Satan, Antichrist, and the false prophet will be the unholy trinity. In heaven, Satan was known as the "morning star" (Isaiah 14:12 NIV), which translates to Lucifer, and he was a cherubim (Ezekiel 28:14), who are among the highest-ranking angels. Isaiah 37:16 says that God sits "enthroned between the cherubim." But that role wasn't good enough for Satan; he didn't want to stand beside the throne of God, he wanted to sit on the throne. He was puffed up over his beauty and his heart was proud; violence began to overtake him so that he was no longer willing to serve under the Creator (Ezekiel 28:16-18; see also Isaiah 14:13-14).

Satan thought himself greater than God, and in his pride (God tells us time and again that He hates pride in verses like Proverbs 6:7, Jeremiah 50:31, Isaiah 2:12, and James 4:6), he hatched a plan to overtake God, trying to set himself up as equal to God (Isaiah 14:13). He even convinced one-third of the angels to join him in his rebellion (Revelation 12:4, 7-8), but God threw him down (Isaiah 14:15, 19; Ezekiel 28:16-19; Revelation 12:9). Jesus was with God from the beginning (John 1:1), and Luke 10:18 says that Jesus saw Satan's fall from heaven.

SATAN'S WOMAN

Once fallen from heaven and realizing that he wasn't powerful enough to usurp God's throne, Satan set his sights on people and turning them away from God. Satan fully understands the purpose of the bride of Christ, and from the beginning, he has sought to have his own woman to help establish his own kingdom. Satan has no love for women as Christ does; Satan only wants to use and abuse, manipulate, deceive, and control women (he started with Eve in Genesis 3). Pastor David Jones says Satan wants to "spiritually rape Christ's Bride in order to satisfy his own diabolic ambitions."[1]

We'll look further into Satan's misuse of women when we learn more about fallen angels, but a simple look into the pages of the Bible reveals that Satan has used women for his purposes throughout history. This will culminate in his "prostitute" during the earth's final years (Revelation 17:1-6). Notice that Satan's woman is not a bride like that of Christ. She is not cherished or adored or worth sacrificing himself for; Satan's woman is a harlot that is always used for his sake. Revelation 17 reveals that this "prostitute" at the end of the age will be the false religious system that will worship and adore Antichrist, leading countless people away from the one true God. In the novel portion of this book, Ubel led the world in worship and praise of Victor Quade, the Antichrist. This "prostitute" will be one of Satan's final weapons to keep people from choosing Christ and for ridding the earth of Christ's saints.

HIS NAMES AND POSITION

Satan wants to keep people from following Christ, so he disguises himself as an angel of light (2 Corinthians 11:14). In reality, however, he is a tempter, thief, destroyer, deceiver of the whole world, murderer, and accuser of the brethren (Matthew 4:3; John 10:10, 2 Corinthians 11:3; Revelation 12:9-10; Zechariah 3:1; John 8:44; Job 2:1-6), among other things. Revelation 12 refers to him as a great red dragon.

As "prince of the power of the air" (Ephesians 2:2), Satan has subjects under him in the atmosphere in the form of evil spirits. Ephesians

6:12 says our battle is against "the rulers, against the authorities, against the cosmic powers over this present darkness, against the spiritual forces of evil in the heavenly places." Those are Satan's subjects in the atmosphere and heavenly places.

In Matthew 12:26, Jesus said Satan has a kingdom. John refers to him as "the ruler of this world" in John 12:31, 14:30, and 16:11. If he's the ruler of this world, of his kingdom, then that means he has subjects under him here just as he does in the atmosphere, and they are the evil men and women on earth who do his work. Adam and Eve gave up their dominion in the Garden of Eden to Satan, and John told us that "the whole world lies in the power of the evil one" (1 John 5:19).

When it seems like the world has gone mad, just remember whose kingdom it is—for now. But God is on His throne and Christ is coming! All those in Christ must never forget that the gates of hell cannot prevail against Christ's church (Matthew 16:18). Keep praying and battling against this present darkness because the light of the whole world is coming!

SATAN'S MOTIVATION

After Adam and Eve's fall in the garden, God told Satan that the seed of the woman "shall bruise your head" (Genesis 3:15). Ever since, Satan's purpose has been to annihilate that seed. One evening, while my husband and I were talking about abortion, my 17-year-old daughter overheard us and said, "It makes sense that Satan wants to destroy children because from the very beginning, God told him that the woman's seed would crush his head." A teenager sees Satan's motivation! Satan knew he had to keep that promised seed from being born in Israel and did everything he could to stop the nation of Israel from existing (see *The Day of Ezekiel's Hope* for a brief history of Israel's formation). If the nation didn't exist, then neither would the seed. Ever since his fall, the destruction of Israel has been Satan's target because without an Israel, there would be no Jesus.

THE GREAT SIGN OF A WOMAN

Revelation 12 pictures a woman clothed with the sun, with the moon under her feet, wearing a garland of 12 stars, and about to give birth. The book of Revelation mentions symbols frequently, and first-century Jews would have recognized this woman as the nation of Israel. The 12 stars represent the 12 sons of Jacob and the 12 tribes of Israel, and in the Old Testament, Israel is frequently portrayed as the wife of Yahweh or a woman in travail.

In verses 3-4, a great red dragon appears, and his hope is that he can devour the woman's child when she gives birth. Jesus was born through the nation of Israel, and Satan's goal is to devour Christ and keep Him from the world, which is why he pursued the woman (Israel—verse 13) and "poured water like a river out of his mouth after the woman, to sweep her away with a flood" (verse 15). Satan has pursued Israel through the ages to destroy it, but he has been unsuccessful.

When Jesus died, Satan thought he had won, but Jesus rose from the grave, and that empty grave means that He's coming back! That enrages Satan because he knows his time is short. Jesus said that He will set up His throne and kingdom in Jerusalem when He returns, for Jerusalem is "the city of the great King" (Matthew 5:35). There was no king in Israel when Jesus spoke those words; He was referring to His future reign. He said that when He comes, He will sit on the throne of His glory (Matthew 25:31). That is why Satan will attempt to pull out all stops in annihilating Israel—so that Jesus will not return.

Satan reasons that without a country to return to, then surely Jesus won't come. In *The Day of Ezekiel's Hope*, I wrote about how the Jews have survived despite fierce persecution and opposition, and Revelation 12:15 reveals Satan's unparalleled attack against Israel in the hopes of sweeping her away. Satan will pursue the total destruction of Israel and the Jews, but he will not succeed. Revelation 12:14 says, "The woman was given the two wings of the great eagle so that she might fly from the serpent into the wilderness, to the place where she is to be nourished."

God will provide a special place of protection for the Jews so that Satan cannot destroy them. Jesus told the people of Judea that when the abomination of desolation (Antichrist) sets himself up in the temple, they are to flee to the mountains (Matthew 24:15-16—we will learn more about those mountains later). God knows the end from the beginning. No matter what move Satan makes, God is always ahead of him. All Satan can do is counterattack, and one day his final attack will take place at the Jezreel Valley in Israel. But we know how that will end for him…because God has already told us.

KICKED OUT OF HEAVEN ONCE AND FOR ALL

From what we are able to determine, after the fallen angels lost the battle in heaven, they have been held in the abyss for millennia (2 Peter 2:4; Jude 6). But Satan has had access to heaven, which was portrayed in the opening chapter of the novel. It is there that he has acted as our accuser (Job 1:6-7; Zechariah 3:1-2; Revelation 12:10). However, he knows that the day is coming when he will be kicked out once and for all. He will no longer be able to accuse us.

> Now war arose in heaven, Michael and his angels fighting against the dragon. And the dragon and his angels fought back, but he was defeated, and there was no longer any place for them in heaven. And the great dragon was thrown down, that ancient serpent, who is called the devil and Satan, the deceiver of the whole world—he was thrown down to the earth, and his angels were thrown down with him. And I heard a loud voice in heaven, saying, "Now the salvation and the power and the kingdom of our God and the authority of his Christ have come, for the accuser of our brothers has been thrown down, who accuses them day and night before our God" (Revelation 12:7-10).

When Satan is cast out of heaven, a warning will be given: "Woe to you, O earth and sea, for the devil has come down to you in great wrath, because he knows that his time is short!" (verse 12).

Satan will be kicked out of heaven for good and come to the earth in great wrath because the clock is ticking. He knows that Jesus is returning, and when that happens, his reign as "the ruler of this world" (John 14:30), "the god of this age" (2 Corinthians 4:4 NIV), and "deceiver of the whole world" (Revelation 12:9) will soon end. He will release the fallen angels from the abyss and, unlike any other time in history, there will be a palpable and visible supernatural evil present in the world. In other words, all hell will literally break loose on the earth (Revelation 9:1-2). Satan will unleash his fury, energizing Antichrist as revealed in Revelation 10:2: "The dragon gave the beast his power and his throne and great authority." In no way could I possibly do an adequate job of describing how frightening that time will be. Nor would our minds be able to fully comprehend the extent of the evil that will be present in those days.

FALSE SIGNS AND LYING WONDERS

Second Thessalonians 2:9 tells us that "the coming of the lawless one [will be] by the activity of Satan with all power and false signs and wonders." Satan will empower the Antichrist to be able to perform "false signs." The King James Version says "lying wonders." The words "false" and "lying" immediately discredit these signs and wonders. Satan can only counterfeit what God does, but his deception will be convincing enough for people to marvel and say, "Who is like the beast?" (Revelation 13:4).

People will be easily deceived during the tribulation, just as many are today. Believers, however, have been equipped with God's Word, and He has told us to resist the devil and he will flee from us (James 4:7). We also know the gates of hell cannot prevail against the church (Matthew 16:18). Things are looking up to Christ's return, and all those who are in Christ have nothing to fear!

THE ANTICHRIST

In John 5:43, Jesus said, "I have come in my Father's name, and you do not receive me. If another comes in his own name, you will receive him."

One day, the earth's final false messiah will come in his own name and the world will fall down in praise before him. He will set himself up inside the temple in Jerusalem (2 Thessalonians 2:4), and many Jews will worship him as their long-awaited messiah. He will be Satan's masterpiece, a counterfeit of Jesus Christ. The prefix *anti* means "against" and "instead of." This coming leader who will dominate the earth will be against Christ and claim to be the savior of the world, and people will follow him (Revelation 13:3-4). You may wonder, *How is that possible? Why would anyone follow a diabolical and evil man?* In a Christ-rejecting and biblically illiterate world, it will happen very easily.

POSSESSED BY SATAN

Nearly 2,000 years ago, Jesus was celebrating His last Passover with the disciples in the upper room when Satan "entered" Judas (Luke 22:3), meaning he took possession of him. Satan is not omnipresent (able to be everywhere) like God; he can only be one place at a time, and at that moment, he saw a way to rid himself of Jesus once and for all by using Judas. But his plan failed. To Satan's great delight, Jesus died on the cross, but to Satan's great horror, Jesus arose from the dead. All through history, Satan has tried time and again to exterminate the Jews and Israel, and I believe that in every era of history, he has prepared himself by possessing a man for that hour in time. His man of the future will be the Antichrist, and Satan will possess him in order to energize him (2 Thessalonians 2:9)—meaning that Antichrist's words, actions, plans, and thoughts will be anointed by Satan.

A MORTAL WOUND IS HEALED

In Revelation 13, John refers to the Antichrist as "the beast" (he uses the term *Antichrist* in 1 and 2 John). Much of Revelation is written using symbolism, and what better word could be used to describe to a first-century persecuted believer a man who is vicious and deadly? Many loved ones of first-century Jews had lost their lives to beasts that had torn them apart within a Roman arena, and the word *beast* clearly identifies that this man will be monstrous, ferocious, vile, and wicked.

In Revelation 13:3, we learn this about the Antichrist: "One of its heads seemed to have a mortal wound, but its mortal wound was healed, and the whole earth marveled as they followed the beast." Does this mean that the Antichrist will sustain a deadly head wound, and Satan will use his power to resurrect him? Or as some believe, does this refer to a revived Roman Empire that has long been dead but will come back to life during the tribulation, and its reemergence will amaze people? Israel became a nation again in 1948, yet no one worshipped the nation, and very few people "marveled" at its reemergence. Instead, several Arab nations quickly started a war against Israel, proving that many people were not amazed, but instead, were angered by its existence. A reformation of nations won't cause people to "follow" that new alignment. People don't follow nations; they follow another person.

Revelation 13:3 says that the beast "seemed to have a mortal wound." Since we know that Satan counterfeits what God does and we've already learned that "false signs and lying wonders" will be performed through Satan, it seems that we can suggest that Antichrist is not actually resurrected, but that this will be one of the false signs and lying wonders that will be used to fool people into worshipping and following him.

However, according to Mark Hitchcock, the word to describe his death are always used to describe a violent death. In Revelation 5:6, the same word is used to describe the death of Jesus:

> Revelation 17:8 says that after the Antichrist is killed he will go to the abyss for a time before reappearing on earth. This doesn't seem to be describing someone who is faking his death. I cannot explain every detail of how this death and resurrection occur, but I do believe these passages lead us to a startling conclusion: God will permit Satan to perform this marvelous feat to further his nefarious parody of Christ and further deceive the world.[1]

Regardless of whether Satan is given power to resurrect Antichrist or if it is one of the greatest false wonders of the world, we know that this event will be used to lead countless souls away from eternity with God. When the lawless one (one of Antichrist's names) is revealed, there will be "wicked deception for those who are perishing," and they will "believe what is false" and "not believe the truth" (2 Thessalonians 2:11-12). People who are alive on earth during this period will follow this prophesied world leader at their peril; their very souls will perish.

MANY NAMES

In the Bible, the Antichrist goes by many names. There are more than 100 passages that refer to him, and these are only some of his many names:

- the "man of sin...the son of perdition" (2 Thessalonians 2:3 NKJV)

- "the lawless one" (2 Thessalonians 2:8)

- the little horn (Daniel 7:8)

- the king of "fierce features, who understands sinister schemes" (Daniel 8:23 NKJV)
- "the prince who is to come" (Daniel 9:26)
- "the king [who] shall do as he wills" (Daniel 11:36)
- "the abomination that makes desolate" (Daniel 12:11) and "the abomination of desolation" (Matthew 24:15)

He is most commonly referred to as Antichrist, a term that is used five times in four verses in the New Testament. The word is used to speak of...

Those who deny the Father and the Son

Who is the liar but he who denies that Jesus is the Christ? This is *the antichrist*, he who denies the Father and the Son (1 John 2:22).

Those who do not declare Jesus

...and every spirit that does not confess Jesus is not from God. This is the spirit of *the antichrist*, which you heard was coming and now is in the world already (1 John 4:3).

The spirit of the antichrist

Many spirits are written about in the Bible and this spirit of the antichrist is one of them; a spirit that was already well entrenched in John's first-century world, one that denies Jesus is from God.

Many deceivers have gone out into the world, those who do not confess the coming of Jesus Christ in the flesh. Such a one is the deceiver and *the antichrist* (2 John 1:7).

The one that Old Testament prophets had warned about would be coming upon the world

Children, it is the last hour, and as you have heard that *antichrist* is coming, so now many *antichrists* have come. Therefore we know that it is the last hour (1 John 2:18).

THE LAST HOUR

In the first century, John said it was "the last hour" and that many antichrists had already come. If it was the last hour in the first century, we must surely be in the last "milliseconds" before Christ's return, and antichrists are plentiful in the world. Recently, on Good Friday and on Resurrection Sunday, the *Los Angeles Times* published two op-eds claiming that "Jesus did not think a person's soul would live on after death,"[2] and praising the country's record godlessness, calling it "good news for the nation."[3] On Easter morning, a US senator tweeted that the meaning of Easter is far more superior than the resurrection of Jesus, and that it's in our commitment to helping one another that we are able to save ourselves.[4] In other words, there is no need for the cross. The backlash was so severe that the tweet was deleted, but not before it had been liked and retweeted thousands of times. Antichrists live and walk among us—and no, they don't look or sound crazy to most of the world. One day, *the* Antichrist will appear on the world stage and seal their fate.

THE COUNTERFEIT

Antichrist's complete opposition to Christ is evident in these descriptions:

Christ	*Antichrist*
The truth	The lie
The holy one	The lawless one
The man of sorrows	The man of sin
The Son of God	The son of destruction
The mystery of godliness	The mystery of iniquity
Cleanses the temple	Desecrates the temple
The Lamb	The beast[5]

Those who come to follow Jesus during the tribulation will recognize Antichrist, but for now, we are not told to look for him. Nowhere in the Bible does it tell us to watch for him. Instead, we are told to wait "for our blessed hope, the appearing of the glory of our great God and Savior Jesus Christ" (Titus 2:13). Our future is secure in Him! Things really are looking up for all those who are in Christ.

ANTICHRIST'S ORIGIN

Daniel 9:26 gives us a clue about Antichrist's origin. It says, in part, that "the people of the prince who is to come shall destroy the city and the sanctuary." The "people" who destroyed the city (Jerusalem) and the "sanctuary" (the temple) were the Romans. They destroyed Jerusalem and the temple in AD 70. This verse says that "the prince who is to come" is from those people—that is, the Romans, meaning he will most likely be of Roman/Western European origin.

SOME CHARACTERISTICS OF THE ANTICHRIST

Entire books have been written about the Antichrist, which go into much greater detail than this book is able, but I will highlight a few of his characteristics.

He Will Be Unlike Any Leader

We know that the Antichrist will rise to power quickly. In Daniel 7, the final kingdom of the earth is described as a beast with ten horns but among them comes a little horn (verse 8) who plucks up three of the horns by their roots. The Antichrist will appear meek (a little horn) among the big horns, but through skill and intrigue (Daniel 8:23; 11:21), he will destroy three powerful leaders (Daniel 7:24). The Antichrist won't subdue them through war but through deception and manipulation. He will ascend to power and deceit will prosper under his rule (Daniel 8:25).

The world will follow and worship Antichrist; he will be unlike any world leader ever known. Revelation 13:8 points out that people all over the world will worship him, even marveling at his remarkable abilities: "Who is like the beast, and who can fight against it?" (verse 4). To garner this kind of awe, he will have to be unlike any leader in human history.

He Will Perform False Signs and Lying Wonders

As mentioned in a previous chapter, the Antichrist will be energized by Satan to perform false signs and lying wonders (2 Thessalonians 2:9), and these will leave most people slack-jawed at what they're seeing. Revelation 17:8 says they will "marvel to see the beast." Along with the false prophet, the Antichrist will perform false healings, false miracles, and other false deeds that will amaze and astonish people. Daniel 8:25 tells us that deception will prosper.

He Will Rule the World Economically, Politically, and Religiously

The Antichrist's rule over the earth will be all-encompassing (Revelation 13:4-8). People will need to receive his mark in order to live freely during his reign (verses 16-18). They will jump in line for that mark so that they can continue to buy groceries, receive a paycheck, pay a bill, buy a tank of gas or new tires, apply to college, run their business, trade in a car, go to the doctor, buy medications, glasses, contact lenses, travel, etc. Nothing will be done without that mark.

He Will "Sound" Like a Leader

Revelation 13:5 says, "The beast was given a mouth uttering haughty and blasphemous words," and Daniel 7 tells us that he will have a mouth that "speaks great things" (verse 8) and "words against the Most High" (verse 25). A.W. Pink says that the Antichrist "will have a perfect command and flow of language. His oratory will not only gain attention but command respect. Revelation 13:2 declares that his mouth is as 'the mouth of a lion' which is a symbolic expression telling of the majesty and awe-producing effects of his voice."[1]

The Antichrist will be so smooth-tongued that he will "make a strong covenant" with the Jews for seven years (Daniel 9:27). The original text of this passage communicates that he will "strengthen" a covenant. That means a covenant will already be in place to confirm. At the time of this writing, there are four countries that have officially signed the Abraham Accords: United Arab Emirates, Bahrain, Morocco, and Sudan.[2] Egypt and Jordan have their own peace plans with Israel, and maybe someday they will also be made part of the Abraham Accords. Perhaps we can suggest that these Accords will be connected in some way to the peace deal that the Antichrist one day strengthens.

He Will Be Worshipped

Cancel culture hasn't seen anything until the Antichrist enters power. He will do his own will, declare himself as god, and exalt himself above every god (Daniel 11:36-38). In other words, during his rule, there will be no other god before Antichrist. He will demolish all worship except that of himself and his lord, Satan. He will attempt to change times and seasons (Daniel 7:25), which means he will cancel long-established thoughts and traditions and, out of fear for their lives, people will kowtow to and follow and worship him. Revelation 13:8 says that "all who dwell on earth will worship it" (the beast), but that doesn't include anyone who is "in Christ," because our citizenship is in heaven, and we will be delivered "from the wrath to come" (1 Thessalonians 1:10). Christ will have already seized us prior to the wrath of God falling in judgment on the world. (For more teaching about being seized by Christ prior to the falling of God's wrath, see my book *The Time of Jacob's Trouble,* pages 243-251.)

He Will Persecute Christ Followers and Jews

Daniel 8:24 says, "His power shall be great—but not by his own power; and he shall cause fearful destruction and shall succeed in what he does, and destroy mighty men and the people who are the saints." The breaking of the covenant with Israel will usher in what Jesus calls the time of "great tribulation" (Matthew 24:21). Persecution and martyrdom will be unlike any other time in human history as the Antichrist makes war with the saints, persecuting and overcoming them (Revelation 13:7; see also Daniel 7:21, 25). Many of them will be beheaded (Revelation 20:4). The Antichrist will be destructive and successful in his persecution because again, his power will come from Satan (2 Thessalonians 2:9-10).

There are many who believe that followers of Jesus will be supernaturally protected from the Antichrist during the tribulation, but the verses we have looked at do not support that. Christ followers and Jews will live in perilous times and experience unprecedented persecution and murder.

When the Antichrist breaks the covenant with Israel, he will make his final push to annihilate the Jews, causing them to run for their lives (Matthew 24:15-22). He will pursue them (Revelation 12:13-17) and kill two-thirds of them (Zechariah 13:8-9).

He Will Have a Strong Military

The Bible tells us that Antichrist will "honor the god of fortresses" (Daniel 11:38), which infers that he will put great stock in the strength of his military. Daniel 7:20 tells us that this beast "seemed greater than its companions," which means "abundant in size, in rank." In the Bible, "this often refers to a captain or chief or lord—a man of high rank or impressive appearance, like Saul in 1 Samuel 9:2, who was head and shoulders above his peers."[3]

All of these characteristics reveal that the Antichrist will be a tremendous leader, one who is utterly incredible (by the world's standards) and worthy of their worship. The world has never seen the likes of him yet.

SOME CHARACTERISTICS OF THE FALSE PROPHET

Let's take a brief look at Antichrist's right-hand man, the false religious leader at the end of the age who John calls the "beast rising out of the earth." John uses two animals to describe him—a lamb and a dragon: "I saw another beast rising out of the earth. It had two horns like a lamb and it spoke like a dragon" (Revelation 13:11).

John refers to him as "the false prophet" three times (Revelation 16:13; 19:20; 20:10). As "a lamb," he will appear gentle, meek, and harmless. Jesus warned us of false teachers like him when He said, "Beware of false prophets, who come to you in sheep's clothing but inwardly are ravenous wolves. You will recognize them by their fruits" (Matthew 7:15-16). As "a dragon," his words will have power as he breathes out the lies of hell. His lamb-like appeal will enable him to emotionally reach the masses, and his dragon-like speech will deceive them to believe that what he says is truth.

He Will Be Persuasive

The false prophet will convince much of the world that the Antichrist must be worshipped: "It exercises all the authority of the first beast in its presence, and makes the earth and its inhabitants worship the first beast, whose mortal wound was healed" (Revelation 13:12).

And it is the signs that he will perform that will deceive them: "It performs great signs, even making fire come down from heaven to earth in front of people, and by the signs that it is allowed to work in the presence of the beast it deceives those who dwell on earth" (verses 13-14).

He Will Be Powerful

In Revelation 13:12-15, we read three times that the false prophet's power will come from the Antichrist. And where does the Antichrist get his power? In verses 2-8, we are told multiple times that his power will come from the dragon, Satan himself. With this power, the false prophet will be able to

- perform great signs and call fire down from heaven (verse 13)

- command an image of Antichrist be built (verse 14)

- give breath to that image so people would worship it (verse 15)

- convince people to take Antichrist's mark on their right hand or forehead (verse 16)

There is no doubt the false prophet will be a powerful man who, because of satanic power, will lead the world in its greatest form of idolatry and deception. Jesus warned us that false prophets like him and others would arise when He said, "False christs and false prophets will arise and perform great signs and wonders, so as to lead astray, if possible, even the elect" (Matthew 24:24).

He Will Be a Great Deceiver and Murderer

In speaking of the false prophet, John writes,

> It deceives those who dwell on earth, telling them to make an image for the beast that was wounded by the sword and yet lived. And it was allowed to give breath to the image of the beast, so that the image of the beast might even speak and might cause those who would not worship the image of the beast to be slain (Revelation 13:14-15).

The false prophet will oversee the creation of an image of the Antichrist, which will be placed inside the temple in Jerusalem. This is what Jesus spoke of in Matthew 24:15-16: "When you see the abomination of desolation spoken of by the prophet Daniel, standing in the holy place (let the reader understand), then let those who are in Judea flee to the mountains."

Every emperor or god in history has had statues or images made of them that were worshipped, and the Antichrist will have the most significant and celebrated one in history. As of now, there isn't a temple standing in Jerusalem, but according to Matthew 24:15 and other passages (Daniel 9:26-27; 11:31; Revelation 11:2), it is clear a temple will be there, and Antichrist's image will be present inside so people can worship him. We don't know what the image will look like, but we do know that the dark power of Satan will enable the image to speak. The false prophet will lead the world in this great deception, this false worship of the Antichrist as god, and he will lead countless souls to their destruction.

Revelation 13:15 tells us that the false prophet will "cause those who would not worship the image of the beast to be slain." He will oversee the murder of Christ followers in earth's final years. Thankfully, his reign of deception will end when Christ returns, and according to Revelation 19:20, his destruction has already been determined. Together with the Antichrist, he will be cast alive into the lake of fire.

As we approach this season of deception, God warns His children to hear His voice and not be fooled by empty words, philosophy, or false teachers (Ephesians 5:6; Colossians 2:8; 2 Thessalonians 2:3). As we get closer each day to Christ's return, pray against any deception that might harm you and your family, and stay in God's Word and listen to what He says.

How Will Antichrist Rise to World Power?

Why would seemingly intelligent people follow one man and worship him as God? Let's answer that question with another question: Why did people follow a madman in Germany who blamed all the world's problems on the Jews and sought to annihilate them all? How is it possible that neighbors and friends turned into monsters under Adolf Hitler's leadership and persecuted and forced out the Jews in their communities? It happened then and it will happen again, but next time, on a global scale. The world will be in upheaval following the snatching away of all those who are in Christ and will be desperate for leadership, security, and peace. Daniel 11:21 tells us that the Antichrist will come heralding peace, and he will seize the kingdom by intrigue.

Note what happens when Jesus breaks the first seal on the scroll in Revelation 6:1-2:

> Now I watched when the Lamb opened one of the seven seals, and I heard one of the four living creatures say with a voice like thunder, "Come!" And I looked, and behold,

a white horse! And its rider had a bow, and a crown was
given to him, and he came out conquering, and to conquer.

The breaking of this seal begins the pouring out of God's judgments
that will come upon the earth during the tribulation period. When the
Lamb (Jesus) opens the first seal, a white horse with a rider who has a
bow and a crown will arise who comes out conquering and to conquer.
I've heard many who believe this is Jesus, but Jesus is in heaven opening the seals at this time, and the word translated "crown" here refers
to the crown of a victor, not a sovereign. The purpose of the rider on
the white horse is to conquer, which is antithetical to Jesus's purpose!
Jesus did not come the first time to conquer, and He will not come the
second time to conquer, but to end the world's rebellion and set up
His peaceful millennial kingdom (Revelation 20). Then later, He will
make all things new (21:5).

Though the rider on the white horse carries a bow, there's no mention of arrows for the bow. The fact there are no arrows and that the
horse is white leads prophecy experts to believe that this man merely
looks like he comes in peace. In Matthew 24, when the disciples asked
Jesus about the signs of the times and the end of the age, His first words
were, "See that no one leads you astray. For many will come in my
name, saying, 'I am the Christ,' and they will lead many astray" (verses
4-5). What is the first judgment to fall during the tribulation period? A
man on a white horse who looks like he's coming in peace and as a savior for the world, but remember, the Bible tells us that Satan disguises
himself as an angel of light (2 Corinthians 11:14).

The Antichrist will look and sound like an angel of light and peace,
but he will lead the world astray. He will wear a cloak of peace but will
actually be a beast beneath it. Today, the world is clamoring for peace
and security, which is what 1 Thessalonians 5:3 said would happen.
Type "peace and security" in your Internet search engine, and see how
many news articles pop up. In a world that will be desperate for peace
and security during the chaos of the tribulation, most people will follow the Antichrist without hesitation because he will look to them like
an angel of light and peace.

THE COVENANT WITH ISRAEL

Daniel 9:27 says the Antichrist "shall confirm a covenant with many for one week" (NKJV). Daniel was writing to his fellow Hebrews that the Antichrist will confirm (again, "confirm" here means "to make strong" or "to strengthen") this covenant with Israel. Imagine anyone being able to strengthen peace with Israel and her neighbors in the Middle East! Conflicts and wars have always broken out in this region. Iran is constantly breathing down Israel's neck. The Bible tells us that in the end, all the nations will come against Israel (Zechariah 12:3). Only someone truly gifted as a persuader will be able to convince the world to have peace with Israel at that time.

We know from the Bible that a temple will be rebuilt in Jerusalem and that the sacrificial system will resume (Daniel 9:27; 2 Thessalonians 2:3-4; Revelation 11:1-2), but we can't imagine how a temple could possibly be built upon the Temple Mount today. Muslims would never allow this to happen; they currently control the Temple Mount, which is home to the Dome of the Rock and a mosque, both of which are highly revered among Muslims. For a temple to be built, it would either have to be put in a different location, or something supernatural will have to happen to convince the Muslims to allow construction on the Temple Mount. (I touched on this in the novel portion of *The Day of Ezekiel's Hope*). One day, the coming world leader will do what no other leader has been able to accomplish. He will bring peace between Israel and her surrounding neighbors, and apparently this will make it possible for the temple to be built and for sacrifices to resume. Only an exceptionally gifted diplomat and negotiator standing on a platform of peace will be able to accomplish that!

WHAT IS THE SIGNIFICANCE OF THE ONE WEEK IN DANIEL 9:27?

The title of this book, *Daniel's Final Week*, is based on Daniel 9:27, which says the Antichrist "shall confirm a covenant with many for one week" (NKJV). There isn't space to write in detail how the 70 weeks of

Daniel 9:24 are broken down, but as prophecy experts explain it, the 70 "weeks" have to do with 70 weeks of *years*, which comes to 490 years.

From the time of Artaxerxes's decree in 444 BC for Nehemiah to rebuild the walls of Jerusalem—which began the 490 years—to the death of Christ on the cross, a total of 69 weeks of years went by, or 483 years. There is still 1 week yet to be fulfilled, which will take place during the future 7-year tribulation. Currently, we are in the "gap" between week 69 and week 70, or the church age. When the Antichrist confirms his covenant with Israel, it will be for 7 *years*. The fact a 7-year covenant has never been made between Israel and any country or leader in history tells us Daniel 9:27 is referring to a still-future event.

Here's what the passage says: "In the middle of the week he shall bring an end to sacrifice and offering. And on the wing of abominations shall be one who makes desolate" (Daniel 9:27 NKJV). In the middle of the "week," which will be three-and-a-half years into the tribulation, the Antichrist will stop the sacrifices and temple worship in Israel, breaking the covenant and turning against Israel. This will begin his attempt to annihilate the Jews once and for all.

SATAN'S THRONE

Revelation 2:13 reveals that Satan has a throne, and at that time, it was in Pergamum. During the tribulation, Satan's throne will be where the Antichrist reigns. For the purpose of the novel, I wrote that he will reign from Italy. Others believe he will reign from a rebuilt Babylon that is located in Iraq. Revelation mentions Babylon six times. Anytime Babylon is mentioned within the Bible it refers to a city that is anti-God, steeped in false religion, rebellion, and corruption. Wherever the Antichrist rules from will be considered Babylon because that is where Satan's throne will be established.

THE MARK

Even those with very limited Bible knowledge are familiar with the number 666, or the mark of the beast, from Revelation 13. In Greek, the word translated "mark" means "a mark or stamp engraved, etched, branded, cut, imprinted."[1] This mark will obviously be visible and permanent and once a person receives it, he is eternally dammed (Revelation 14:9-10). Those who refuse to receive the mark will be put to death by the Antichrist and the false prophet, but will live eternally with Jesus and reign with Him during His millennial kingdom (Revelation 20:4).

Revelation 13:17 states that "no one can buy or sell unless he has the mark, that is, the name of the beast or the number of its name." Again, because Satan has to counterfeit everything that God does, this mark will counterfeit the seal that God will place on the foreheads of the 144,000 servants of Christ during the tribulation. God's seal will protect them from any harm. (I explore this seal and the identity of the 144,000 in the first book in this series, *The Time of Jacob's Trouble*—see pages 216-222.)

There are some who claim that all the prophecies in the book of Revelation have already been fulfilled. They say that the Roman emperor Nero was the beast, and that he used a mark. However, here are some prophecies about the beast (Antichrist) that Nero did *not* fulfill, nor did any other leaders in history:

- Neither Nero nor anyone else has been worshipped by the entire world (Revelation 13:8)

- No one has ever forced the people of the world to take their mark on their right hand or forehead (verse 16)

- Nero never was presumed dead only to come back to life (verse 3)

This tells us the beast will be a *future* world leader who will utilize technology that already exists today (some of this is covered in *The Day of Ezekiel's Hope*) to mark those who vow allegiance to him. In Antichrist's one-world economy, those with the mark on their right hand or forehead will be able to buy and sell in his kingdom. He will be the object of their worship, not Jesus, and God will send them a strong delusion so that they will believe the lie (2 Thessalonians 2:11). And what is that lie? That Antichrist is God and can save them. But those who "are wise" at that time will understand what is happening (Daniel 12:10) and will not receive the mark.

Revelation 13:17-18 tells us how the wise will understand: "No one can buy or sell unless he has the mark, that is, the name of the beast or the number of its name. This calls for wisdom: let the one who has understanding calculate the number of the beast, for it is the number of a man, and his number is 666."

This tells us some sort of numerical value will be attached to Antichrist's name so those who are alive at that time can figure out who he is. "Whatever the personal name of the Antichrist will be, if his name is spelled out in Hebrew characters, the numerical value of his name will be 666. Those who are wise (verse 18) at that time will be able to point him out."[2]

ANTICHRIST'S END

The Antichrist will rule for three-and-a-half years (Revelation 13:5), murdering Jews and Christ followers alike (Daniel 7:25; Revelation 11:7; 13:7). Daniel 7 says the beast's kingdom will "devour the whole earth, and trample it down, and break it to pieces…and his dominion shall be taken away, to be consumed and destroyed in the end" (verses 23, 26).

When Christ returns, He will bring an end to the Antichrist. Second Thessalonians 2:8 says Jesus will "kill [him] with the breath of his mouth," and the word translated "kill" means "to abolish or take away." The Antichrist and the false prophet will be captured and thrown alive into the lake of fire (Revelation 19:20), where they will be tormented forever (20:10).

At the end of Jesus's 1,000-year reign (mentioned six times in Revelation 20:1-7), Satan will be released for a short time from the bottomless pit, where he will have been held during Christ's 1,000-year kingdom. After Christ puts down Satan's final rebellion, Satan will join the Antichrist and the false prophet in the lake of fire, bringing a final end to this unholy trinity.

WHERE ARE THE WARNINGS?

Is Antichrist alive today? It's possible. We know we are in the season of the return of Christ, but no one knows the day or hour, not even the angels nor Jesus Himself. Only God the Father knows (Matthew 24:36). We know we are living in a time when many end-time signs are converging, which means our redemption is near (Luke 21:27), so perhaps the Antichrist is a young boy or young man at this time. He could even be an adult; we don't know. Many people throughout history have tried to identify who the Antichrist will be, but again, we are never told to look for or to try to recognize him. Rather, we are told to look for our "blessed hope, the appearing of the glory of our great God and Savior Jesus Christ" (Titus 2:13).

If the bride of Christ was going to remain on earth during the tribulation, then Paul and the other New Testament writers who wrote of Christ's coming would have told us how to survive the mark of the beast. They would have warned us about how to live off the grid and gather food and water. They would have told us to be waiting and watching for the Antichrist and to be very, very afraid. *But they didn't say that!* Not once. We're told to live in anticipation of Christ's return:

> When Christ, who is your life, appears, then you also will appear with him in glory. Put to death, therefore, whatever belongs to your earthly nature: sexual immorality, impurity, lust, evil desires and greed, which is idolatry (Colossians 3:4-5 NIV).

> It teaches us to say "No" to ungodliness and worldly passions, and to live self-controlled, upright and godly lives in this present age, while we wait for the blessed hope—the appearing of the glory of our great God and Savior, Jesus Christ (Titus 2:12-13 NIV).

> Everyone who has this hope in Him purifies himself, just as He is pure (1 John 3:2-3 NKJV).

The early church looked for and anticipated the coming of the true Christ, not the emergence of the Antichrist. The closest any passage comes to providing instructions for living during the tribulation is Matthew 24:15-18, when Jesus told the Jews to flee to the mountains when the abomination of desolation is set up in the temple. That will happen at the beginning of what Jesus calls "great tribulation, such as has not been from the beginning of the world until now, no, and never will be" (Matthew 24:21).

The Greek word *megas*, which translates to "great," doesn't mean many, large, or more than, but is defined as violent, mighty, strong.[3] The chaos to come will be so intense and horrific that Jesus warns His listeners to flee. But He gave no instructions about how to live in that world, the world of the Antichrist. We're only told to be ready for Christ's coming. Jesus should be our focus, our hope, and our redemption—so let's keep looking up!

Fallen Angels and Demons

When Satan rebelled and was kicked out of heaven, he had a following of angels who left with him—Revelation 12:4 says, "His tail swept down a third of the stars of heaven and cast them to the earth." In the Bible, the word translated "stars," or heavenly host, often refers to the angels in heaven. In Genesis 6, we read about the fallen angels, referred to as "sons of God" (in the Old Testament "sons of God" always referred to supernatural beings), who procreated with women, which resulted in the birth of giants. I mentioned earlier that Satan only wants to use and abuse women, and Genesis 6 tells us that the "sons of God" married any woman they chose. These women weren't valued or treasured. The result of these abhorrent unions were the giant Nephilim, or mighty men with demonically charged supernatural strength who would advance Satan's kingdom. This was among the reasons God destroyed the earth in the worldwide flood. The Bible later tells us these fallen angels are being kept in eternal chains of darkness until the judgment (2 Peter 2:4; Jude 6).

Likewise, we know that many demons dwell in the abyss because in Luke 8:30-31, when Jesus encountered a man possessed by demons, He asked the man, "What is your name?" and the answer was, "'Legion,' for many demons had entered him. And they begged him not to command them to depart into the abyss."

SATAN RELEASES DEMONIC FORCES

In Revelation 9, when Satan is kicked out of heaven once and for all, the bottomless pit will be opened, releasing demonic forces throughout the earth:

> The fifth angel blew his trumpet, and I saw a star fallen from heaven to earth, and he was given the key to the shaft of the bottomless pit. He opened the shaft of the bottomless pit, and from the shaft rose smoke like the smoke of a great furnace, and the sun and the air were darkened with the smoke from the shaft (verses 1-2).

A swarm of locusts can cover the land like a black cloud, and these demonic forces will darken the earth's atmosphere as evil spreads throughout the world during the tribulation.

FIVE MONTHS OF TORTURE

Revelation 9 then goes on to tell us what these demonic forces will do:

> They were told not to harm the grass of the earth or any green plant or any tree, but only those people who do not have the seal of God on their foreheads. They were allowed to torment them for five months, but not to kill them, and their torment was like the torment of a scorpion when it stings someone. And in those days people will seek death and will not find it. They will long to die, but death will flee from them…They have as king over them the angel of the bottomless pit. His name in Hebrew is Abaddon, and in Greek he is called Apollyon (verses 4-6, 11).

In the Bible, locusts are among the ways God sends judgment on a rebellious and wicked world. The locusts in Revelation 9 will be Satan's horde loosed from the abyss. Verse 11 tells us their king is named Abaddon, which means "destroyer." His name tells us what this satanic swarm is going to do on the earth.

Unlike normal locusts, these demonic creatures won't harm vegetation; rather, they will afflict those who aren't sealed by God. But like normal locusts, they won't live long for carrying out their assignment—only five months. During that brief time, they will torment those with the mark, and those people will want to kill themselves, but death will flee from them. I believe we can suggest that this is an act of mercy from God on all those unbelievers who have not yet taken the mark. Those five months will provide an opportunity for them to hear the gospel and choose to follow Jesus, rather than the Antichrist. Even in the time of greatest darkness God will show His mercy.

AN ARMY OF 200 MILLION

Next in Revelation 9 we read this:

> "Release the four angels who are bound at the great river Euphrates." So the four angels, who had been prepared for the hour, the day, the month, and the year, were released to kill a third of mankind. The number of mounted troops was twice ten thousand times ten thousand; I heard their number *(*verses 14-16).

The fact these angels are described as being "bound" reveals they are not God's holy angels. God's angels are sent out to serve those who will inherit salvation (Hebrews 1:14). Bound angels are fallen angels, and during the great tribulation, four of them will be released at the Euphrates River. Apparently they will lead a satanically charged army of 200 million troops, and their mission is horror, destruction, and death—so much so that verse 18 says "a third of mankind [will be] killed, by the fire and smoke and sulfur coming out of their mouths." One-third of earth's population will perish due to this wicked satanic throng.

Does this mean there will be more than 200 million demonic creatures across the planet? There is no way to know the number of angels that fell from heaven or how many demons Jesus has sent to the abyss, but we know this destroying army will comprise 200 million fighters.

We cannot comprehend what this demonic battalion will do to the world, but it will be horrendous and terrifying. Along with Antichrist and the false prophet, this satanic force will thrust unprecedented evil onto the world during the tribulation.

DEMONIC POSSESSION

Matthew 8 tells the account of Jesus casting demons out of two men and into a herd of pigs who then run over a cliff to their deaths. Verse 28 says, "When [Jesus] came to the other side, to the country of the Gadarenes, two demon-possessed men met him, coming out of the tombs, so fierce that no one could pass that way."

According to Strong's Concordance, the word "fierce" here means "dangerous, furious, fierce, savage, perilous."[1] Strong's points out that the same definition applies to 2 Timothy 3, where Paul is describing the characteristics of the last days.[2] In 2 Timothy 3:3, he says that in the last days people will be "brutal." The exact term for demon-possessed men in Matthew 8 is used here to describe people in the last days. They will be savage, dangerous, furious, and fierce because demons won't be rare during the tribulation but will be commonplace and will find plenty of bodies to possess. As I stated earlier, when we study Bible prophecy and what God has told us will happen at the end of the age, we know that we don't want anyone to go through the horror of the tribulation. Studying God's Word gives us an urgency to share the gospel message of salvation with others so they can be in Christ and live with Him forever. Because we know that things are looking up to His return, we are compelled to point people to Christ while there is still time.

WHERE ARE THE MOUNTAINS THE JEWS WILL FLEE TO?

In Matthew 24:15-18, Jesus said, "When you see the abomination of desolation spoken of by the prophet Daniel, standing in the holy place (let the reader understand), then let those who are in Judea flee to the mountains. Let the one who is on the housetop not go down to take what is in his house, and let the one who is in the field not turn back to take his cloak."

Jesus warned the Jews that wherever they are at the time Antichrist sets himself up as god inside the temple in Jerusalem, they should flee to the mountains. He told them not to pack or even grab a jacket on the way out. That's how urgent and dangerous it will be for the Jews in Israel at that time! The mountains located in Israel are unable to provide the protection that is necessary for millions of people, and many suggest that it is in the mountains of Jordan—specifically in Petra, 120 miles southeast of Jerusalem—that the Jews will find safety.

When speaking of the warrior-leader of the end times, Daniel says this of his great military takeover of the world: "He shall come into the glorious land. And tens of thousands shall fall, but these shall be delivered out of his hand: Edom and Moab and the main part of the Ammonites" (Daniel 11:41). This verse tells us that the ancient countries of Edom, Moab, and the place of the Ammonites won't be reached by Antichrist, and these are part of the present-day country of Jordan.[1] This rugged, mountainous area is now called Petra and is seen in the Bible as far back as the book of Genesis. It's the region where Jacob's brother Esau and his descendants lived. At that time, it was called Mt. Hor, Mt. Seir, and the Valley of Salt. Roughly 20 square miles in size, this is a rocky area where an ancient city was literally carved into tall sandstone cliffs. There are thousands of centuries-old chambers and cave dwellings in this mountain area; some of them are enormous and can hold hundreds of people. There is an amphitheater carved into the side of one mountain that can hold 7,000 people.[2]

Still present today are conduits, dams, and cisterns that were carved out of the rocks for rainwater and for the water that flowed from the high mountains. A spring called the Spring of Moses still flows from a rock formation near the entrance and will enable anyone to draw water from the outside of the city to the inside. The Jews who hide here will have water for themselves, for their goats and sheep, and for any crops they raise.

An earthquake in AD 363 is believed to have created the nearly mile-long entrance called the Siq, which contributes to this nearly impregnable fortress of rock.[3] By the middle of the seventh century, the area was mostly abandoned and remains so to this day. Besides visitors, Petra is a ghost town and could hold the millions of Jews who flee Israel when Antichrist begins his murderous spree—it would serve well as a place where God can protect and provide for them (Revelation 12:6). In the novel portion of this book, I suggested that God will once again feed them manna from heaven. He did that when His people were wandering in the wilderness long ago and could certainly do it again today. We don't know how God will feed and care for them during that future time, but we know that He is faithful and will do as He has said.

WILL THEY SURVIVE?

Zephaniah 1:15-16 calls that future time

a day of wrath…
 a day of distress and anguish,
a day of ruin and devastation,
 a day of darkness and gloom,
a day of clouds and thick darkness,
 a day of trumpet blast and battle cry.

How many Jews could possibly survive such a time of wrath, devastation, and anguish on earth? Zechariah 13 says,

It shall come to pass, that in all the land, saith the LORD, two parts therein shall be cut off and die; but the third shall be left therein. And I will bring the third part through the fire, and will refine them as silver is refined, and will try them as gold is tried: they shall call on my name, and I will hear them: I will say, It is my people: and they shall say, The LORD is my God (verses 8-9 KJV).

This verse says that God will bring one-third of the Jews through the fire. Can one-third of the Jews live in this location for three-and-a-half years in safety? Whichever mountains it is that the Jews flee to, the Bible says that Israel will be nourished (Revelation 12:6) in this hiding place. The word "nourished," in the original Greek text, means "to cherish, feed, fatten, nourish."[4] They will be cared for by God Himself. The Jews have a long history of survival. An estimated two-and-a-half million came out of Egypt with Moses and lived in the wilderness for 40 years. For 70 years they were in captivity in Babylon. The Romans sacked Jerusalem in AD 70, scattering the Jews across the world, but a remnant remained and survived for 2,000 years. The Jews were largely exterminated as a race under Hitler, but again, a remnant survived, and there are roughly 14.8 million Jewish people today.[5] So, do I believe they can survive the fury of the Antichrist and stay hidden among mountains for three-and-a-half years? Yes!

WILL THERE BE CHILDREN ON EARTH DURING THE TRIBULATION?

This is the subject of the greatest number of emails I have received after people read *The Time of Jacob's Trouble* and *The Day of Ezekiel's Hope*. One woman angrily wrote, "You are wrong. Children will not be in the tribulation!" This question isn't addressed in the Bible, but we can be sure that God is loving and just and will work all this out for good. We also know that God will not send anyone to hell who shouldn't be there.

For help with this, I spoke with pastor Tom Hughes of 4/12 Church in San Jacinto, California, and he said, "God doesn't clearly define this in the Bible. We know about the Antichrist, false prophet, and others, but not this. We do know that when God destroyed the world in the flood that that included children. They weren't spared when Sodom and Gomorrah were destroyed. In the battles that Joshua led, in every battle, God instructed them to leave no one alive and take no captives, not even children."

I would add here that in Korah's rebellion in Numbers 16, the entire clan was killed, even "their little ones" (verse 27). When the plagues of Egypt began to fall on the Egyptians in Exodus 7, they fell on the children as well. The death of the firstborn would include small children, too, not just adults. No child was preserved in any of these acts of God's wrath. But there are trusted Bible scholars who say that the child who is incapable of deciding what it means to choose and follow God will go into God's presence at the time of death. They point out, for example, that when King David's infant son died, David said that he would "go to him, but he will not return to me" (2 Samuel 12:23). David knew his infant son was with the Lord.

THE CHILDREN OF UNBELIEVERS

The people who are left on earth after the rapture are those who have rejected Christ. They are unbelievers, and they will go through the tribulation. The tribulation will be a time of God's wrath, but as I said earlier, even during this time God will show His mercy to people. I believe that it is in His mercy that He will leave the children of unbelievers here (more on believers' children in a moment). God is good and gracious, merciful and loving, and it would be a heinous act if every child disappeared from the planet. Imagine waking up each day in a world without your children. Or for a pregnant woman to no longer be pregnant. What indescribable horror that would be! That would cause many parents an extraordinary amount of anxiety, even to the point of becoming suicidal. The tribulation years would be spent trying to locate their children instead of finding Christ. Being responsible for a child during the tribulation could very well lead a mother or father to discover the truth about what is happening because they would want to protect and defend their child. Sadly, there will be many people who will abandon their children, but there will also be many who will do everything they possibly can to care for them. I and others believe that if a child dies during the tribulation, and that child is truly unable to distinguish what it means to choose Jesus as Lord or reject Him, he or she will go to heaven.

IS THERE AN AGE OF ACCOUNTABILITY?

The question is always asked, "At what age is a child accountable for his or her salvation?" Many people refer to this as the age of accountability, a concept that is not found in the Bible with regard to salvation. There is no way to know that age. Every child and culture is different. Here in America, in our age of cell phones, computers, movies, TV, social media, music, Internet access, and more, a child learns about sex, drugs, perversion, and other sins that are contrary to God's Word much sooner than children of previous generations. Most of this information is right at a child's fingertips. This has resulted in speeding up the age of accountability. A ten-year-old now is exposed to far more ungodliness than a ten-year-old in 1950. In 1950, false teachers and rejection of God and His Word were not as rampant as they are today. Today, false teachers and their teachings appear in movies, TV shows, podcasts, social media feeds, and other places. These days, children know about rebellion and disobedience sooner than children in any age prior.

THE CHILDREN OF THOSE SNATCHED AWAY BY JESUS

What about the children of believers who are seized by Jesus prior to the wrath of God falling? "They are sanctified by their believing parents when they are young," Pastor Hughes says.

For help with this, let's look at 1 Corinthians 7:15: "The unbelieving husband is made holy because of his wife, and the unbelieving wife is made holy because of her husband. Otherwise your children would be unclean, but as it is, they are holy." Does that mean an unbelieving spouse or a grown child gets a free pass into heaven? No, of course not. The Bible says that *all* have sinned and fall short of the glory of God (Romans 3:23), and *no one* comes to the Father except through Jesus (John 14:6). If a person is mentally capable of understanding what it means to seek salvation in Christ, he or she is responsible for making that decision (Romans 10:9-13). "It does seem to indicate that a child is sanctified by his believing parents until the age when he is accountable for his decisions," pastor Hughes says. "And we don't know what that is; that age will be different for each child."

In this noisy, distracting world, we should be living our lives for Christ now and teaching our children about salvation in Jesus alone. Again, no one will be in hell who shouldn't be there; only those who have consciously decided to reject God's gift of grace. Let's make sure everyone we know accepts that gift today!

CHRIST WILL RETURN!

Right now, Jesus sits at God the Father's right hand in heaven (Acts 7:55; Romans 8:34; Ephesians 1:20). David spoke of Him at the right hand of God in Psalm 110:1:

> The LORD says to my lord:
> "Sit at my right hand
>   until I make your enemies
>   a footstool for your feet" (NIV).

One day, God will make the enemies of Jesus His footstool. Verse five goes on to say, "He shall execute kings in the day of His wrath" (NKJV). Concerning that day of wrath, Isaiah wrote that people will

> Enter into the rock
>   and hide in the dust
> from before the terror of the LORD,
>   and from the splendor of his majesty.
> The haughty looks of man shall be brought low,
>   and the lofty pride of men shall be humbled,
> and the LORD alone will be exalted in that day...

> And people shall enter the caves of the rocks
>   and the holes of the ground,
> from before the terror of the LORD,
>   and from the splendor of his majesty,
>   when he rises to terrify the earth (Isaiah 2:10-11, 19).

That day of wrath is coming. Christ the Lord will return as a warrior executing kings and exacting vengeance (Revelation 19:11-21). This will bring fear to many. Though we may prefer to think of Christ in terms of the gospel message of salvation, we must acknowledge that He is also coming to judge the world of sin. If there were no final judgment of sin, that would mean evil would never come to an end. How could we call God good if He failed to put an end to evil when He makes all things right in the world?

FEAR OR ANTICIPATION?

Believers are never told to dread, fear, or mourn Christ's coming. Why not? As we learned in *The Time of Jacob's Trouble*, when Christ comes to snatch up His bride, He will do so to take us to heaven. It's not until after the tribulation that the second coming will occur, when He returns to earth in judgment. There are two aspects to Christ's return, and those who are believers are not destined for judgment. Rather, we'll be taken up to heaven. That's why we have no reason to shirk away from the thought of or to be anxious about His coming. Instead, just like those in the early church, we're encouraged to

"eagerly await a Savior from [heaven], the Lord Jesus Christ" (Philippians 3:20 NIV)

"look up and lift up your heads" (Luke 21:28 NKJV)

"eagerly wait for Him" (Hebrews 9:28 NKJV)

"be always on the watch" (Luke 21:36 NIV; see also Matthew 24:42; 25:13, Mark 13:35-37)

wait and be ready (Luke 12:35-40)

keep watch and be prepared because He returns as a bridegroom (Matthew 25:1-13)

"set your hearts on things above" for when "Christ, who is your life, appears" (Colossians 3:1, 4 NIV)

"be awake and sober" (1 Thessalonians 5:6 NIV)

We're told to anticipate Christ's coming as the bridegroom to receive His bride as spoken by Jesus in John 14:3: "If I go and prepare a place for you, I will come again and will take you to myself, that where I am you may be also" (*The Time of Jacob's Trouble* digs deeper into this truth).

Jesus said He is coming back. That's awesome news! According to John 14:3, He's coming to take all of those who are in Him. Concerning Christ's return, I have been emphasizing in each book in this series that things are looking up!

WHAT'S NEXT?

I'm so honored you took the time to read *Daniel's Final Week*. My prayer is that this book has encouraged your faith, answered some questions, or piqued your desire to know more about Christ so you can enter into a personal relationship with Him. If you don't know Him, you can, and upon receiving Him as your Savior and Lord, He will guide and lead you for the rest of your life.

The Bible says,

> If you declare with your mouth, "Jesus is Lord," and believe in your heart that God raised him from the dead, you will be saved. For it is with your heart that you believe and are justified, and it is with your mouth that you profess your faith and are saved. As Scripture says, "Anyone who believes in him will never be put to shame." For there is no difference between Jew and Gentile—the same Lord is Lord of all and richly blesses all who call on him, for, "Everyone who calls on the name of the Lord will be saved" (Romans 10:9-13).

St. Augustine said that God gives where He finds empty hands. Would you open your hands today and surrender to Him the sin that has separated you from Him so that He can fill your hands with His good gifts, including the gift of salvation? Would you ask Him to guide and lead your life?

God knows our hearts and whether we're truly repentant, confessing and turning from our sin; He knows when we are honestly seeking Him. If you want to know Him, tell Him that. Tell Him that you believe that He raised Jesus from the dead and proclaim with your mouth that Jesus is Lord, and you will be saved. And once you've become a child of God, you'll want to ask for His help every day as you read His Word and walk with Him.

In this book we've gotten a glimpse of what the Bible says about God's plan for our world. I encourage you to read the Bible, with the help of the Holy Spirit, to learn more about the season we are living in. And I pray that you are encouraged as you come to realize that things are looking up!

As I said at the end of the first two books in this series, I pray that God will bless you, keep you, and make His face shine on you, being gracious to you. May the Lord fill you with His peace—in Jesus's name.

NOTES

WHERE IN THE WORD? DEEP WATERS

1. See the Blue Letter Bible at https://www.blueletterbible.org/lang/lexicon/lexicon.cfm?Strongs=G2347&t=CSB.
2. J. Dwight Pentecost, *Things to Come* (Grand Rapids, MI: Zondervan, 1958), 235.

WHERE IN THE WORD? SATAN

1. David Jones, "The Coming Bride," Royston Bethel Community Church, Bride Ministries, 2014), 219.

WHERE IN THE WORD? THE ANTICHRIST

1. Mark Hitchcock, *101 Answers to the Most Asked Questions About the End Times* (Colorado Springs, CO: Multnomah Books, 2001), 138.
2. Bart D. Ehrman, "Op-Ed: How Christians came to believe in heaven, hell and the immortal soul," *Los Angeles Times*, April 4, 2021, https://www.latimes.com/opinion/story/2021-04-04/christians-heaven-hell-soul?utm_medium=email&_hsmi=119834967&_hsenc=p2ANqtz-2H1C88kFMowE8zqEfh2x85TaN7DVbRop4Ggr5A9LXHqt-_Sd5gXcqJ7xwrm386UWf-8c99EcFFra_mE_YYJgc8DMg&utm_content=119834967&utm_source=hs_email.
3. Phil Zuckerman, "Op-Ed: Why America's record godlessness is good news for the nation" *Los Angeles Times*, April 2, 2021, https://www.latimes.com/opinion/story/2021-04-02/godlessness-america-religion-secularization?utm_medium=email&_hsmi=119834967&_hsenc=p2ANqtz-8XJHtqpwLZ5HVkDyawylSJIch2i4NA7GO5qAb00M-H_JKJBp_5578zQT_JI_0MNQ-wHvURcMdAdhaoT9pmZ-mb1OxqTA&utm_content=119834967&utm_source=hs_email.
4. Tré Goins-Phillips, "'This Is Literal Heresy': Sen. Raphael Warnock Posts Troubling 'Meaning of Easter' Tweet," *Faithwire*, April 4, 2021, https://www.faithwire.com/2021/04/04/this-is-literal-heresy-sen-raphael-warnock-posts-troubling-meaning-of-easter-tweet/.
5. Hitchcock, *101 Answers to the Most Asked Questions About the End Times*, 120.

WHERE IN THE WORD? ANTICHRIST'S ORIGIN

1. Arthur W. Pink, *The Antichrist* (1923; repr., Grand Rapids, MI: Kregel, 1988), 8.

2. Reuters staff, "Sudan quietly signs Abraham Accords weeks after Israel deal," *Reuters*, January 6, 2021, https://www.reuters.com/article/uk-sudan-usa-israel-idUSKBN29C0Q5.

3. David Jeremiah, *Agents of the Apocalypse* (Carol Stream, IL: Tyndale, 2014), 147.

WHERE IN THE WORD? HOW WILL ANTICHRIST RISE TO WORLD POWER?

1. William F. Arndt and F.W. Gingrich, *A Greek-English Lexicon of the New Testament* (Chicago, IL: University of Chicago Press, 1957), 876.

2. Arnold G. Fruchtenbaum, *The Footsteps of the Messiah*, rev. ed. (Tustin, CA: Ariel Ministries, 2003), 255.

3. See the Blue Letter Bible at https://www.blueletterbible.org/lang/lexicon/lexicon.cfm?Strongs=G3173&t=CSB.

WHERE IN THE WORD? FALLEN ANGELS AND DEMONS

1. Blue Letter Bible, https://www.blueletterbible.org/lang/lexicon/lexicon.cfm?Strongs=G5467&t=CSB.

2. Blue Letter Bible, https://www.blueletterbible.org/lang/lexicon/lexicon.cfm?Strongs=G5467&t=CSB.

WHERE IN THE WORD? WHERE ARE THE MOUNTAINS THE JEWS WILL FLEE TO?

1. Bryan Windle, "Biblical Places on Modern Maps: Jordan," *Bible Archaeology Report*, April 7, 2018, https://biblearchaeologyreport.com/2018/04/07/biblical-places-on-modern-maps-jordan/.

2. Kiran Bisht, "Petra Caves in Jordan: A Rose-Red City Half as Old as Time," *Travel Triangle*, https://traveltriangle.com/blog/petra-caves-in-jordan/.

3. "Petra: One of 7 Wonders," *Visit Petra*, https://visitpetra.jo/DetailsPage/VisitPetra/LocationsIn-PetraDetailsEn.aspx?PID=5.

4. See the Blue Letter Bible at https://www.blueletterbible.org/lang/lexicon/lexicon.cfm?Strongs=G5142&t=CSB.

5. Shlomi Ella, "How Many Jews There Are in the Whole World?," *Jewish Business News*, September 29, 2019, https://jewishbusinessnews.com/2019/09/29/how-many-jews-there-are-in-the-whole-world/.

ALSO BY DONNA VANLIERE

BOOK 1

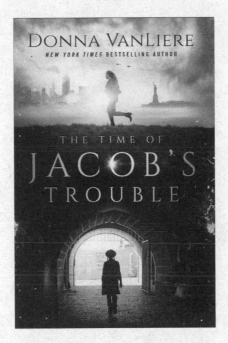

A typical day at work turns into a nightmare for Emma Grady when her favorite patient and several colleagues vanish in front of her. Fear turns to chaos as Emma begins the frantic race from Brooklyn to Queens, anxious to discover if her boyfriend is safe. Subways are closed, graves are open, and countless people have inexplicably disappeared. Mayhem erupts as terror grips the residents of New York City.

What could make so many vanish in a moment? And not just in New York, but all over the globe? Emma wonders if this is the predicted end of the world and begins a desperate search for answers.

This page-turning story will take you on a riveting journey from New York City to Israel, and in the final chapters, Donna turns to the pages of the Bible, where you'll learn that God has made known to us "the end from the beginning," and that things aren't spiraling downward but are actually looking up.

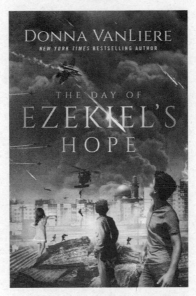

BOOK 2

Millions have vanished…
War has erupted around the globe…
Cities have been ransacked and overrun with lawlessness…
Yet this is only the beginning of the chaos that is to come.

Emma Grady has seen civilization collapse and New York gutted by nuclear attack. Amidst this international crisis, she and her growing family of outcasts must unravel the meaning of these strange and horrifying events, even as they struggle to survive.

On the other side of the world, Zerah Adler finds Israel surrounded by invaders intent on total annihilation. In Jerusalem, two men have the power to stop the rain and call down plagues of every kind. Are they sorcerers, or do they have the power of God? And a magnetic new leader has emerged, promising to provide peace and even salvation to the globe.

In the gripping follow-up to *The Time of Jacob's Trouble*, bestselling author Donna VanLiere explores the end times through the journeys of Emma, Zerah, and others who face unprecedented danger. In the final chapters, you'll discover what God's Word says about our world's future and yours—and realize that things aren't spiraling downward but are actually looking up!

THINGS ARE
LOOKING
UP
PODCAST
Donna VanLiere

Does Bible prophecy often leave you confused and frightened? You're not alone. There are some strange and mystifying Bible passages that have bewildered generations of Christ-followers. Many aspects of Bible prophecy could never be understood by our parents and grandparents simply because the signs of the end times had not yet become apparent.

But did you know that the meanings of many of these same Bible verses are being revealed before our very eyes? It is our generation that is seeing end-time prophecies being fulfilled.

Join Donna VanLiere and listen to her free podcast *Things Are Looking Up*, in which she shares significant and specific prophecies that only our generation has been able to understand, and discusses the very real connection between Bible prophecy and our world today.

www.DonnaVanLiere.com/LookingUp

To learn more about our Harvest Prophecy resources, please visit:

www.HarvestProphecyHQ.com